THE ITALIAN HOUSE

THE ITALIAN HOUSE

Teresa Crane

St. Martin's Press ♊ New York

Library of Congress Cataloging-in-Publication
Data

Crane, Teresa.
The Italian house / by Teresa Crane.
p.   cm.
ISBN 0-312-13992-6 (hardcover)
I. Title.
PR6053.R356I83   1996
823'.914—dc20   95-26049   CIP

First published in Great Britain by
Little, Brown and Company

First U.S. Edition: March 1996
10   9   8   7   6   5   4   3   2   1

Prologue

The storm had raged for a night and a day. A bitter wind gusted from the north, from the mountains of the Garfagnana. It shrieked about the treeless peaks above the house, buffeted the wooded hillsides, drove rain in drenching sheets against roof and wall and shuttered window. It shredded the ragged, fast-moving clouds that streamed about the hilltops and boiled down into the valleys; it whispered through the house like a chill breath, stirring a paper here, a silken fringe there. A shutter banged, monotonously, clattering back and forth with a manic, metronomic regularity. This was a gentle house, built for quiet sunshine and summer breezes; now it loomed dark upon the hillside grimly braving the onslaught, the single light that gleamed fitfully in an upstairs window the only sign of life.

The figure at the window was so still he might have been carved from stone. The smoke from the cigarette that he held between slim, nicotine-stained fingers wreathed about him. He had been standing for some time now, his attention upon a donkey-cart that

1

toiled up the winding track below in the half-light of the stormy evening, its small lamps glimmering through the streaming rain. Every so often it would disappear beneath the wildly tossing branches of a stand of chestnut trees, to emerge moments later, plodding at a dogged and dispirited pace, inching up the hillside, closer to that spot where the mountain track forked sharply to come up to the house. In the days that he had been here no one had turned at that fork – the hamlet of San Marco lay a half-mile or so further on, and it was to there that most traffic on this little-used way would be heading – but something held him now, watching, as the ancient vehicle struggled on. When, on reaching the fork, the driver swung the shambling donkey in an awkward, muddy arc and set him at the final climb to the house the man at the window stirred at last, the neat head lifting sharply, narrow eyes narrowing further. He stood for a single, suspended moment, poised and still, before turning swiftly, stubbing out his cigarette, reaching for the lamp that stood upon the table behind him and extinguishing its glow.

The wind, that had eased for a moment, buffeted again, and somewhere within the dark house a door slammed in the sudden draught.

Chapter One

Hastings, England. December 1922

Carrie Stowe, head down against the gale-driven rain, battled around the corner of Barrymore Walk, one hand grabbing at the flying skirts of her coat, the other awkwardly clamping her small hat to her head. Thank the Lord that number 11 was only a short way down the long, straight street that seemed to funnel the Channel winds and increase their strength fivefold. Street lamps glimmered in the dusk. The windows in the smart new brick façades of the houses of the Walk glared with garish and self-confident electric light, the neat, clean interiors glimpsed from the pavement appearing like a series of bright-lit pictures, almost clinical behind their glass, somehow safely set apart from the elements. Carrie's cheeks stung with the cold. She was surprisingly tired. The train ride back from London had seemed interminable; the effort to contain her excitement, to prevent herself from hoping too much, had all but exhausted her.

'You mean – the house is mine?' she had asked, the thing so much beyond her grasp that the words had verged on the disbelieving. 'Mine?'

Mr Bagshaw of Bagshaw, Bagshaw and Stott, Solicitors, had nodded, patiently. 'As I said. Yours, Mrs Stowe. Entirely yours, under the conditions which I hope I have made clear to you?'

'Yes. Yes, of course.' Far from making the conditions clear, Mr Bagshaw had given the distinct impression that the arcane workings of Italian law were as much beyond him as they were beyond Carrie herself. His every disapproving sniff had indicated just how low was his opinion of such alien if apparently legal skulduggery. But still – Yes, he had said. Yes, the house is yours.

The Italian house. The Villa Castellini. Hers.

She leaned into the wind, struggled the last few steps to the small wooden gate that was set in the low, clipped privet hedge of number 11. The concrete path led, neat and uncompromising, directly to the front door. She swung the gate behind her, then, realising that the latch had not caught, turned wearily back to secure it; she would not hear the last of it if Arthur came home to find the gate swinging on its hinges in the wind.

She fumbled with cold fingers for the key. Even here in the small, relatively sheltered porch the December wind swirled, bone-chillingly cold.

Inside at last she leaned against the front door, shutting out the noise and the spiteful weather; turned on the overhead light. The long, narrow hall with its oak coatstand, its small mirror, its polished brown lino was as cold as the grave. The light was bright

4

and unforgiving. She stood for a moment, her arms wrapped across her body, narrow shoulders hunched.

'You mean the house is mine? Mine?'

'Yours, Mrs Stowe. Entirely yours.'

She stood unmoving for a long time, a slight figure of medium height, muffled in woollen coat and little, nondescript felt hat. The weather sounds were muted now, the small house very still. Carrie reached for another switch. The landing light clicked on, throwing angular shadows down the steep and narrow stairway.

Mine. Entirely mine.

The third and the seventh stair creaked, as they always did, like new shoes, as she mounted them. Why did she always notice it? Would the day ever come when she didn't?

The boxroom door, at the end of the small, L-shaped landing, was closed. She pushed it open. She had never been able to fathom whether it was called a boxroom because it was a place only fit to store boxes, or because, in itself, it so much resembled a box. Other people, in other houses, she supposed might use it for babies, or for visitors; but since both were in exceptionally short supply at number 11, this one was used for nothing but storage.

At least, that is what Arthur thought. The time that Carrie spent alone in this tiny, cheerless room was her own secret; she had always known that Arthur would be of the opinion that no rational woman, given the neat comfort and convenience of number 11 Barrymore Walk, would feel the need to escape to the furthest, smallest, coldest corner of the house to gaze at two old pictures and to dream.

The room was icy. The curtains stirred in the draught from the windows. She pulled off her hat and tossed it onto the bed, extracted the clutch of hairpins with which she had half-heartedly attempted to secure her heavy, dark hair and rubbed ruefully at her aching scalp. It was ridiculous; if only Arthur would allow her to have it cut – to a bob perhaps, or even a shingle.

Still wearing her coat she walked to the tiny, empty fireplace. Above it upon carelessly fixed nails hung two small oil paintings, side by side, quite spectacularly incongruous in this bleak little room. Carrie had known these pictures all of her life; until her mother's death a couple of years before they had always held pride of place over the cluttered mantelpiece in her sitting room. On Carrie's inheriting them Arthur had insisted – with nothing less than absolute good sense, Carrie herself would not dispute it – that they were entirely unsuited to the brisk and modern decor of number 11. And so they had been banished, with the broken tennis racquets and the silk cushions that Carrie had embroidered with fanciful flowers, that Arthur had decreed too frivolous for use, to the boxroom. She stood now, as she had stood so often, absently picking up a cushion and hugging it to her for warmth, looking at them.

The Villa Castellini – a large, square house with a small tower set into one corner, its ancient tiled roofs a series of slopes and angles – pictured perched within its tumbling gardens on a hillside in northern Tuscany, bathed in sunlight, golden and warm. She remembered

6

it as an enchanted childhood dream. It had seemed huge on those joyous occasions before the war when she had been taken to visit her grandmother, the high ceilings vaulting above her, the dim, cool interiors of the rooms cluttered with a fascinating collection of the picturesque and the absurd; strange and wonderful artefacts collected by her grandfather on his travels side by side with the charming and whimsical treasures her eccentric grandmother had spent her life collecting, a few valuable, most – at least in the eyes of the world – worthless. But always interesting, always beautiful. She remembered a fragile, pearly shell, brought from a far island, in which a child could clearly hear the shifting roar of the sea. She remembered a shining brass box full of tiny heavy glass beads, jewel-coloured. She remembered books, and pictures and tiny figurines. She remembered the garden, the wonderful garden, full of steep twisting paths and secret corners; a paradise for the child that the young Carrie had been.

The thought drew her attention to the other picture. It was of her favourite place in the garden of the villa. This it was that brought her so often to this room, to read, or to sew, or simply to daydream within sight of that magical, hidden arbour. There were times when she fancied she could feel the sun, hear the sound of the water splashing in the fountain, feel the smoothness of stone, warm almost as skin beneath her hand as she touched the statues that stood in the dappled shadows beside the water.

She stirred a little. Her wet feet were so cold she could barely feel them, and despite her coat she was

7

shivering. A gust of wind hit the window, rattling the
panes. She tightened her grip on the cushion, burying
her chin in it. She should go downstairs, light the fire,
start the tea. Arthur would be put out if he came home
to a cold house.

She did not move.

Arthur would make her sell the house, of course. She
knew it. His only interest when the letter had arrived
from the solicitor had been in how much this unexpected
bequest might be worth. He had been extremely annoyed
that at the last moment, owing to a suddenly arranged
meeting at the bank, Carrie had had to make the
trip to London on her own. Indeed, had there been
time she knew he would have rearranged it; he had
made it perfectly clear, as he always did, that in his
firm opinion she was neither competent nor capable
enough to handle something like this on her own. He
was probably right. His last instructions as he had left
her at the station had been a set of comprehensive
and intelligent questions that she should bring up in
her meeting with Mr Bagshaw; questions, she realised
now, that she had of course completely forgotten to ask.
Yes, Arthur was undoubtedly right; she was hopeless at
such things. And, no, he obviously had no intention of
allowing her to keep the Italian house; indeed, Carrie
herself was ready enough to admit that all that could
be done, in the end, was to sell it. What good was an
old house halfway up a mountainside in Tuscany to a
very English bank clerk and his wife – wryly, hearing
Arthur's sharp, precise voice as clearly as if he had
been standing beside her, she amended that thought –

a very English chief bank clerk and his wife? She would have to sell it, she understood that. But first – she drew a sudden, sharp breath, fighting against the lifting of excitement, the stirring of hope – first, Mr Bagshaw had said, looking down a disapproving nose, first she must go to Italy. Until she did, the house could not be transferred into her name.

Oddly, it had only been later, whilst she sat on the train staring sightlessly out at the drenched and dreary winter landscape that the thought had finally penetrated. She would have to go to Italy. Alone. The bank would surely never let Arthur go for that length of time? Three weeks, Mr Bagshaw had said. At least. Perhaps four – another repressive sniff – knowing these foreigners and their ways.

Arthur, surely, would have to make the choice; to let her go, and to glean what profit they could make on the sale, or to refuse, and to lose it.

She turned now and walked to the window, stood looking down into the long, narrow garden that marched side by side with the other long, narrow gardens of Barrymore Walk in neat, regimented, clearly defined plots. If the fence posts were your side, then the fence was yours and you maintained and mended it. If the fence posts were in your neighbour's garden then the fence was his responsibility.

When first they had moved to number 11 she had consoled herself with the thought that at least she might make something of the garden. A winding path, perhaps, with shrubs and trees and small drifts of colour to beguile the eye, to suggest that, small as the area was,

9

something waited around the corner, just out of view. They were fortunate that there was already an old apple tree standing, legacy of the orchard that once had been here. It had been the only one in the length of the brand new street that had somehow survived the builders and their efficient machinery. At first, when diffidently she had suggested that she might take some interest in the garden Arthur had seemed pleased. Once he had seen her intentions, however, once the first tentative lines were in place he had changed his mind. Argument, as always, had served her ill. Within a month order had been restored and reason had reigned. Delphiniums, lupins, dahlias, all had been planted in acceptable rows, singly, staked out and straight as soldiers on parade. The apple tree had been cut down – very sensibly, since it had stood in the most inconvenient place possible, just where the washing line should be. A nice, straight, clean concrete path ran the length of the garden now, edged with square lawn and regular, tidy flower beds. It was very easy to maintain.

The gale gusted, and for a moment she imagined the old tree, creaking and protesting, flinching against the salt wind.

She turned back to the pictures.

Mine. Entirely mine.

So strange – almost surreal – had been the day that she could still think the words without entirely taking them in. And yet, somewhere, somewhere in the passive, subdued place that was her heart, something was stirring.

He'll have to let me go. Just this once. He'll have to.

Downstairs a clock chimed, briskly and regularly. One. Two. Three. Four. Five.

She blinked. Five o'clock. Half an hour, just half an hour before Arthur came home. There was the fire to light, the tea to make – she felt a small, queasy twist of apprehension. Arthur hated to wait for his tea.

—For goodness' sake, Carrie, what have you been *doing*? Is it too much to ask that, occupied as I'm sure you must be, home all of the day and with this new and – I must say – highly efficient house to run, you manage to produce a meal on time? And please, *please*, do remember that we have separate knives and forks for fish. You can surely see, my dear, the sense in that? Fish – wholesome as I am certain it is – does taint things so.

She could hear his voice, see the very expression on his face. She breathed a long, silent breath and turned. At the door she looked back, for the briefest of moments, before turning out the light.

'I'm sorry, my dear,' Arthur adjusted his angular frame to the small armchair beside the fire, 'but you surely must see it's quite out of the question? To travel to Italy, alone? Have you any idea – any idea at all – what such a journey would involve?'

Carrie considered, briefly, pointing out that of the two of them she, as a child, had in fact made the journey several times with her disorganised scatterbrain of a mother and had somehow survived unscathed, whereas Arthur himself had never been out of the country. She remained silent.

'No, no. Apart from anything else the political situation in Italy is still unstable. These Fascist chappies don't do things by half measures by all accounts. Mind you, they're just what the country needs, if you ask me. But for you to go there alone?' Arthur shook his head, put his cup very precisely back on to the saucer, set it upon the cork mat that rested upon the small table beside him. 'Quite out of the question. There must be some other way.'

Carrie looked down into her own cup. The tea had cooled. It looked dark, and muddy and utterly unappetising. 'No,' she said. 'There isn't. Not according to Mr Bagshaw. And he mentioned the political situation too; he said the trouble had been almost entirely confined to the cities, and that anyway since the march on Rome and the defeat of the Socialists earlier this year everything had quietened down. The new government have everything under control, he said.' She leaned forward and put her own cup on the table; it sat awkwardly half on and half off the mat. 'I'm sure he said there was no other way except to go in person.'

Arthur tutted, his thin mouth tightening in irritation, and reached with a long, bony hand to set her carelessly placed cup straight. 'I'm sure that can't be so, my dear. You must have got it wrong.'

In face of Arthur's relentless and dismissive certainties Carrie was coming to believe it herself. 'Perhaps,' she said.

'I'll go and see the man myself. Get some sense out of him. If the house is ours, it's ours. It's absolute nonsense to suggest that we cannot simply take possession of it from here.'

She tried once more. 'I'm sorry, Arthur, I don't think I've explained very well. It's the Italian law. It's different from ours. Something to do with Napoleon,' she blinked a little at the swift impatience of his movement, 'you can't just leave something to someone. Everyone in the family has a right to a part of it. I'm sure that's what he said.'

'But you don't have any family since your mother and her brothers died.'

'Yes I do. At least, I think I may have. My cousin, Leo, remember? Uncle John's son.'

'Him? You haven't heard from him for years. Not since the war. He's surely dead.'

Fresh from the recollections of those childhood summers she would not let him see her flinch at the brisk brutality of that. 'He may be. But he may not. And if he were alive, had Grandmother not made these provisions the house would have been divided between us. By law, you see. And she didn't want that. She wanted me to have it.'

'Us.' Arthur said.

'Yes. Of course. Us.'

There was a small and slightly dangerous silence. Carrie glanced at her husband's face unable to disguise her open anxiety. It was Tuesday. Above all things she did not want to anger him. She would surely suffer for it later if she did. A small, unpleasant sensation, something between fear and aversion, twisted in her stomach. 'Would you like some more tea?'

13

He shook his head. 'So, tell me about this mumbo jumbo again.'

Carrie sighed. 'I'm sorry. I really can't remember all the legal terms he used. Something like *usu frutto* was one, I remember – and there was something else—' she felt the colour rising in her face as he lifted sharp, impatient eyes to hers. 'Anyway, what it means is that Grandmother gave the property into the hands of someone else, a close friend of hers. He, I assume it's a he – Mr Bagshaw didn't know exactly who it was – held the house in trust whilst Uncle Henry lived there. Now I have to pay a small sum of money and, according to Grandmother's wishes, the house becomes mine. Ours,' she amended, hastily.

'What an unutterable shambles.' Distaste for foreigners and all their works was in his precise voice.

'Yes, Arthur. I'm sorry.'

He leaned forward, poked a long, large-knuckled finger at her. 'Tell me this: what is to stop this, this so-called friend from keeping the place, eh? Eh? What makes you think he'll let it go now he's got his hands on it?' He nodded sharply, an oddly smug gesture. 'You tell me that.'

Carrie folded her hands in her lap. Glanced down at them. Small sallow-skinned paws, undistinguished and unladylike. Her wedding ring, that had been Arthur's mother's, hung loose and heavy upon her finger. 'I don't know, Arthur. Truly I don't. All I know is what Mr Bagshaw told me. He said I would have to go to Lucca, to Grandmother's Italian lawyer, and he would put me in touch with the person who's holding the

14

house for me.' She lifted her shoulder a little, flicked a glance at him, decided against calling attention to her slip by correcting it. 'It apparently isn't an unusual arrangement in Italy.'

'I'm sure it isn't,' Arthur said, repressively. He sat for a moment, thoughtful, a strong nail clicking against his teeth. Carrie watched him warily. 'The house,' he said at last, 'it must be worth something?'

'I suppose so.'

'This Bagshaw, he didn't have any idea how much?'

She shook her head.

'And the contents?'

She shrugged. 'I don't know if there are any. The house has been empty for months. And Uncle Henry – well, you know he wasn't quite—' she hesitated.

'There was no "not quite" about it, my dear. From what I gather your uncle was as simple-minded as a two year old and there's an end.' There was another moment's silence. When her husband straightened in his chair Carrie almost jumped. 'I shall go to see this Bagshaw myself,' Arthur said, firmly. 'I'll get the right of it from him. We shouldn't look a gift horse in the mouth. Inconvenient it might be, but the thing must be worth something and we might as well have the benefit of it. Yes. That's what I'll do. I'll see the man myself.'

'Yes Arthur. Of course.'

'If worse comes to worst – who knows? – perhaps I'll take some time from the bank and accompany you to Italy. Could make something of a jaunt of it.'

The small, subversive spark of hope that had been kindled that afternoon flickered and died. 'Yes, Arthur.'

15

He stood up, came to the chair, laid a bony hand upon her shoulder. 'And Carrie—'

She looked up. A faint, dark colour had lifted in his long face. 'It's Tuesday, my dear. You won't forget to bathe, will you?'

She shook her head, numbly. 'No, Arthur. I won't forget.'

Arthur arrived home from his interview with Mr Bagshaw in chancy temper. 'Pompous ass. The man's an incompetent idiot.'

'Oh?' Carrie lifted her head, added mildly, 'I thought he was quite nice.'

'You think everyone's nice, Carrie.' The comment was not intended as a compliment and Carrie did not take it as such.

Arthur paced the room thoughtfully, hands clasped behind his back. 'He absolutely insists that this ridiculous arrangement has to stand. We have to go to Italy. It really is very inconvenient.'

'Yes, Arthur.'

'I don't know how much time I can get off from the bank.'

'No. I realise that. It must be very difficult.'

'Blasted idiots.'

'Who?'

'The Italians. Napoleon conquers them, imposes his laws, and here we are a hundred years later still suffering them. A totally foolish system that does nothing but break up the holdings of a family—'

'I think that was what it was designed to do.'

He ignored her interruption – 'and instead of changing the law they find devious ways around it. It's absurd.'

She smiled the smallest of smiles. 'It's Italian,' she said.

He had come to rest in front of the fireplace, rocking a little on his heels, looking into the flames. 'Three to four weeks, Bagshaw said.'

'Yes. That was what he told me. And there's the house to clear, if we're going to sell it. If there is anything left it may take longer.'

He shook his head. 'I can't take that amount of time off from the bank, of course. Even if I could get permission Cranshaw would be bound to take advantage of such a long absence.'

She sat very still, hardly daring to move. Hope whispered, and stirred again.

He clicked his tongue in sharp irritation.

Carrie reached calmly for another skein of wool.

He turned again, paced to the window. Stopped, his eye caught by a small, brightly painted china bowl. He contemplated it, frowning a little. 'This is new, isn't it?'

'Yes. I found it in the market. The little stall in the corner that sells second-hand goods.' Collectedly she arranged the wool, teased the end from the skein.

'Second-hand?' The word expressed distaste. 'How much did you pay for it?'

'One and sixpence.' In some part of her heart she marvelled; how easily, how automatically, she lied. 'I thought it quite a bargain. It's pretty, don't you think?'

17

'At the price, I suppose so.' He picked it up, turned it in his hands, set it back absently upon the table. 'There must surely be someone we can call upon?'

'Call upon?'

'To accompany you. Perfectly obviously it is out of the question that you should travel alone to Italy. And as for coping with an Italian lawyer—' he shook his head sharply.

She contemplated him with tranquil eyes. The rage that suddenly shook her quite genuinely surprised her. 'There's no one,' she said, quietly. 'Arthur, it seems the choice is clear. Either I go alone, or I don't go at all. If I go, the house is ours, and we can keep it or sell it as you see fit. If I don't go, then presumably Grandmother's friend benefits. As I say, it's a simple choice.' She picked up the wool and shook it, separating the strands. 'It seems a pity to let such a chance for profit go.' She saw, as she had so often seen lately, the house and the garden, dreaming in the soft Tuscan sunshine. 'It may not be worth a fortune, but it surely must be worth something?'

Fretfully he turned. 'But, Carrie – my dear – how will you manage?'

To be strictly honest, the same question had occurred to her, many times. 'I have made the journey before, as a child. I'm sure it can't be too difficult. And of course there's a large English community in Bagni di Lucca. I'm sure I'll find someone ready to help when I get there. Grandmother – and Uncle Henry – must have had friends and contacts in the village.' She watched him, covertly, her breath suspended; saw the battle

18

between greed and propriety, between the desire for profit and the desire to keep her here, under his eye. Saw, suddenly and certainly, the moment that avarice won. She lowered her eyes and waited.

He clicked his fingers suddenly. 'Thomas Cook,' he said. 'Of course, that's the ticket! Thomas Cook. They'll arrange everything for you, I'm sure.'

'Yes. I'm sure they would.' Freedom. A few, precious weeks of freedom. Freedom from number 11 Barrymore Walk. Freedom from Arthur's parsimony, his constant, critical attention. Freedom from the tyranny of Tuesdays, Thursdays and Saturdays.

'You'll have to be careful about what you spend. I can't afford to let you have much, you know that.'

'Yes. Of course.'

'You'll presumably live in the house, that will save hotel bills.'

'Yes,' she said again. 'Of course.'

'With the travelling time – three weeks, the man said.'

'He did say it might take a little longer.'

'Three weeks should certainly be enough.' His voice was firm.

She said nothing.

'Once the place is legally ours you can come home. We can sell it from England.'

'Yes.'

'Well.' He rubbed his long hands together. 'That's settled.'

Carrie bent her head. Smoothed the material of her skirt over her knees. 'Yes,' she said again.

'I'll go into Cook's for you tomorrow. See what I can arrange.'

'Thank you.'

'Your grandmother might have been a rather strange old bird, but she was a character, and Bagshaw tells me she wasn't ill thought of in some circles.'

'No.'

'Her bits and pieces might fetch something.'

She took a small, steadying breath. Repressed rage could so easily become a stab of hatred. 'We don't know that there's anything there.'

'No, of course not. But if there is – well she had enough contacts in the artistic world to make it worth while trying.' He looked at her then, sharply, almost in irritation. 'I don't like this, you know. I don't like the thought of your going off on your own. I shall worry about you.'

'I'll manage, Arthur. I'm sure I'll manage.' She lifted her head, smiling. 'Would you like a cup of tea?'

Arthur, as always with good sense and practicality on his side, decided for her that it was not appropriate to travel in the worst of the winter months. Letters were written, arrangements made. March. She would go to Italy in late March.

The knowledge shone in her head, in her heart, like a lamp in darkness.

March. In March I'll go to the Italian house again. Alone. She gazed at the pictures in the boxroom, picked over the newly aroused and precious memories – not just of the Villa Castellini but of the family house in

Hampstead, forever associated with Christmas, forever associated with her grandmother, Beatrice Swann, dead now these ten years yet still vivid in her mind. Vivid too, she suspected, in the mind of anyone who had known her. The Hampstead house was gone, sold many years before the war, when Beatrice's carelessly managed money had begun to run out. Carrie's own mother Victoria had bewailed that loss. Carrie remembered it still. 'What on earth does Mother think she's doing? For goodness' sake, where will we go if she doesn't keep the Hampstead house? She can't – she surely can't – be thinking of living in Italy? Not even she could be thinking of that!'

But, characteristically, that was exactly what she had done, with Henry, her handsome eldest, handicapped and best-loved son. And then, for Carrie, there had followed those summers, magical times of sunshine and delight, spiced by her cousin Leo's beguiling and perilous presence and blessed by the gleam of her grandmother's capricious interest – the child had always hesitated to call it love – occasionally blithely and impulsively intent, usually absent-minded, always sought-after.

Then all had changed; Beatrice had died unexpectedly in 1912, leaving Henry to live in the Villa Castellini alone. And then, suddenly and shockingly, the war had come; and with it privation, young adulthood, her mother's sickness, and the terrible responsibility that it had brought. Leo – his father, her Uncle John, dead a mere two years after his mother – had disappeared into the trenches with so very many of the country's young men, and she had heard neither from him nor of him since. Italy had seemed a lost world away. Carrie had been eighteen years old when the war had ended, living hand to mouth in a rented apartment in Islington with a demanding and querulous invalid of a mother and very little money. Arthur Stowe's correct and conventional attentions had offered an escape that her mother had been firm in accepting on her daughter's behalf. Carrie, never a fighter, always anxious to please, had acquiesced. What else was there to do?

And now, by some quirk, perhaps some remembered regard, some tie of blood, the Italian house had come to her. She would see it again, this one last time, wander its rooms, explore its gardens. Without Arthur. Her one adventure in an unadventurous life. She would come back to Hastings, to Arthur, and to the bank, she knew it. Nothing would change. Not in the long run. How could it? But at least she would have a memory. A dream, of sorts, to sustain and protect her.

In late March 1923, her outward calm concealing an apprehensive excitement that dried her mouth and unsettled her stomach, she allowed Arthur to install her in a 'Ladies Only' carriage, fuss about her luggage and her tickets, oppress her with a stream of last-minute instructions and orders and then sat quite still, watching his tall, gaunt figure recede as the boat-train pulled out of a noisy, steam-filled Victoria Station.

She often wondered, afterwards, where she had found the courage not to return his wave.

Chapter Two

When she thought about it later Carrie supposed that she should have foreseen that the journey, that started with so much anticipation, might end as something of a nightmare. On grounds of economy Arthur had eschewed the efficiency – as he saw it – of the Belgian and German rail networks and had opted for the French, which were cheaper if a little slower; the extra cost of a sleeper had predictably outraged him, but not even he could bring himself to suggest that Carrie sit up all night. He had booked her a second-class ticket through France to Switzerland and then on to Milan and to Parma, where she would change to the branch line that ran through the mountains to Bagni di Lucca. It was a route that, in the summer, was much frequented by the British going to Bagni to take the waters; but this, of course, was March.

The crossing to Calais was stormy; Carrie never forgot that first acquaintance with the wretched embarrassment of seasickness. The boat was late; by the time they were ready to board the train the cold afternoon was darkening. Still feeling wretchedly queasy she settled into her corner seat and resigned herself to the relentless chatter of her apparently inescapable travelling companions; for by this time the Pilkingtons had found her.

They had sat opposite her as Arthur had fussed and advised and settled her into her seat at Victoria, the three of them the only occupants of the carriage. She had studiously managed to avoid the woman's small, inquisitive eyes for the first twenty minutes of the journey; it was with a sinking heart that she had returned the beaming smile that the first crossing of glances brought forth. The plump, middle-aged woman leaned forward confidingly. 'I see you're travelling alone, my dear. How very brave of you.'

Carrie's smile grew, if possible, fainter. 'Not really. It was – unavoidable.'

'How far are you going? To Calais? You have relatives there, perhaps?'

Carrie shook her head. 'I have to go to Italy for—' she hesitated 'for family reasons.'

'Italy! Clarence, did you hear that? The lamb is going to *Italy* all alone!' The woman settled in her seat, cosily. 'Well, my dear, at least we can accompany you as far as Switzerland. We're going to Lucerne, you see, to visit friends – very dear friends – the Peter Thorncrofts, Doctor Peter Thorncroft that is. He and Clarence were in practice together before they retired, weren't you Clarence? As a matter of fact, my dear, I remarked to Clarence on the marked physical resemblance between your husband – he was your husband, I take it?

– and Doctor Thorncroft. Remarkable. Really quite remarkable. Wasn't it, Clarence? Didn't I say— ?'

Her voice, Carrie found herself thinking, was like the sound of cutlery clattering in a sink, loud, soulless and sharp.

'And you're going to Italy! All alone. Well, my dear, I must say you have my admiration. Why, I never stir a step without Clarence. Do I, Clarence?'

Her name was Milly. They had three children, two boys and a girl, all properly and advantageously married, all with offspring – Carrie had admired endless photographs long before they reached the grey, storm-tossed Channel. They lived in Maidstone. Their house had four bedrooms, three reception rooms and a newly modernised kitchen. They had two cats and what sounded like a decidedly ill-behaved spaniel. Mrs Pilkington was a stalwart of the Women's Institute, the Tory Party and the local bridge club. Carrie smiled, and nodded, and contemplated in some despair the prospect of this ordeal all the way to Switzerland. The one relief afforded by the dreadful crossing was that Milly Pilkington was as incapacitated as anyone. The moment she stepped on to dry land, however, she was her unrelentingly loquacious self again. 'Honestly, my dear – the French! The French! We never set foot in the country without some *contretemps*.' She beamed happily at her own aptness. 'Do we, Clarence?'

Carrie actually rather liked Clarence; she imagined that had they had a chance to exchange more than three or four words at a time they might have constructed an interesting conversation. But Milly was unflagging.

She complained about the trains. She complained about the sleeping accommodation, which admittedly was less than comfortable; she complained – at length and vociferously – about the toilet facilities. She complained about the food, that Carrie actually rather liked. As in the dusk the countryside of France streamed past the window, and as Carrie tried to watch it, beguiled by the vast, rural landscapes, the tiny villages, the odd, intriguing sight of a château nestling, slate-roofed, amidst groves of trees and the roll of picturesque parkland, Milly talked, mercilessly. She was last into her narrow bunk and first out of it in the morning. She talked all the way through breakfast.

Then they were, at last and thankfully, steaming through the snow-shrouded mountains of Switzerland. 'What a pity, my dear,' Milly Pilkington said. 'We must part. You are certain you can't take a few days' break from your journey to stay with us? The Thorncrofts have plenty of room, and I know they'd welcome another house-guest.'

'No. Thank you, but no. I can't.' Carrie was exhausted. They had slept fully clothed; she felt rumpled and grubby. She had spent the night in an uneasy, dozing half-sleep, the rhythmic clacking of wheel and rail always on the edge of consciousness, the narrow bunk hard and uncomfortable, the small, airless cabin too hot. She waved the Pilkingtons off with what she knew to be an ungrateful relief.

She was glad to travel through the majestic mountains in daylight, even though the day was grey, the light dull. Free at last from Milly Pilkington's exhausting attentions she allowed herself now the indulgence of contemplating her journey's end. The house was waiting for her, nestling in the chestnut woods on its hillside above Bagni. Safely tucked into an envelope in her bag was the key the Italian lawyer – a Signor Bellini – had sent to Mr Bagshaw; a simple iron key, black painted and worn. She loved the feel of it in her hand. As through torrential mountain rain the train slid smoothly into the Swiss side of the St Gotthard Tunnel, she felt the rise of excitement; the next skies she saw would be the skies of Italy. A couple of hours later they would be past the lakes and in Milan. And surely, as they moved on south, the weather would improve, at least a little?

It did not; in fact, if anything, it got worse. She saw little or nothing of the lakes; the view was lost in shifting sheets of windswept rain, the waters were grey and stormy. Villages huddled in sodden misery beneath the downpour, oxcarts and donkeys plodded along the streaming lanes and tracks, their stoically hunched drivers or riders quite often swathed in sacking in a futile attempt to keep dry.

Tired, and with the beginnings of a faint but nagging headache, she dozed, fitfully.

The train steamed noisily into the industrial sprawl of Milan early in the afternoon, scheduled to stop for ten minutes before continuing on to Parma and Bologna. The station was busy, noisy with announcements she could barely hear through the closed window, and would not have been able to understand if she had. Ten minutes passed. Then another ten. Half an hour

27

later the train still had not moved. Opposite her sat a smartly dressed, middle-aged Englishman who had disclosed in the few words of stilted conversation they had exchanged since the Swiss border that he was bound for Bologna on business. He frowned now, leaning towards the window, peering along the platform.

'Is something wrong, do you think?' Carrie asked, hesitantly.

'My dear, this is Italy. And this is a train. I would be extremely surprised if there weren't something wrong. As a matter of fact I'm surprised we've got this far. I'd better go and find out what's happening.'

She waited for him, a little nervously. Rain dripped from the canopies above the station, pooled muddily on the platform. People jostled ill-temperedly.

Five minutes later her travelling companion was back, his expression a mixture of resignation and exasperation. 'We have to change trains, I'm afraid.'

'But – my ticket was booked through to Parma. I was told there were no connections after Lucerne—'

'My dear, as I said before, this is Italy. What someone tells you in a nice cosy ticket office in London tends to have about as much relevance to what actually happens within the Italian rail network as it has to the price of fish or the length of a piece of string. Don't worry. If there's a train, we'll find it. Come, they're unloading the baggage – best to be there.'

'If?' Carrie asked, faintly. '*If* there's a train?'

He smiled at her encouragingly. 'Don't worry,' he said again, 'I'm sure there is. Somewhere.'

The next two hours were amongst the most miserable

Carrie had ever spent anywhere. The station, for no obvious reason, was in chaos. They were shuffled from pillar to post, from one cold and draughty platform to another. Had it not been for the fortunate circumstance that her new friend – for certainly, after the first exhausting hour that was how she came to view him – had a very reasonable working knowledge of the Italian language she would have had little idea of what was going on, or why; as it was there was little by way of excuse or explanation for the delay. A lifted shoulder, an expressive wave of a hand was all that most enquiries elicited.

'Don't worry,' her companion, whom she now knew to be a Mr Robert Gowrie, reassured her for at least the sixth time and over yet another thick, dark coffee purchased from the trolley that trundled dispiritedly up and down the long platforms. 'We'll get you to Parma. Eventually.' He smiled, drily. 'Perhaps even today.'

She did not like to tell him that what now bothered her most was what she would do, alone and unaided, after she reached Parma. It had seemed a simple matter, to disembark from one train and to join another that would take her to her final destination; now, suddenly, nothing was that straightforward. In the fly-spotted and damp-marked mirror in the Ladies' Waiting Room she gazed at her reflection in near despair. Her reflection gazed back; sallow, dishevelled and weary. Her eyes ached abominably; she felt as if she had not slept in a week. It hardly seemed possible that it was a bare twenty-four hours since she had left Arthur standing on the platform of safe, sane Victoria Station.

Half-heartedly she tried to tuck the dark, straight strands of hair that had fallen about her face back under the rim of her hat; abandoned the attempt as a miserable failure. She took a long breath. Here she was. There was no way but forward. She lifted her chin, and with a bravado she had not known she possessed made no further attempt to tidy herself but pushed her way back through the crowds to rejoin Mr Gowrie.

'We're in luck,' he said, briskly. 'It seems there is a train. In the inevitable ten minutes. Fingers crossed, my dear; we may be on our way.'

Half an hour later they were, though slowly. The train meandered in its own time through the drenched, flat and uninteresting landscape of the Po Valley, stopping at the most wayward of halts. Occasionally, towards the south and through the steady rain, Carrie caught a glimpse of the distant Apennines, the mountain range that stood between this wide, pancake-flat, fertile valley and her destination. They loomed in moving mist, and disappeared like an enchantment, by turn enticing and terrifying.

'Mrs Stowe?' Mr Gowrie leaned forward and tapped her knee. She jerked awake. 'Parma,' he said, gently. 'We're nearly there.'

'Ah.' Clearly, her panic must have shown upon her face.

'It's all right.' The words carried the affection of camaraderie, of dangers and confusions shared. 'If I have to keep this damned train waiting for an hour I'll see you on your way.'

He was as good as his word. He armed her with timetables, platform numbers, lists of phrases. He enlisted the help of a small, cheerful and rotund porter who had a blessed if sketchy vocabulary of English, checked her baggage, bought her ticket. 'At La Spezia you take the train for Bagni di Lucca. You won't be there before late evening, I'm afraid. You can manage now?'

'Yes. Thank you. I'm so grateful.'

He smiled, lifted his hat. 'It's no trouble, Mrs Stowe. No trouble at all. Good luck.'

She watched his retreating figure as an exile must watch the retreating shores of home.

'Signora?' Her rotund porter beamed at her, jerked his head. '*Il treno* ees 'ere.'

'Thank you. Yes. I'm coming.'

The mountains, like the lakes, were hidden from her by the rain. With a self-possession born of desperation she manoeuvred herself and her suitcases from one train to another at La Spezia; and for once the gods smiled upon her. This time there really was a train in ten minutes. It was a very slow train. It stopped at all stations down the long, winding valley: tiny village halts, road crossings, the odd small town that spread, clinging like ivy, up the mountainside. A river ran, churning and muddied over its rocky bed, in full spate alongside the tracks. Wind battered the windows and the mountaintops were lost in cloud. Totally exhausted Carrie dozed, and jumped awake, frightened, fearful she had missed her stop.

And then, at last, there it was. Bagni di Lucca. Not

a large station, but well lit and somehow welcoming, despite the weather. The end of the journey.

She stood by her two scuffed and dilapidated suitcases, buffeted by the wind, as the train, hissing and steaming, pulled away into the gathering dusk.

'Signora?'

She turned. A tall thin man in something approximating a uniform executed a small and sloppy salute. 'You want to get to hotel,' he said; a statement rather than a question. 'It's late, but I help. My brother, he waits outside.'

'No,' she said. 'No, I'm not going to a hotel.'

He raised his eyebrows and cocked his head enquiringly, waiting.

'But, if your brother would take me to the house— ?'

'He will take you anywhere, Signora. Anywhere.' He spread long hands and smiled disarmingly, 'For a small fee of course.'

'Yes. Yes, of course.'

He picked up her suitcases as if they weighed nothing at all. 'Where you go? You stay with the good Mrs Johnston-Smith? Many young ladies from England stay with Mrs Johnston-Smith, or perhaps Signora Webber? Ah yes, she too has many visitors.'

She hurried along the platform beside him. She had long since given up trying to keep her hat on, and had stuffed it into her pocket. The wind whipped her flying hair across her face. 'No. No, I want to go to the Villa Castellini. It's near San Marco. Do you know it?'

They had entered the small, bright booking hall. He

stopped, looking at her in surprise. 'You go up the mountain? Tonight?'

'Yes.'

He shook his head. 'Not a good idea, Signora. The weather – it's wild.'

'I can see that.' The words were wry.

'And the mountain tracks – they're dangerous in the rain. You go to hotel. For tonight. Then, tomorrow, you go up the mountain to this house.' He looked pleased with himself to have solved her dilemma so satisfactorily. 'I fetch my brother.'

'No, please—' she put out a hand to detain him. The journey had cost her much more than she – or rather Arthur – had budgeted for; to spend even one night in a hotel would stretch her sketchy resources even further. Before she had boarded the train at La Spezia she had purchased bread and cheese, cooked meat and fruit. 'I really must go to the house tonight.'

'Signora, I know a good hotel. Very cheap.' He spoke as a reasonable man in an unreasonable world. 'Believe me. It's not good to go up the mountain tonight.'

Quite unexpectedly, her patience snapped. She was tired, and cold, and not a little scared at the prospect of arriving at the empty house in the dark. To stand and argue about it with a stranger, however well meaning, was the last thing she needed. 'Good or not,' she said, shortly, 'I'm going.' She reached a hand for her suitcase.

He somehow managed to hold on to the suitcase and shrug at the same time. 'Very well, Signora, if you insist.

Come. We talk to my brother. But I tell you, he will say the same.'

They stepped outside into the teeth of the gale. Rain swept along the empty street. Shutters clattered and crashed. A wooden bench set outside a bar had overturned, and an empty can rattled along the pavement, as if kicked by an invisible child. Water ran bubbling in the gutters. Within a few steps Carrie was drenched. She turned her collar up about her ears, pulled the scarf from around her neck and battled to tie it over her blowing hair. The man led her a little way along the street, shouldered open a door. 'Eh, Mario!'

Carrie followed him, and found herself in a small bar, where several men were sitting around an oilcloth-covered table playing cards.

'Eh, Mario,' her escort said again. '*Una cliente.*'

One of the players turned; a burly, unshaven man with wiry dark hair.

Carrie's self-appointed guardian spoke swiftly in Italian, indicating Carrie with a jerk of his head as he spoke. The cardplayers watched her. Self-consciously she scraped the sodden strands of hair from her cheeks. Mario listened, grunted, shook his head.

The other man put down the suitcases the better to use his hands as he spoke again.

Mario flicked a glance at Carrie, shrugged, and shook his head again, answering his brother in a few sharp words.

The man turned to Carrie. 'He says – you see – the weather, it's too bad. It's not good to go up the mountain tonight.'

34

Suddenly, infuriatingly, Carrie felt the unwelcome and embarrassing rise of tears. In all her dreams of her arrival at the Villa Castellini nothing like this had ever figured. The stresses of the past twenty-four hours had been bad enough; to find herself now stranded here, alone, with little money and with no readily apparent means of reaching the house was almost too much for her. Obstinately she gritted her teeth. 'Please,' she said, 'tell him I'll pay.'

He shook his head. 'He won't.'

A chair scraped as one of the cardplayers stood up. He was an older man, thick-set, his square face lined and weather beaten. 'I take her,' he said, unsmiling.

Relief almost made Carrie dizzy. 'You will? Oh, thank you. Thank you so much.'

He held out a large, dirty hand, palm up.

It took Carrie a moment to understand what the gesture meant. Then, hastily, she opened her bag, took a handful of coins from her purse, dropped them into the calloused palm. The stubby fingers curled a little, encouragingly. The hand remained outstretched. She reached into her purse again.

Mario spoke explosively, making a fierce, almost threatening movement with his hand. The older man ignored him. Calmly he stowed the money in his pocket, picked up the cases.

'Come,' he said to Carrie, as he passed her.

The weather on the mountain was indeed wild. Carrie huddled within the oilskin cape provided by her taciturn driver as the donkey, an animal of skin and bone, toiled up the steep and winding track. Beneath them the lights of Bagni glittered wetly through the tossing branches of the trees, strung out along the churning river like a bright necklace. The wind was bitterly cold.

'How far?' Carrie turned her wet face to the driver, raising her voice above the storm. It was almost completely dark now. The lamps on either side of the little cart guttered and gleamed.

The man shrugged.

'Where is the house? Can we see it from here?'

He shook his head. 'No. In a moment, perhaps.'

She subsided, shivering, beneath the cold, heavy oilskin that smelled mustily of donkey.

'There,' the driver called. 'The Villa Castellini.' He lifted an arm, pointed upwards. She turned her head. They had come to a fork in the track. Ahead she could see the dim, clustered lights of San Marco. Above her the hillside climbed steeply, and against it she saw the dark bulk of the house. For a moment, through the storm-tossed woodlands she imagined she saw a light; but when she had rubbed the streaming rain from her eyes and looked again, it was gone. It must, she thought, have been a reflection – perhaps of the lamplit village ahead.

The whip cracked. The tired animal turned in a wide arc, head down, and began to pull up the steep and slippery stony track. A few moments later they were swinging through tall, rusted wrought-iron gates, set permanently ajar. Water gushed like a stream about the donkey's hooves. The wind shrieked, and a shutter banged monotonously. Carrie's silent companion manoeuvred the cart expertly in the small area in front of the house and drew up at the foot of the steps that led to the front door. Stiffly Carrie clambered from her seat. The driver made no attempt to assist her, but splashed down onto the gravel himself, swinging her suitcases from the cart and setting them on the step.

'Thank you.' With fingers that were clumsy with cold Carrie fumbled in her bag for the key. 'Would you, would you wait for a moment – just until I get the door open?' She hated the tremor in her voice, knew how close it came to a plea.

He grunted something that did not sound too unhelpful, then unhitched one of the lamps from the cart and brought it to the door. By its light Carrie fitted the key into the lock, and the door swung open. She stepped into the high-ceilinged hall, grateful to be out of the wind, though draughts whispered coldly. The driver held up the light. On a nearby table stood a lamp. Unspeaking he fished in his pocket, pulled out a box of matches. Carrie watched as with short, stubby fingers he removed the glass shade and set a match to the wick. To her surprise and relief the flame caught immediately, flared, and steadied. He set the shade back upon it, started to put the matches back in his pocket and then, abruptly, offered them to her.

'Th—thank you.' Why hadn't she thought of matches? 'Thank you,' she said, again. And then, a little shyly, '*Grazie.*'

'*Prego.*' He turned to the door, hesitated for a moment, turned his square, lined face to her. 'You sure? You stay here?'

'Yes. I'm sure.' She wasn't sure. She wasn't sure at all.

He nodded. 'Then I go.'

'Yes. Thank you. Thank you for bringing me.' There was a smell – a tang – in the air that she could not identify. She looked around. Four doors and a curving staircase that swept into darkness; the entrance hall at least was just as she remembered it. The door behind the staircase led to the small hallway that in turn led to the kitchen, she was certain of it. Her companion went back to the door, hesitated again.

'It's all right,' she said, gently, more certainly.

He grunted again. 'Arrivederci, Signora.'

'Arrivederci.'

The door closed behind him, muffling at last the noise of the storm. She heard the sound of the heavy wheels on the gravel before they were lost as he swung out onto the track again. The house whispered around her. She sniffed the air again, puzzled, still unable to identify the faint, vaguely familiar, scent in the air. After a moment she tucked the matches the driver had given her into her pocket and, leaving her suitcases where they stood, picked up the lamp and walked to the door behind the staircase, pushing it open.

The lamplight threw dancing shadows on wall and ceiling. The shutter banged still, somewhere at the top of the house, rhythmic and monotonous.

The short, flagstoned passage that led to the kitchen was exactly as she remembered it, the old stones worn and uneven beneath her feet. She recalled that, as a child, utilising this floor, she had invented an arcane and complicated game involving marbles and ball bearings, that had kept her occupied for hours but had been perilously dangerous for anyone using the passage who might step upon the things.

She was smiling at the thought and reaching a hand to the kitchen door when suddenly, like a pistol shot just above her head, a door slammed, the noise loud in the comparative quiet of the house. She started so violently that she almost dropped the lamp, then froze, straining her ears, her heart pounding in her throat. It was a full minute before she could bring herself to move.

The wind. It was the wind. What else could it be?

Moving suddenly and briskly she pushed open the kitchen door, stepped through it. Stopped, staring; and once more the heavy, frightened thudding of her heart all but choked her. Again she could see by the trembling light of the lamp she carried that the room was as she remembered it: large and uncluttered, an iron range occupying one side, a huge dresser the other, in the centre of the tiled floor a large table, with a disparate assortment of chairs about it.

And on the table the fresh remains of a simple meal. Bread, cheese, a bottle of wine.

She stood rooted to the spot.

The room was comfortably warm; the range gave off a mellow heat. And now, suddenly, she identified the smell she had detected in the air when first she had entered the hall.

Cigarette smoke.

There was someone in the house.

She was trembling so that she could barely trust

39

herself to move. Very, very carefully she set the lamp upon the table. The flame steadied. There was a three-branched wooden candelabra on the table; with hands she had to force herself to control she lit it, grateful for its flaring light.

From behind her came an utterly unmistakable sound; quick, light footsteps, coming from beyond the door through which she had just entered.

Catching her breath she turned, pressing herself back against the table, her hands gripping the edge. In her fear she felt as if every last drop of blood had drained from her body.

The door opened to reveal the slender figure of a young man. He hesitated in the doorway for a moment then came on swiftly into the room, stopping a few feet from her, exposing his face deliberately to the full blaze of the lamp and the candles. A thin, clever face beneath fine, tousled hair; narrow eyes, gleaming blue and bright in the light; a straight, shadowed mouth. In one hand he held a small torch, the other was held towards her, open, in a quick gesture of reassurance. There was a moment of silence. Then 'Carrie—' he said, 'Carrie, don't be frightened. It's me. Don't you recognise me?'

The sound that she made was something between a sob of relief and laughter. 'Leo! Oh, Leo – of course I recognise you! How could I not? Leo, Leo! What are you doing here?' In two quick steps she was fast in her cousin's arms. He was at the most only a couple of inches taller than she, but the slight body was wiry and strong, the arms that hugged her so fiercely to him crushed the breath from her body as he all but lifted her from her feet, rocking her back and forth.

'Carrie, Carrie! What in the world are you thinking of – coming here alone, and on such a night? I could have been anyone. Anyone!' He put her from him. Tilted her face towards him. 'Tears? Oh, sweetheart, don't cry.'

She sniffed valiantly. 'I'm not crying. Not really. It's just, oh it's been such a horrible journey – and I was – was very frightened when I realised there was someone here.' The tears rolled on, unchecked, down her cheeks.

With a half smile and a gesture so tender that it entirely vanquished what little was left of her fragile self-control he brushed her wet face with his fingers, pulled her to him again and held her, gently, as she sobbed against his shoulder. When at last she quietened he released her, holding her hand, drawing her to the table. 'Come on. Sit down. Have a glass of wine – don't be silly,' she had shaken her head, 'believe me it's exactly what you need. When did you last eat? I've bread, and cheese and some chicken.' He slipped her coat from her shoulders, guided her firmly to a chair, talking quietly, giving her time to collect herself. 'Eat, Carrie. It will do you good.' He grinned, suddenly, wide and boyish, a smile she remembered so well it almost brought the tears again. 'And while you're eating I'll explain what I'm doing in your house. It is your house, isn't it?'

She nodded.

He turned, walked to the door, hung her coat on a hook on the back of it. 'I thought it might be,' he said, his back to her, his voice calm, almost expressionless. 'After what happened between Grandmother and my father – well, you can't blame her, can you?'

She watched him, a suddenly shadowy figure beyond the circle of light. 'Leo, what did happen between Grandmother and Uncle John? Why did she—' she hesitated, realising that she had been going to use the word 'hate', 'dislike him so much? He was her son, after all.'

Leo shrugged. 'Who knows? I never did. Just one of those things.' He came back to the table, leaned against it, looking down at her, relaxed and smiling again, the slightly uncomfortable moment past. 'You know how these family feuds are. Love turns to hate, and all that. There's no one can hurt us as much as those we love.'

The thought rose in her mind, utterly unbidden; that's why Arthur, no matter what he may think or how hard he tries, can never really hurt me.

He leaned to pour the dark wine into the glass he had set for her. 'Do you mind if I smoke?'

'No. Of course not.' She nibbled a piece of chicken, picked up the glass, watched him as he pulled a worn and dully gleaming silver cigarette case from his breast pocket and extracted a cigarette with long, brown-stained fingers. Her tears had dried, her reason was asserting itself. 'So, what are you doing here?' she asked, undisguised curiosity in her voice.

He shrugged narrow shoulders. 'I saw a report in one of the papers at home about Uncle Henry's death. As I said, I guessed that Grandmother would have moved heaven and earth to prevent me from touching anything of hers.' His voice now was matter of fact, held no rancour. He tilted his head for a moment, blowing smoke to the ceiling. She studied the sharp line of his jaw, the slant of his cheekbone; he had, she remembered, been a handsome child; the harder lines of maturity suited him even better. She recognised suddenly that for all the familiarity of him this was not – could not be – the Leo she had once known so well. The best part of half a lifetime and the survival of the brutality of war separated the two. If she had changed from the child she once had been, how much more must he have done?

He glanced down, caught her looking at him. 'I adored her, you know,' he said, simply, and making no attempt to disguise the sudden glint of pain in his narrow eyes. 'I really did.'

'Yes.' Carrie said. She was certain it was no less than the truth; there were not many who had come within the sphere of Beatrice Swann's complex and brilliant personality and had remained untouched. Why should the grandson who in some ways so much resembled her but whose relationship with her had always been marred by the enmity between mother and son, be different?

'So,' he slid from the table, walked to the dresser, took down another glass, 'I decided to come and steal something.' He grinned again, suddenly and teasingly, lightening the mood. 'Not a very valuable something, I promise you. But just – a little something. Something to remind me of her. I assumed that if you had inherited the place you'd sell it as it stood, goods and chattels included so to speak. I didn't think you'd miss one small thing. A keepsake. Oh, I'm afraid I had to prise the shutters apart in the tower room to get in. That's why they're banging.' He poured himself wine, lifted the glass to his lips.

She was staring at him. 'Leo! How could you? How *could* you?'

The bright eyes widened and flickered at her, startled and flaring with a sudden and intemperate flash of anger. The smiling mouth straightened.

She did not notice his misinterpretation of her words. 'Why didn't you contact me? Why come here like this? *Steal* did you say? Oh, Leo for goodness' sake you must know me better than that? If you'd asked – just asked – well, of course, you can have anything. Anything you want.' She reached for his hand. 'Leo, I didn't even know if you were alive or dead. You could have contacted me. Why didn't you? We're all the family either of us has.'

The sudden, savage glitter had died. He controlled the faint tremor of his fingers with concentrated will. 'I – haven't been in England.'

'Where have you been?'

The narrow shoulders lifted again. 'Oh, here and there. After the war,' he tilted his head and drained his glass, reached for the bottle again, 'I found it hard to settle.' He smiled again, but this time with little humour. 'I'm not alone in that I think.'

'No.'

He half filled his own glass, leaned to pour the last of the wine into hers.

'Oh no, really—'

'I insist. It will, if nothing else, help you to sleep. Take it from one who knows.'

Carrie broke off a piece of bread and picked up a chunk of cheese. She had not realised just how hungry she was; few things had ever tasted so good, and the wine was inducing feelings that were quite alarmingly pleasant. 'Where were you? In the war?'

'Just about everywhere. Ypres, mostly. The Somme. The Marne at one point, with the French. They had it tough.'

'And afterwards? Where did you go?'

He made a small, dismissive gesture. 'We can talk about that later. Never mind about me, tell me about you. What are you doing here, alone?' He glanced at her ring finger. 'You've married? Why isn't he with you?'

She sipped her wine. 'He couldn't get away.' She lifted her eyes to his. 'Oh, Leo, I can't tell you how good it is to see you! I was so afraid you'd been killed. Arthur was certain of it.'

He grinned, gracelessly. 'Well Arthur, as you can clearly see, was wrong.' He picked up the empty bottle. 'They're making these things smaller and smaller, you know that? I'll open another.'

'So,' she lifted her glass, surveyed the guttering light of the candles through its dark depths. He was laughing; she had been surprised at how funny she had managed to make the difficulties of the journey sound, 'here I am. More by luck than judgement, I have to admit. It well might have been a case of the lamb to the slaughter, I fear.' She sipped the wine, settled her chin on her hand,

45

turning her head to look into his face. 'I've come to the conclusion that I'm perhaps not one of the world's great adventurers.'

He lifted his glass to her. 'With your forebears? Of course you are. You just haven't found your own adventure yet.'

She thought about that for a moment. Smiled, delightedly. 'Do you think that's it?'

'I'm sure of it.'

She yawned.

'I should go,' he said.

Carrie blinked. 'Go? Go where?'

'There's a bar in San Marco. They have a couple of rooms.'

'But, why? Why should you go?'

He spread his hands, smiling a little.

She blushed. 'Oh, Leo – don't be silly! For goodness' sake. We're cousins. We've known each other since we were children. We're as good as brother and sister. Oh, of course you must stay. You wouldn't – surely you wouldn't – leave me here alone?'

'You were ready to stay here alone before you knew I was here.'

'Well, yes. Of course I was. But now – well now I know you're here, and it's different.'

'A fine piece of feminine logic,' he said.

She yawned again, and blinked. 'Oh dear. I am sorry.' She bowed her head and pulled the last of the pins from her hair, shaking her aching head. Her heavy, straight hair slid untidily about her shoulders. She rested her face for a moment in the cup of her hands. 'I

46

haven't asked. Is there much left? I remember the place as a positive Aladdin's cave. Childhood exaggeration, I suppose. Is there anything left?'

The silence was long enough to penetrate her dazed and wine-muddled tiredness. She lifted her head. He had picked up the lamp and was holding out his hand to her. 'Come and see. Come and see your inheritance.'

He simply led her from room to room, standing at the door, holding up the lamp to illuminate the interiors.

'Leo! What in the name of heaven am I going to do with all this stuff?' She sat on the top stair of the curving staircase, surveyed in wonder the carved ivory ball she held in her hand, picked up at random in the swift tour of the house. Within the tracery of the intricately carved outer shell was another, within that another, and so on down to the tiniest carved sphere, bead sized, just visible within the complexities some master craftsman had produced in a place so removed, both in distance and in time that she could hardly comprehend it. 'It will take me a month of Sundays to sort this lot out.'

'Grandmother was certainly something of a collector.' The wind still buffeted the house, though with a little less vigour. The loose shutter still banged. He lifted his head. 'Perhaps I can fix that for you before I leave.'

She closed her eyes, rubbed the back of her neck tiredly. 'I wish you wouldn't. Leave, I mean. Really I do.'

'You're asleep on your feet.'

'Yes.' She blinked her eyes open, laughing a little. 'Except I'm not even on my feet. I'm sitting down.'

He hesitated for a moment longer. 'All right,' he said. 'I'll stay. Just for tonight. Come on, back down to the kitchen with you. I'll make up a bed – no,' he held up a hand at her half-hearted protest, 'I've had a chance to find where everything is. Come on; there's tea in the cupboard beside the sink. Go and make us a pot. I'll make up a bed for you in the main bedroom. But tomorrow I'll move down to the village.'

He offered a hand to help her to stand up. She held on to it. 'You'll help me? You'll stay and help me sort the place out?'

He shook his head. 'I don't know, Carrie. I think not.' His voice was gentle.

She was too tired to argue. 'Don't talk about it now. We'll talk about it tomorrow.'

'Yes. Tomorrow.'

A bare half-hour later, aching and exhausted, she fell into a huge wooden bed that felt the most wonderfully comfortable she had ever occupied. The sheets were damp, a little coarse. The pillow was vast, and very soft. The small night light that flickered on the washstand illuminated a musty room vast in its proportions and cluttered, as was the rest of the house, with all manner of odds and ends. A huge bookcase overflowing with books made up one side of the room and in one corner stood a large and ornate oriental jar filled with ancient, mouldering pot pourri.

She snuggled sleepily beneath the covers, grateful for the comfort, grateful above all to have the great bed to herself; not once since her marriage to Arthur had she slept alone. In some odd corner of her brain she registered the fact that it was Tuesday. She smiled, sleepily and burrowed deeper, aware that, at last, the wind was dropping, and that the rain had ceased to hammer against the closed shutters. The last thing she heard in the quiet of the house was the door of the tower room, along the corridor from the bedroom Leo had chosen for her, clicking shut.

During the night she jumped awake once, thinking she heard someone cry out. She lay for a moment, disorientated, listening.

But the house was still. The storm had died. All was silent.

She slept again.

Chapter Three

Carrie woke next morning in the large, shadowed room and for a sleepy moment could recall neither where she was, nor why she was there. Light glinted through the shutters. The house was very quiet. Somewhere beyond the window a cockerel crowed, challenging the world.

She stirred and stretched; looked up at the high, plastered ceiling, remembering.

Leo. Leo was here. She was not, after all, alone.

With a sudden happy burst of energy she threw back the bed clothes and on bare feet ran across the cold tiles of the floor to the window, wrestling impatiently with the unfamiliar catches of the shutters, throwing them open with a protesting shriek from the rusty hinges.

She stood quite still, her breath held.

The foothills of the Garfagnana rolled before her beneath the palest and clearest of skies. The sun had not yet topped the high rise to the east, but the air was sweet and brilliant with its light. Stormwater still cascaded down the hillsides, gleaming and sparkling, streaming from rock to ravine in glittering ribbons, disappearing into the rainwashed woodlands to join the swollen, foaming waters of the river below. The clay-tiled roofs of San Marco tumbled down the mountainside beneath her. Somewhere a woman was singing. Woodsmoke hung fragrantly in the calm air.

She rested her elbows on the sill, leaned out of the window, her hair swinging about her face like a child's.

Bagni di Lucca nestled in its valley beneath her, the tree-shaded houses and their gardens scattered like childrens' toys along the banks of the flooding River Lima and up the green sides of the valley. She could see the road that ran alongside the river; could trace, too, the winding track up which she had come last night as it meandered through the trees. Arched bridges spanned the torrent that was the storm-swollen Lima, the waters dashing themselves against the ancient stone supports that had stood against them for so long.

From the hilltop in the east, as she watched, the first glittering rays of the sun struck in blades of light across the valley.

She smiled in sheer delight.

'Hey, sleepyhead. Aren't you ever coming down to breakfast?'

She looked down. Beneath her, standing on the gravel drive, hands on hips, head flung back as he laughed up at her stood Leo, in shirtsleeves and flannels, his slight figure foreshortened by the height.

She waved. 'I'm coming! Wait – I'm coming.'

She flew to her cases, flung one of them on to the bed and opened it, grabbed slacks and a jumper, tumbling the carefully folded clothes in her haste, slamming the lid back down, leaving the sleeve of a blouse trailing. Almost dancing with excitement and energy she pulled the clothes on, dragged a brush through her hair, shoved her feet into a scuffed pair of sandals, hopping in her impatience as she struggled to buckle the narrow strap. Then she was out of the room and running down the stairs. 'Leo? Leo, where are you?'

He was in the kitchen. He looked up, smiling, as she burst in. The remains of last night's meal had been cleared away. There was fresh bread on the table, and a chunk of cheese. Coffee bubbled on the black stove, filling the air with its fragrance, making her mouth water.

'Good morning,' she said. 'Good morning, Good morning, Good morning!'

His smile widened. 'That's a lot of mornings?'

She swung around the table to plant a light kiss on his cheek. 'It's a lot of "goods", actually. Gosh, I'm hungry. As a hunter.' She broke a chunk of warm bread from the loaf, bit into it. 'This is wonderful. And fresh!'

'There's a baker's in San Marco. Only a little place, but the bread's good.'

'You've been out already?'

'Already?' He came to the table with the coffee, laughing at her. 'Do you know what the time is?'

She shook her head.

'It's ten o' clock.'

She stared at him, her mouth full. Swallowed. 'It can't be.'

'It is.'

She put a hand to her mouth, stifling laughter. 'I've slept till *ten o' clock*? Oh, Leo, I can't have. It's outrageous! Whatever would Arthur think? *And* I haven't so much as washed my face or cleaned my teeth. Oh, I'm sorry—' she stopped, ducked her head, sudden colour lifting in her cheeks, 'I'm acting like a child.'

He put out a carelessly affectionate hand to ruffle her hair. 'What's wrong with that?'

The silence was a long one. She put down her bread, took the coffee he offered her, not looking at him. She set the steaming cup on the table, and self-consciously smoothed her hair, twisting it into a knot that immediately fell apart.

'Carrie? What's wrong?'

She shook her head. Nothing would have persuaded her to tell him Arthur's reaction to what he deemed to be childish. 'Nothing. Honestly, nothing. It's just – this isn't real, is it?' She lifted a sober face to his. 'It's silly to enjoy something too much. It only gets taken away from you. Or, well, you have to give it up.'

He pulled a chair to the table, the scrape of the legs on the tiled floor loud in the quiet. Sunshine flooded the room.

Carrie picked up the piece of bread again, shredded it absently into crumbs that spilled untidily upon the table-top.

'Real?' he asked at last, very quietly, 'What does that mean? And who takes things from you?'

She shook her head, unexpectedly unable to speak.

'I'll tell you what's real, Carrie.'

She glanced up at him. He was not looking at her. She

53

found herself noticing the curl of the fine brown lashes that, gilded in the light, guarded his eyes.

'Now is real. This is real. What we can touch is real.' The lashes lifted. 'Death is real. Death is very real indeed. If the war taught me nothing else it taught me that. When you think about it, death is the only reality that in the end we all, inevitably, share.'

'That's horrible,' she said, after a moment.

'It's the truth. The simple truth.'

For a second or two it was as if the blue gleam of his eyes had mesmerised her. She sat silent, watching him. 'It's still horrible,' she said, and had the oddest feeling that they were not the words that she had wanted to say.

'So's this coffee,' he said, after the briefest of silences.

'No, it's not.'

'It's stewed. Remind me not to trust you to make the coffee if this is the way you like it. I'll make some more.' Briskly he stood, and the mood, as he had obviously intended, was broken. 'I called in at the bar at San Marco this morning,' he said, over his shoulder. 'They have a room. I'll move down there today.'

'Leo—'

He turned. 'Carrie – I'm sorry, but I insist. I'll only be just down the road if you need me. I'll stay for—' he hesitated, 'a day or two.'

'A day or two?' She spread helpless hands. 'Leo, please. From what I saw last night it's going to take weeks to sort this place out. I mean – where am I going to start? What on earth am I going to do with everything?'

'There's an attic full of tea chests upstairs.' He was soothing. 'And I'll help you – I will help you. For a couple of days. We'll get more done than you imagine.'

'But, I have to go to Lucca – to see the lawyer – won't you wait? Won't you please stay?'

'A day or two, Carrie. Then we'll see.'

After breakfast they went into the garden, the two or three acres of which scrambled up the hillside behind the house in a series of varying sized terraces. It was, as Carrie had expected, sadly neglected. Ivy-smothered walls were crumbling, steps and paths were uneven and overgrown – some indeed had disappeared altogether beneath the invasion of grass and weeds, heather and brambles. Self-rooted trees grew at odd angles in the terrace banking, some of which had deteriorated so badly it no longer served its original purpose at all; in many places one terrace had slid into another in a jumble of bricks and stony soil, muddy still from the recent rain. Here and there, however, patches recognisable as a cultivated garden survived: an arbour of roses, run wild and woody, a semi-circular box hedge with a stone seat overlooking the valley, the odd flowering shrub, and everywhere the ornamental trees of which Beatrice Swann had been so fond. Many of them were old now, and past their prime; but most still stood, tall and beautiful, fresh-budded in the sunshine.

'There's a place,' Carrie stopped, looking up the hillside, hand shading her eyes, 'that I particularly want to find. I have a picture of it at home. A sort

55

of arbour. With a fountain. You must remember it. We used to play there as children. Have you found it?'

Beside her Leo shook his head. 'I've hardly been out here.'

'I think,' she nibbled her lip, searching her memory, 'in fact I'm sure – it's somewhere over there.' She pointed. 'There was a large tree – an acacia, I think. There, you see? Surely that's it? Let's go and look.'

'Can you get up there in those shoes?'

She grimaced down at her feet, already filthy from the mud and dirt. 'Not very practical, are they? Never mind. Let's try.'

Slipping and sliding they scrambled up a steep bank, to find themselves on a fairly level strip of terrace, at the back of which was a small flight of stone steps curving into an overgrown shrubbery. 'This is the way, I'm sure it is.' Excitedly Carrie pushed through the shrubbery, winced as a small branch whipped across her face.

'Careful. Why don't you let me go first?'

'I'm all right, honestly. Watch your step here, it's a bit slippery. Oh, Leo, look! There – I said it was here.'

They had emerged into a paved area several square yards wide, sheltered on one side by a sheer, dripping rock face upon which grew ferns and lichens and tiny wild flowers and enclosed on the other three by the overgrown shrubbery through which they had just come. Above them the graceful acacia lifted its arms to the sunlit sky.

'The fountain.' Carrie said softly. 'Oh, Leo – you must remember it?'

The water in the pool was dark and stagnant. The graceful nymph in whose hands once the water had splashed and danced stood, dirty, lichen covered, empty handed, but still, to Carrie's eyes, heart-wrenchingly beautiful. The playful dolphins that tumbled at her feet had a bright life of their own, despite the dirt and slime that caked them.

'Oh, and look at this one!' Carrie ran to a small statue that stood by the rock wall; a young boy, naked, holding a jar from which the natural water still ran into a clogged pool at his feet. 'We used to call him George. Why did we call him George, for goodness' sake?'

Leo shook his head, smiling.

'It was always so cool here in the summer.' Carrie perched on a rock, arms linked around her knees. 'You surely remember that? We used to spend so much time here—' she trailed off, her dark eyes suddenly thoughtful.

Leo, still silent, still watching her affectionately, reached into his pocket for his cigarette case.

'But then again, perhaps we didn't,' Carrie said. 'Spend as much time up here as I think we did, I mean. This is the picture, you see. The one I have at home.' She tilted her head to look at him. The sun was behind his head, sheening the sharp planes of his face, turning the fine, straight hair that constantly fell across his forehead to gold. For a disconcerting instant he was the image of the boy she remembered. Then he moved, tapping the cigarette on the case, turning his head to look at the fountain, and the impression was lost. 'I've looked at it so often. Dreamed about it so much. Perhaps that's it?'

'I certainly don't recall it as well as you seem to. As a matter of fact, I'm not sure I'd ever have remembered it was here at all.' He leaned beside her. In the silence a bird sang, and water ran musically amongst the shadowed, fern-cloaked rocks.

'Leo?'

'Hmm?'

She rested her chin on her knees. 'Can I ask you something?'

'Well, of course.'

'Why didn't you come down to greet me when I first arrived last night? Why did you give me such a fright?'

The silence was a long one.

'I'm not – not complaining, you understand,' she said at last, a little timidly, fearful she had angered him, spoiled the ease between them. 'I just – wondered that's all.'

'Don't be silly. You have every right to complain.' He turned, moving lightly, hunkered down beside her so that he was looking up into her face, the usually narrow eyes were wide and very blue in the sunlight. 'First – I didn't know it was you until you got out of the cart and the lamp shone on your face. Second—' he hesitated. Pulled a small, self-deprecating face. 'Second – well, to be honest my first inclination was to leave the house in the same way as I had entered it. Clandestinely through the window of the tower room.'

58

'You mean, you would have gone? Without even talking to me?'

'It crossed my mind.' The words were dry.

'But why? Oh, Leo, why would you have done that?'

He stood up, shaking his head, half-smiling. 'Perhaps, my Carrie, because I didn't much fancy being caught stealing your property?' There was a certain sardonic defiance in the set of his head, the sudden steadiness of his veiled gaze.

'Oh, for heaven's sake! I wish you'd stop using that silly word.' She scrambled from the rock, walked to the fountain, tossed a small stone into the still water and watched the ripples widening, glimmering, in the dappled light. 'I told you. You can have anything you want. You're as entitled to it as I am.'

He grinned suddenly. 'How would your Arthur feel about that? You haven't told me much about him, but from what little you have said—' he spread his hands and shrugged a little, questioningly.

For a moment her stomach churned unpleasantly. 'What Arthur doesn't know,' she said, composedly, 'Arthur doesn't have to feel anything about. Does he?' and was astonished at the sheer, wilful delight of simply speaking the words. Ridiculously, she wanted to say them again.

He laughed. 'True. Now – come on, cousin. We really can't waste all day, you know. You said yourself that the house could take weeks to clear and you haven't seen the half of it yet. Just wait till you see it in daylight. It's a cross between a museum and one of those lucky dip barrels you get at village fêtes.'

As she turned to follow him something caught her eye. She bent to pick it up. 'Leo, you've dropped a packet of cigarettes.' She held them out to him. 'Funny. They're soaking wet.'

He took the unopened cardboard pack from her, tucked it in his pocket. 'Damn it. They must have fallen from my pocket. Never mind, I've some in my case and more in the house.' His smile was disarming, 'Not a habit I will ever be able to overcome, I fear. Here – take my hand – this bit's awfully slippery.'

They decided, sensibly, that the only thing to do was to catalogue everything, room by room, and for Carrie to decide as she went along what to keep and what to dispose of.

'But what will I do with the stuff I can't keep?'

'Sell it,' he said, promptly. 'Ship it back to England, and let one of the auction houses have it. Carrie, we took it all very much for granted but before the war Grandmother was quite a celebrated figure in artistic circles, you know. She had a lot of friends who were famous then, or have since become so. Writers, artists, musicians. It could make these bits and pieces very collectable. Advertise. Get a couple of magazine or newspaper articles written. Nostalgia's all the thing, you know. I once met Henry James at the Hampstead house. I believe that Joseph Conrad lived there for several weeks. Shaw was one of her closest friends.'

'Yes. I do remember that.' They were in the drawing room, a large and charming room, cluttered in unlikely fashion with the kind of furniture that might have graced an English Victorian country house, right down to the grand piano over which was draped, like a faded cobweb, a disintegrating silk shawl. Every dust-filmed surface held its quota of statues, vases, dishes, pieces of glass and of silver. A filthy but particularly fine marble bust of a child gazed dreamily into space from one of the three or four small tables scattered about the room. As in so many of the rooms of the Villa Castellini a huge bookcase stuffed full of volumes of every size, shape and age took up an entire wall. Of the other three walls one was graced by the four tall windows that opened on to the shady verandah outside and the other two were all but entirely covered in pictures, some so dark and smoke stained that it was difficult if not impossible to tell from any distance what their subject might be. Carrie was sitting on the floor, her legs tucked beneath her, surrounded by heaps of books. 'Ouch!' With some difficulty she stood up, stretching, 'My foot's gone to sleep.' She rubbed it vigorously, then flexed it, strolled shoeless to the window, stood looking out across the hills. With the afternoon a few wisps of cloud had appeared in the sky, high and unthreatening and their shadows chased swift across the hillsides. The light was golden. In the blue distance of the mountain air a bird wheeled, gracefully, wings outstretched, gliding on the wind, too tiny, too distant to be identified. She watched its flight with something close to longing. 'I met him once, I think. Shaw, that is. So Mother always said.' She stood with her head thrown back, watching the bird. 'What was it he said? About the two great tragedies of life?' Her eyes followed still the great, free

61

arcs of movement above her. 'One is not to get your heart's desire. And the other—'

'Is to get it,' he said, from the shadows behind her.

'Yes.' She turned, quickly, shrugging. 'Silly, isn't it?'

He did not reply. He was standing at a table, his back to her. She heard the clink of glass. He turned, two glasses in his hand. The subdued light gleamed in their contents, almost exactly the same ruby red as the ancient velvet curtains that draped the windows.

'An excellent port,' he said. 'The perfect antidote, I find, to philosophising.'

She laughed. 'I had a glass of wine at lunch time.' He, she could not help noticing, had finished the bottle.

'Why so you did.' His voice was light, and equable. He held out the glass. 'So it's only reasonable to carry on as you started.'

She took it. Sipped it. It was mellow, and sweet. She watched as he wandered across the room and stood looking up at a small picture. 'Have you seen this?'

She joined him. Light from the window fell upon the painting.

'The only picture of her ever painted.' Leo said. 'She had an aversion to being painted or photographed, I believe.'

'I can understand that. I don't much like it myself.' Carrie grinned, quickly, 'Photos, that is. No one's ever suggested a portrait.' She studied the picture with interest.

'Do you realise how like her you are?'

Carrie turned truly startled eyes to his. He nodded

back at the painting of Beatrice Swann. 'Look at it. Can't you see it?'

She stepped closer. The hair was certainly the same, she could see it at once, recognise despite the artist's light and flattering touch the heavy, uncontrollable, slippery weight of it. And suddenly she could see it: her grandmother's habit of constantly, almost absently, touching and tucking her hair into pins, into combs, beneath scarves. Her own habit.

The face was wide at the cheekbones, perhaps a little too narrow about the mouth. The smooth skin was the colour of olives – Beatrice Swann's mother had been Italian – the dark eyes large and expressive.

'Here. Try this.' With a swift and deft movement Leo unhooked the painting from the wall and took it to where a mirror was set upon the piano. 'There,' he said, holding it.

There could be no denying the likeness. It was not simply the hair. The skin colour – that Arthur had always referred to, dismissively, as 'sallow' – the shape of the face, of the brows, of the eyes. 'How extraordinary,' she said. 'It hadn't occurred to me.' She looked back at the picture. No classic beauty this, by any manner of means. But – interesting. She had never thought of herself as having an interesting face. However, there was a difference. She leaned forward, studying the picture. Feature by feature she could see the likeness. But, indefinably, something was different. It took a moment to see what it was.

She turned away. 'You can see how strong she was,' she said. 'Something about the eyes.'

Leo was studying the picture intently. 'Yes. But it's more than that, isn't it? The set of the head, perhaps. Just look at her.' He smiled. 'She looks like a queen.'

'Yes. She does.' Carrie looked back out of the long, velvet-draped window. The sun still shone. The bird still climbed and spiralled above the peaks. But somehow, indefinably, some part of the magic had gone from the afternoon. She gulped the last of her port; all but choked.

Laughing now he set the picture down and came to pat her on the back.

'I think,' she said, 'that I need some air.'

As Leo had already pointed out, the only way to get down into Bagni was either to hire a donkey, or to walk, as the locals did.

'You can often hitch a lift back. There's always someone coming up to San Marco. You're sure you won't wait? I haven't a lot to pack; it would take no time to drop my bag off at the bar.'

'No.' A little alarmingly she realised that, above all things, she did not want to be here when he left. 'I'm happy to go alone.'

'Right.' He checked his watch. 'You'll be back here by five?'

'Yes.'

He tugged her hair. 'I'll be back by then. Don't worry about supper. I'll arrange it.'

She dismissed the thought of Arthur, and tea at five thirty sharp; the tightened lips and tapping fingers if it were five minutes late, or if the sugar bowl were not set upon the tray in just the manner he liked it. 'Thank you.'

The English Cemetery at Bagni di Lucca lay on a slope on the south side of the river, a quiet enclosure surrounded and guarded by tall cypress trees. A small Chapel of Rest, at the top of the hill, presided over the peaceful tombs and memorials, most of them neatly and carefully kept, some imposing, some simple. Carrie pushed open the big wrought-iron gates and stood for a moment looking around her. In the far corner someone tended a new grave, the flowers a bright splash of colour in the clear spring sunlight. Birds sang, and the faintest of breezes whispered in the branches of the trees. Two bright butterflies danced dizzily about a stand of tall, yellow flowers. Behind her the Lima still ran in spate, foaming and churning about the white rocks of the riverbed. She climbed the shallow steps that led through a cypress-lined avenue up the hillside, stopping now and again to examine the memorials that lined it.

Sacred to the memory of the best of wives, the most affectionate of mothers – snatched after a short illness from her disconsolate family

She had always rather liked graveyards; liked the serenity of them, the stories that sprang to mind from even the simplest of inscriptions. She stopped at another.

Frederick Charles Philips, Esq. 13th King's Hussars. Battle of Waterloo

She puzzled a little over that one. Was poor Frederick

actually killed in the battle? Or had he merely wished the world to be reminded that he had been there?

Baron Julius de Sass Now there indeed was a name to conjure with, *Privy Counsellor to HIM the Emperor of Russia.*

Beatrice was certainly buried amongst exalted company.

She made her way to the Chapel, pausing by the door to read yet another simple but telling inscription.

Nelly Erickson. Died of Spanish fever November 15th 1918, while working for the relief of the refugees in the Great War

Poor Nelly. November 1918. Less than five years ago. Carrie wondered how old she had been when she died. Carrie herself, born with the century, had been eighteen years old when the war finished, and a year off marrying Arthur. Why had she done it? Why hadn't she done what Nelly Erickson and the woman buried beside her – Rose Elizabeth Cleveland who had died within a week of her – had done? She stood for a long time, head bent, staring sightlessly at the two inscriptions.

You married Arthur because, quite simply, you weren't strong enough – brave enough – to do anything else. Lie to the world, Carrie Stowe, but don't lie to yourself. You could not have done what these women did. You don't have the courage.

From the corner of her eye she saw movement. She lifted her head, suddenly and uncomfortably certain that she was being watched. On the far side of the cemetery, a shadow in shadows, a small figure stood, very still, black clad and veiled. As Carrie looked towards her the old woman turned, walking slowly and with difficulty towards the gate. Carrie followed her with her eyes, intrigued. At the gate the woman glanced back, and seeing Carrie watching stood for a moment, quite still, before turning away.

'You must be Mrs Stowe?' The light, busy voice took her entirely by surprise. 'Beatrice's granddaughter?'

Carrie turned. A large lady in a floral dress and a wide, battered straw hat was beaming at her.

'I – yes. That's right.'

'Mary Webber. So pleased to meet you.' A square, capable hand was extended. 'You've come to see your grandmother's grave, of course.'

'Yes. And Uncle Henry's.'

'Of course, of course. Yes. Poor Henry.' Mary Webber leaned close, confidentially. 'He wasn't quite – as others are, you know.'

'Yes. I do know.'

Completely unembarrassed the other woman beamed again. 'Oh, well, certainly you do. How silly of me.'

'Could you tell me where Grandmother's grave is? I had intended to ask my cousin, but I forgot.'

'It's over there, next to her brother's. She had insisted that the plot be saved. By the large tree, you see?' Mary Webber turned surprised eyes upon her. 'Your cousin?'

'My cousin Leo. He's been staying at the Villa for a few days.'

'Has he indeed?' Nondescript brows climbed almost to an equally nondescript hairline. 'I don't think we knew that? And you say he's been to the cemetery?'

'Yes.' Leo had told her that morning, when she had mentioned her own intention of visiting Beatrice's grave. 'He was very fond of our grandmother.'

'Well, well. How odd. I spend a lot of time here, you see. My dear Cyril – he's over there' she gestured, vaguely. 'I don't recall any strange young men around.'

Carrie laughed a little. 'He's not that strange.'

The woman looked at her blankly, then snorted with laughter. 'Oh, good. Very good. Of course not. But, you see my dear, we're a very small community here – the British community that is – and we all tend to know each other rather well. That's how we knew you'd be coming. Dear Mr Fawcett is very friendly with a colleague of the lawyer you've come to see. Signor Bellini – a lovely man – you'll like him. So word has gone round, you understand? You must come to supper. Soon. How long will you be staying?' Mary Webber seemed to have perfected the art of talking without taking a breath.

'I – don't know.'

'I'm at the Continentiale – a permanent resident, you know – just look me up if you need anything. Anything at all.'

'I will, Mrs Webber. Thank you very much.'

'No trouble. No trouble at all.'

Carrie pointed. 'There was an old lady over there a moment ago. By my grandmother's grave. Do you know who she was?'

'Oh, that'll be Maria. She comes most days. She was nurse and companion to Beatrice, and to her brother, when they were children – oh, donkeys' years ago. She

68

must be pushing ninety if she's a day. She was devoted to Beatrice. Quite devoted.'

Carrie glanced over to the gate through which the old woman had disappeared. 'Why, of course. I remember Grandmother mentioning her, often. I had no idea she could still be alive. Where does she live? Do you know?'

'Oh, yes, everyone knows old Maria. She lives in one of the houses down by the Ponte di Serraglio.'

'I'd like to meet her.'

'I'm sure you will, my dear, I'm sure you will. I'll arrange it for you if you like. She's a cantankerous old thing, mind.'

'Well – thank you.' A little awkwardly Carrie put out her hand again. 'It's been very nice to meet you.'

The other woman smiled, comfortably, and instead of taking the proffered hand slipped her arm companionably through Carrie's. 'No trouble, my dear, no trouble at all. We're all friends here, you know. Come, I'll show you the graves. Oh, and before you leave you really must see our most famous tomb – over there, see it? The small recumbent figure with the dog at its feet? Louise de la Ramée – otherwise known as 'Ouida' – a very famous novelist; she was born in Bury St Edmunds, can you believe it? Lived most of her life here surrounded by dogs – well, there's no accounting for tastes, I always say. To each his own and all that.'

Carrie allowed herself to be escorted, via the novelist's grave, that certainly was the most outstanding in the cemetery, to the quiet corner under a vast, budding chestnut tree where three tombs, obviously of varying ages, stood above ground. The oldest was weathered and dark, covered in lichen. The inscription was brusque and unrevealing. *Leonard Johnstone. b. 1842. d. 1867.*

'Johnstone?' Carrie asked.

'Why, your grandmother's maiden name, my dear. Johnstone. Her father was an Englishman married to an Italian. Very beautiful, so everyone says. Beatrice became a Swann when she married.'

'Oh. Of course. Silly of me.' Leonard Johnstone. 1842 to 1867. Beatrice's brother had died tragically young. 'What did he die of, do you know?'

There was a short but somehow significant silence. Carrie glanced at her companion. She was standing with pursed lips, looking at the tomb. 'We-ell. It's said—'

'What?'

'It's said in the village that there was something—' the woman hesitated, 'well, that there was something a little strange about his death. Did no one in the family ever say anything?' she threw a sideways glance at Carrie that was sharp with curiosity.

Carrie shook her head. 'No one ever mentioned him so far as I remember. I knew of his existence, of course. That's about all.'

'Very close they were, he and your grandmother. He died, oh, only a few months before she married your grandfather.'

Carrie turned amused eyes upon her. 'And people still talk about it? Why, that was more than fifty years ago!'

70

Mary Webber laughed. 'Oh, yesterday, my dear, yesterday so far as Bagni di Lucca is concerned.'

'So, what does Bagni di Lucca say about his death? Why was it – strange?'

The woman leaned a little closer, spoke quietly, for all the world, Carrie thought exasperatedly, as if they were surrounded by people instead of being entirely alone on a sunny Tuscan hillside. 'He was, it seems, a very sensitive young man. People mention – suicide.'

'Oh. How awful.' Sobered, she looked again at the tomb with its stark inscription. 'How awful,' she said again, softly.

'It's just a rumour, of course,' the other woman said. 'I don't know anyone who would say it was the proven truth. Just a rumour.'

Carrie had moved to the middle tomb. Beatrice's last resting place was small and made of marble, wreathed and decorated with carved vine leaves. Like her brother's, the inscription was less than flowery. *Beatrice Swann. Born 1846. Died 1912.*

'They none of them went in much for epitaphs,' Mary Webber said, beside her. 'See, here's Henry. The same. *Henry Swann. Born 1868. Died 1922.*'

'Three lives,' Carrie said, quietly.

The other woman bent to pull up a stand of straggling weeds. 'We all come to it, my dear. We all come to it.' She straightened. 'Well, I'll leave you then. Don't forget; the Continentiale. You can't miss it, it's in the main street. Anything you want – anything at all.'

'Thank you.'

Carrie stood for a long time after the other woman

had moved off into the graveyard, shoulders hunched a little, her hands in her cardigan pockets. The breeze whispered about her, stirring her hair. She rested a gentle hand upon the cool marble of her grandmother's tomb, tracing the simple words.

Thank you, she said in her mind. Thank you.

As she left the cemetery, Mary Webber waved cheerfully.

As Leo had said, it was easy enough to get a lift up the mountain; within minutes of starting up the track a cart drawn by a plodding mule had stopped beside her. She returned the gleaming smile of the young man who drove it. On the seat next to him sat a pretty young woman, advanced in pregnancy, obviously his wife, a small child on her lap.

'San Marco?' the young man asked, pleasantly.

'Oh, yes. Please.'

He spoke rapidly in Italian, waving his free hand.

'I'm terribly sorry.' She was embarrassed. 'I don't speak Italian.' She tried the one sentence she had mastered. '*Mi scusi. Non parlo italiano.*'

His grin widened. He turned in his seat, indicated the empty cart. Made a sweeping, courteously welcoming gesture with his hand, obviously inviting her to climb aboard.

She laughed. '*Molte grazie.*'

'*Prego.*'

She scrambled on to the tailboard, sat with her legs swinging as the mule toiled on and the springless cart rattled up the winding track. Behind her she could hear the two young people talking softly. Before her, as they climbed, vistas opened, and shifted with each turn. The air was clear and cool and smelled still of the storm. Steadily diminishing streams ran and bubbled down the hillsides and across the track, washing away the soil and leaving the rock exposed, clean and bare as bone. The mule's hooves splashed in water. They passed small huts and houses, doors and shutters open to the evening air. Chickens scratched and strutted about the yards. Dogs barked as the cart laboured noisily past. A lean cat slept upon a stone wall. A small, handsome boy in ragged shirt and trousers, a bright scarf tied gypsy-style about his neck, sat upon a rock, his herd of black goats quietly cropping around him. He lifted a hand. The driver called something and laughed, and the boy replied, laughing too.

The sun was low over the mountains now. One side of the valley was already in shadow. The woodlands were still, and shady, and smelled of wet earth and of the sweet, unfurling buds of spring.

Carrie took a long breath. As they turned a bend in the track she glanced up and caught a glimpse of the Villa Castellini above her; it must have been from here that she had first seen it last night. Last night! She smiled a little. It seemed a lifetime ago.

The sun had dipped behind the mountain, leaving the sky still radiant with light.

Leo was waiting for her. Leo, and supper, and the long, cool evening.

As they passed the turn for the house she jumped from the cart, calling her thanks. '*Grazie. Molte grazie!*'

'*Prego*.' The young couple smiled and waved. She stood for a moment watching them move out of sight round the corner then turned and set off with a light heart up the path to the house.

Leo had laid supper on the kitchen table; meat, and cheese and bread and butter, with a jar of pickled vegetables. 'Hardly a feast, I'm afraid.'

'It's wonderful.' She broke off a piece of cheese and popped it in her mouth, watching as he poured wine into two glasses. 'What a fascinating place the cemetery is. Don't you think?'

'Hm? Oh yes.'

'All those people, all those stories. The writer who lived with all the dogs – what was the name?'

He shook his head, smiling. 'He can't have been all that well known if neither of us can remember.'

She glanced at him, surprised. 'He? No – I mean the woman – the woman with the little dog at her feet. You must have seen her? She stands out above all the others.' She clicked her fingers. 'Louise. That was it. Louise Someone-or-other. She was born in Bury St Edmunds. And then there are the two nurses who died of Spanish flu.'

'I didn't see that.'

'They're right by the chapel. What a tragedy, to come here to help people, and then to die so young.'

'Yes.'

She nibbled thoughtfully at the cheese. 'Strange, the inscriptions for Grandmother, and Uncle Henry, and Great-Uncle Leonard.'

74

He stood leaning gracefully against the table, sipping his wine, his eyes veiled, almost wary. 'Strange? How, strange?'

She shrugged. 'Well everyone else seems to have gone in for full-scale and flowery epitaphs; life stories, some of them. And there are our three; just their names and the dates.'

He watched her for a moment. 'What else do you need?'

'I don't know.' Absently she took the glass he was offering, sipped it. 'Something. Some memory, perhaps? Some word of love?'

He said nothing.

'Leo?' she asked, after a moment.

He looked at her, waiting. She lifted her eyes to his. And for a startling moment could neither speak nor look away.

'Yes?' he prompted.

She blinked. Her heart was beating in a most peculiar, almost alarming, fashion. She cleared her throat. 'I met a woman in the cemetery. A Mary Webber. Leo – had you ever heard a rumour that Great-Uncle Leonard killed himself?'

He shook his head. 'No.'

'Apparently that's what people think.'

He laughed a little. 'Gossip,' he said. 'Pure gossip. If it had been so, surely we would have known it? Even family secrets can't be kept forever and – for goodness' sake – it must be fifty or so years ago.'

'Yes.'

He pushed himself away from the table. 'Come on.

Eat. Then I've got something to show you. Something I found this afternoon.'

'Oh? What is it?'

He grinned, mischievous and affectionate, and once more her heartbeat quickened, treacherously. 'Wait. I'll show you later.'

'There.' He had pushed the remains of the meal to the far end of the table to clear a space in front of her.

'What are they?' She looked at the battered books he had laid before her.

'Take a look.'

There were four of them, leather bound, with no legend on the spine, nor on the cover. Gingerly she opened one. It was handwritten in scrawled copperplate. On the first page there was a pencil sketch, very creditably executed, of the Villa Castellini. And beneath it the words *Beatrice Johnstone. Her Journal. 1864*

'Leo!'

He smiled, watching her excitement.

She turned the pages. This was, she saw at once, no meticulous, day-by-day diary, but an erratic, lucid account, punctuated by drawings and some small water-colours, of the eighteen-year-old Beatrice's enthusiasms and discoveries.

'*We went up the mountain today. The weather was simply glorious, the air as intoxicating as wine. The flowers spread across the meadows like a perfumed cloak.* "And 'tis my faith that every flower Enjoys the air it breathes" *Wordsworth – and I take no credit; Leonard quoted it at me – of course—*'

She turned another page. A small watercolour of a hill village, nestling on a vine-covered slope, was accompanied by the brief caption '*6th June. Visited San Antonio. Most marvellous church. The Madonna made me cry. I wonder why?*' Then, in different ink, '*Leonard says because of the tears she sheds for us. Perhaps he's right?*'

'Leo – these are wonderful!'

'Aren't they?' He pulled one of the journals towards him, opened it at random. '"*9th September*" – this is –' he turned to the front of the book '1866. "*Papa is here. He took us to Siena. What a city it is! How full of ghosts, of violence and of beauty! Poor Leonard found it difficult. I loved it.*" There's a picture, look – isn't it marvellous?'

Carrie had lined the books up, with the front covers open. 'There's one missing.'

'Oh?'

He came to stand behind her, looking over her shoulder. She could sense his excitement, his pleasure, sparking from hers. She resisted the all but overpowering urge to reach up and take his hand. She pointed. '1864. 1865. You've got 1866. And there's 1868. Where's 1867?'

He shook his head. Reached for the book inscribed as being the journal for 1866. 'Perhaps she condensed two years into one book?' He flicked through. Shook his head again. 'No. This ends in early November '66. They went back to the London house for the winter.'

'There weren't any others?'

'No. Not unless it's been put on another shelf. We

77

can look tomorrow.' He moved away, set his glass on the table. 'Well, I should be going, I think. Do you need some help clearing this away?'

She could not conceal her dismay. 'You're going? Already?'

He turned. Studied her, suddenly intent. Helpless colour flooded her face. 'Yes, Carrie,' he said, gently, 'I'm going. You surely cannot have failed to realise what a very small community this is? I will not – *will not*' he emphasised, 'compromise you. Believe me, I know these people. They have nothing better to do with their time but to talk and to speculate.'

'But we're cousins! We've known each other since we were children. And no one even knew you were here!'

'But they know now.' He smiled, gentle still. 'Don't they?'

She nodded.

'It's best that I go. I'll be back in the morning. When are you going to Lucca?'

'Thursday.'

'Right. If it suits you I'll stay around at least until then.'

She fought, and won, the battle to prevent herself from pleading with him. 'All right. Until Thursday.'

Two more days. At least two more days.

He picked up his jacket, shrugged it on to his narrow shoulders, tossed his hair away from his eyes. 'Don't forget. If you need me I'm at the bar, just down the way there. Don't worry; you're perfectly safe here.'

'I'm not worried.' She was surprised to realise it was nothing less than the truth.

She called him as he reached the door; just to see him turn, just, once more, to have the narrow, blue gleam of his gaze rest on her. She smiled, very brightly. 'You haven't chosen your keepsake.'

'Tomorrow,' he said. 'Tomorrow will do.'

She stood for a long time, leaning against the table, watching the door that had closed very quietly behind him. Then, briskly, she turned, looked first at the dirty plates, then at the journals.

And with no qualms at all settled down to read.

Chapter Four

'I've been thinking,' Carrie said, next morning at breakfast. 'The missing journal – it's from the year Leonard died. I wonder if that's significant?'

'Significant?' Leo sent her a quick, questioning look. 'In what way?' He looked tired, she thought, his thin face drawn and oddly shadowed, as if he had not slept well.

'Well – doesn't it strike you as at all strange?'

He shook his head. 'Not really. Have you looked for it?'

Carrie finished her mouthful of bread and cheese. 'Yes. I spent an hour or so this morning, before you came, going through the bookshelves in the drawing room. It isn't there, that I can see.'

'Perhaps it's in another room? There are books all over the house.'

'Could be. Perhaps it will turn up. I hope so.' She put her elbows on the table, pushed her hair behind her ears. 'You must read them, Leo. They're fascinating. It's as if—' she hesitated, 'well, I know it's a bit fanciful, but it's as if Grandmother – Beatrice – is talking to you. She's eighteen years old, and full of life. Full of questions. Full of happiness. Devoted to Leonard – she obviously adored him – cosseted by Maria. It must have been a quite marvellous life. She loved this house so much, even then. You can see why she finally came here to live.' She got up from the table, wandered to the door, stood, hands linked in front of her, looking out towards the mountains. Morning mist wreathed them, rolling down into the valley, cloaking the woods and hiding the rooftops. The sun shone from a sky of patchy, spacious blue and billowing cloud. 'I'm much afraid that I'm coming to love it myself,' she said, very quietly.

She heard his movement behind her, sensed as he came to stand beside her, but did not turn. His silence was sympathetic. They both knew there was nothing to be said.

'Here be dragons,' Carrie said, softly, after a moment.

'I'm sorry?'

She smiled. 'Here be dragons. They used to write it on maps in ancient times. The mysterious and perilous edges of the world. Places of enchantment. Here be dragons.' She pointed to where cloud wisped about the high rock. 'Don't you think it looks as if there might be dragons up there in the mountains?'

'Yes,' he said. 'It does.'

She turned. He was standing very close, their faces almost level. She was suddenly aware of her heartbeat, steady and strong, a drumbeat he must surely hear. His

81

eyes, half closed as he looked at her, were blue as the sunlit skies. 'I wish,' she said, 'that there were such things. As dragons, I mean.'

He smiled a little, the disturbing eyes still searching her face. 'You haven't changed, in all these years, you know that? Not a bit.'

She managed at last to tear her gaze from his. Looked down at her hands. 'You mean I was odd then and I'm as odd as ever now?'

His narrow hand moved to tug her hair lightly, teasingly. 'Something like that.'

She lifted her head, spoke quickly. 'Leo – please – will you come to Lucca with me tomorrow? You needn't come to the lawyer's with me if you don't want to, but I should so like your company.'

He hesitated for the briefest of moments. Then he smiled, the intent look gone from his face. 'All right. If you want me to.'

'And – you won't leave just yet? You'll stay and help me?'

The hesitation was longer this time.

'Leo? Please?' She did not care that she was pleading; it came to her suddenly that she had never wanted anything so much as this. 'Please stay for a while. I'll never manage on my own.'

'I'm sure you would. Whatever you may think it strikes me that a girl who contrives to travel halfway across Europe on her own and then laugh about it wouldn't be put off by this—' he waved a hand, indicating the house and its contents, 'but—' In that last precarious moment's hesitation she held her breath, 'but, all right. If you really want me to, I'll stay. For a little while anyway.'

They spent the morning in the drawing room, making lists, gathering like items together, dusting and cleaning glass and silver and intricate little statuettes.

'Oh, Leo – just look at this. Isn't she gorgeous?' Carrie held up a figure of a girl, less than six inches tall. The figure, a jug in her hand, bent gracefully as if to a pool of water, her hair swinging about her face. 'Oh, I must keep this! I couldn't let her go. Leo?' She looked up, realising he had not replied. 'What's that you've found?' She scrambled to her feet, wiping her hands on her skirt and, still holding the little figurine, joined him at the table where he was bent over a sheaf of sketches, studying them intently. 'Oh, Leo. They're lovely.'

'Aren't they? Bakst I would guess.'

'Who?'

'Leon Bakst. He's a Russian artist – designs costumes and settings for the Ballet Russe in France – you must have heard of him?'

'Vaguely.' She bent beside him, looking at the pictures. A few lines, the odd, violent splash of colour and a figure moved upon the page, the essence of dance, savagely beautiful in a barbaric costume of bright-patterned fabric that served to emphasise rather than to hide the elegant, athletic, oddly androgynous grace of the body of the dancer. Leo touched the sketch gently with a long finger. 'Nijinsky,' he said, 'I think this must be Nijinsky.' There was a note in his voice that was almost reverence.

She smiled. 'Even I've heard of him.' She looked at Leo with curiosity in her eyes. 'You like the ballet?'

'Oh, yes. I'd go so far as to say I love it. As a matter of fact I once actually saw Nijinsky dance – in Paris, just before the war. *L'Après-Midi d'une Faune*. It was an utterly unforgettable experience. His problems since have been tragic, for the world as well as for himself; the man is undoubtedly the greatest dancer who's ever lived. I wonder how these came to be here?'

'Knowing Beatrice, this Bakst person probably gave them to her himself,' Carrie said, only half joking. 'Keep them. Please keep them.'

He shook his head. 'I couldn't possibly.'

'You must. I want you to. You obviously love them. I insist. You said you wanted a memento.'

He looked at her with that sudden, unguarded smile that so transformed his face. 'May I?'

'Of course. And anything else you see. Leo – I told you – you're as entitled to these things as I am.'

He folded the portfolio carefully, tied the ribbon that secured it. Shook his head. 'No, Carrie. That wasn't the way Beatrice saw it.'

Thoughtfully Carrie rubbed a thumb over the grubby porcelain of the small figure she still held. 'I wonder why? I wonder why she so hated your father?'

He shrugged. 'It's old history. They're both dead. We'll never know.'

'I suppose not.' She flexed her shoulders a little. 'Gosh, I'm stiff. Time for a break. Lunch? I think it's warm enough to eat outside.'

'Wonderful idea.'

'Carry on the good work in here. I'll give you a shout when it's ready.'

They lunched on the terrace outside the kitchen, a small sunny corner shaded by a large pear tree and with a view across the valley that was nothing short of breathtaking. They talked, easily and companionably, touching on one subject and then another, interrupting themselves and each other with laughter. Leo argued against her concern at the Fascist ideas that were taking such strong root in Europe, especially in Italy and in Germany. She took him to task for his views on the bright young women who were, in small but growing numbers, making their mark on a world that had finally been forced by war to admit to their capabilities.

He toasted her with a half-empty glass. 'But a woman's place, surely, is in the home, isn't it?' he asked, innocently, lazily smiling.

She pulled a face at him. 'You sound like Arthur.'

He looked at her for a long, pensive moment, the smile gone. 'That's bad?'

She had splashed wine onto the table. Absently she dipped her finger in it, drew a circle on the table-top. Raised her eyes to his, frankly and defiantly, aware that perhaps she had drunk just a little too much of the tongue-loosening stuff. 'Yes,' she said. 'It is. Very bad indeed, actually.'

The silence was thoughtful. She drew a square with her wet finger, avoiding his eyes now, too aware of them upon her. Too aware that she had broken on to perilous ground. Her cheeks grew warm.

'Carrie?' His voice was soft. 'What is it?'

She shook her head, nibbling her lip. In all their conversations until now she had, as far as was possible, avoided talking about Arthur.

He leaned forward in his chair, looking down into his wine. His straight, fine hair fell across his eyes. He tossed it back with a sharp movement of his head, an unconscious, habitual, somehow nervy gesture. 'What's he like?' he asked after a moment, an edge of real curiosity in his voice.

She looked at him. This was her only living relative. The closest thing she had to a brother. Why shouldn't she confide in him? What had Arthur ever done to deserve her loyalty? 'Arthur?' She forced herself to keep her eyes upon his face. 'He's respectable, ambitious, and very capable. He's also humourless, prudish, parsimonious. Meanspirited.' She could not sustain her defiance when those eyes lifted to hers so suddenly. She turned from him, wiped fiercely at the winestain on the table. 'And cruel,' she added, very softly.

The silence was long, and awkward.

'I'm sorry,' she said, at last. 'I shouldn't have said that.'

'There's no earthly reason why not, if it's true.'

'It's true.' The terrible bitterness rang in her own ears like a knell.

'Why did you marry him?'

She leaned back in her chair, drawing a long breath, looking up into the fresh-budding branches above her. 'Leo – you can't know what it's like to be young and not very brave, alone with an ailing mother, no money

86

and no prospects. Living from hand to mouth. The pawn shop – oh, how I hated the pawn shop! There was an old man,' she shook her head, grimacing. 'It was horrible. And mother was so demanding – and sick – I was worried about her all the time—' her voice trailed to silence. She discovered that her fingers were tangled fiercely in her hair. She disentangled them, flinching a little as she pulled sharply at her scalp.

He waited in silence.

'When Arthur came along Mother simply pounced on him. Leo, I was eighteen years old! I couldn't hold out against both of them. I couldn't. He's older than me – a good deal older. And for Mother a gift from heaven. As I said, he's respectable – a bank clerk—' she smiled, totally without humour, 'I beg his pardon. A chief bank clerk. One day he'll be manager.' Her eyes flickered to his and away, 'That'll be nice, won't it?' Something very strange was happening; and it had, she was certain, absolutely nothing to do with the wine. She felt a sudden, subversive sense of release. Not once, in five years of misery, had she spoken like this; there had been no one to speak to, no one to care. Any protest had been so comprehensively and brutally dealt with that she had simply, and quickly, stopped protesting. She had taken herself at Arthur's own valuation of her. Weak-willed. Submissive. A coward. It had taken distance to change the perspective. 'I think I hate him,' she said, pensively, the words brutal in the tranquil day. 'I truly think I do.' She had never admitted as much to herself before, let alone to anyone else. She felt an unpleasant stirring in the pit of her stomach at the shock of it.

He reached a hand to hers. 'Carrie. I'm so sorry.'

She shook her head, shrugged. 'A self-inflicted injury,' she said, wryly. 'You aren't supposed to feel sorry for them, are you?'

He laughed a little. 'You know something?'

'What?'

'You underestimate yourself. All the time.'

She shook her head.

'Oh, yes. I recognise. it all too well. I saw it during the war. Often. It wasn't the gung-ho lads with the loud voices and the bravado who were the heroes. It was those who recognised fear, and faced it. Who knew their own weaknesses and overcame them. The ones who wanted to run, and didn't. They were the brave ones.'

'And were you one of them?'

Blue, oddly secretive, veiled again by the curling lashes, his eyes glinted with wayward laughter. 'Oh, no. I enjoyed it. Ask anyone.' He reached into his breast pocket for his cigarette case.

She watched him. 'I'm not sure I believe that.'

'Believe it.' His voice was cool.

'You were wounded, weren't you?'

'Mm-hmm.' Blue smoke wreathed about him. 'Twice. You couldn't get through the whole show without getting scratched occasionally.'

'Were you never afraid?'

Again the flash of laughter, almost, she thought, of excitement. 'I didn't say that. Did I?'

'No. You didn't.'

He stared across the valley. The high sun filtered through the branches and turned the air to gold

88

about them. 'Funny thing, war,' he said, very softly.

'That's putting it mildly, I would have thought.'

In the silence a bird sang above them.

She frowned a little. 'Leo? You didn't really? Enjoy
it, I mean?'

He took a long time to answer. 'No. Of course
not. It was bloody; everyone knows how bloody it
was. But, Carrie, even the bloodiest of things you
have to learn to live with. To—' he hesitated 'to
adapt to, if you like. It's either that or you go
under.'

'Yes,' she said.

'So. I learned to live with it. I learned to keep the
odds on my side. I taught myself to enjoy the risks. The
challenges.' He grinned swiftly. 'Excitement – danger –
can act like a drug, you know. The more you get the
more you want.'

'What, exactly, did you do?'

He shrugged. 'This and that. The odd foray across
the lines. Taking the fight to the enemy was what I seem
to remember they called it.' He smiled again, the very
ghost of a self-deprecating smile. 'Quietly, and never in
broad daylight, of course. Be fair. If you remember, I
could always dodge the column. I discovered very early
that I wasn't one for ploughing off across no-man's-land
with a whistle and an officer's revolver and a pack of
scared squaddies at my back when the opposition was
an extremely efficient Hun with a machine-gun. I found
a quiet word in the middle of the night worked very
efficiently, and was much more fun. For most of the

duration I was – let's just say – more independent than most.'

She found herself looking at his hands, lying quiet upon the table – had they killed, in the quiet, the dark of night? Was that what he was saying? For an instant she tried to imagine it; the intensity, the barbarity of it. And could not.

He poured more wine. 'What will you do?'

She jumped from her reverie. 'I'm sorry?'

'What will you do? About Arthur?'

She looked at him in true surprise. 'Why nothing,' she said. 'What can I do? I'll finish what needs to be done here, and then—' the very thought was like a dead weight on her heart 'and then, I suppose, I'll go home.'

For the first time it occurred to her; she had no idea where his home was. And where, now, she found herself wondering, was hers?

'Of course.' He handed her her glass. Lifted his own. 'Well.' He smiled. 'Perhaps we should drink to today?'

She looked across the valley, and then up, to the bright-lit peaks. The bird was there again, wheeling in the clear air.

'To today,' she agreed.

They went to Lucca the next day. Carrie was enchanted. 'Leo – it's like stepping back in time!'

Set on its plain beyond the foothills within the circle of its ancient walls the little city had hardly changed since it had reached the height of its power as a City State in the Middle Ages. It was a busy and attractive place; its narrow streets and alleyways, its handsome piazzas and small courtyards teemed with life; the lovely buildings, tall and decorative and well proportioned, effortlessly harmonised the styles of several centuries. With an hour to spare before Carrie's appointment with Signor Bellini there was plenty of time to explore the centre of the city; to admire the lovely black and white façade of the cathedral, the fascinating, multi-arched Gothic front of the Church of San Michele with its huge statue of the archangel vanquishing the dragon.

'I'll meet you back here,' Leo said. 'At half past three. Is that okay?'

'It's fine.' Carrie looked up at the church front. 'What a wonderful building.'

'Yes. Isn't it? I'll meet you back here on the steps at three thirty. We can go inside then. You'll like it. There's a wonderful Madonna and Child.'

'Right.' She checked her watch. 'I'd better go.' They had already ascertained the whereabouts of Signor Bellini's office. 'I'll see you later.'

'Good luck.'

She flashed him a smile. 'Thanks.'

The building that housed the office of *P. D. Bellini, Procuratore Legale* was in the Via Fillungo, not far from the clock tower. A little tentatively she pushed open the great carved wooden door to find herself in an atrium; a well-proportioned, enclosed courtyard of black and white marble in which a small fountain played and from which a wide marble staircase rose to the first floor. The polished wood of the banister was like satin beneath her

91

hand. At the top of the stairs a wide, arched hallway ran from the back to the front of the building. She found the door with Signor Bellini's nameplate beside it and tapped, hesitantly.

The door opened to reveal a dapper, middle-aged man in the most elegantly cut suit Carrie had ever seen. The hand he extended was small and soft. A diamond gleamed in gold on his little finger.

'Signora Stowe. Welcome.'

'Thank you.' She followed him into a large office, the long windows of which looked down the narrow street outside, towards the clock tower. There was a huge, leather-covered desk, and several comfortable leather armchairs. The walls were covered in pictures.

'Coffee?' he said, in his flawless, attractively accented English. 'Or no – tea, of course. Your grandmother always preferred tea.'

She turned to him, smiling at that. 'Did she? You knew her well?'

He waved a hand. The diamond flashed. 'But of course. I saw to all of her affairs in the last ten years of her life, and then to those of her son. Such a gentle man.' He made a courteous gesture towards one of the armchairs. 'I hope to serve her granddaughter as well. You must know, Signora Stowe, how very like her you look? Please. Make yourself comfortable. I'll organise some tea.'

He left the room. She wandered to the window, looking down with pleasure into the busy street below. The Via Fillungo was very narrow; it was lined with the tall, shuttered, balconied houses that so characterised the city; in one place the overhanging roofs almost touched. The ancient clock tower was silhouetted against a pale, spring sky. The street itself was in shadow.

'There. It will be only a moment.' The lawyer came to stand beside her. 'A good view, yes?'

'Lovely.'

'The tower is the only one left in Lucca. There were once many more, so they say.'

'Oh?'

'In past times there were many families here, powerful families, you understand. There was much struggle between them. They built the towers, for protection, and for power. Higher and higher they built them—'

Carrie, her breath held suddenly in her throat, had stopped listening. In the street below, in the shadow of the tower, two figures stood, in intent and absorbed conversation. One was unmistakably her cousin. The other was a woman, tall and very slim. Even from here Carrie could see from her carriage, and from the paleness of her skin, the raven's wing of her hair that she must be beautiful. What held her was the inexplicable intimacy of the picture they made together, standing in the busy street as if they were alone, oblivious to the tide of humanity that parted about them, unheeded, like water about a rock. The woman was talking animatedly, waving her hands. Leo stood, shoulders hunched a little, his hands in his pockets, head tilted towards her. Carrie knew, with a cruel clarity, exactly what the expression on his face would be. '– I'm, I'm sorry?'

Signor Bellini looked at her a little questioningly.

'The towers,' he said, gently. 'I apologise. You are not interested.'

Carried flushed furiously. 'Oh, but of course I am. I was distracted, that's all. I thought I saw someone I knew—' She looked back into the street. The woman had a hand on Leo's arm. Leo turned, jerked his head to flick the hair from his forehead. Together they started to walk, quickly, down the street.

'—so to prevent such riots and public dangers the Comune of Lucca decreed that the rivalries must stop and the towers must come down. The clock tower is the only one to survive.'

'I see.'

Leo and the woman had gone, swallowed up in the crowds. A donkey laden with pots, pans and terracotta jars plodded down the street.

Carrie turned to smile brightly at Signor Bellini. Why shouldn't Leo know a woman – any number of women, come to that – in Lucca? What business was it of hers?

Why hadn't he mentioned her?

'Now, Signora Stowe – if you'll take a seat – we'll talk of what must be done. Tell me, how much did Signor Bagshaw explain?'

She drank her tea and listened to it all again. Her grandmother had sold something called the 'nuda proprieta' of the property to someone she trusted, keeping the use and occupation, the 'usu frutto' for herself and for Henry. On Henry's death Carrie, by paying a small sum – literally 'buying back' the property – became sole owner of the house and of all its contents.

94

'When do I do that?' She could still see it in her head, that strangely intimate picture, the neat brown head bowed to the sleek dark one—

'Why, today,' he consulted a gold watch. 'I had hoped that Signora Carina would be here by now. She's old. She becomes forgetful, I'm afraid—'

'Signora? It's a woman?'

'Why, yes. Your grandmother's—' his words were interrupted by a sharp rap upon the door. 'Ah! That surely must be her.'

He went to the outer door, opened it. Carrie stood up expectantly.

And found herself facing the diminutive, black-veiled figure she had seen watching her in the cemetery.

'Signora Stowe, this is Signora Carina. Your grand-mother's nurse and companion from childhood. She it is who has guarded the property for you.'

With tiny, black-gloved hands the woman lifted the veil, and Carrie found herself looking into a face as brown and wrinkled as an ancient walnut, dominated by a pair of the smallest, brightest and possibly the most hostile eyes she had ever seen.

She stepped forward, hand outstretched. 'Signora Carina. I saw you at my grandmother's grave yesterday, didn't I? I am so very pleased to meet you.'

Leo was waiting for her on the steps – why had she even begun to imagine that he would not be there? – when she hurried, breathless, across the Piazza San Michele to the church. He leaned to kiss her lightly on the cheek. 'How did it go?'

'Fine. I'm sorry I'm late.'

'That's all right. So, it's all settled?'

'Yes. It was Maria. The person who was holding the house for me. It was Maria Carina. Grandmother's childhood nurse. I told you, I saw her at the grave yesterday.'

'Oh, of course.' He had taken her arm and was walking her slowly up the wide steps that led to the huge door of the church.

'I suppose I should have guessed. Signor Bellini persuaded her to let me visit her. Tomorrow. She lives in Bagni. She speaks English, of course, though a little rustily. She's a rather strange old lady.'

'In what way?'

Carrie shrugged. 'I don't know. She seemed – suspicious of me, somehow. It took all of Signor Bellini's considerable tact and charm to persuade her to agree to see me tomorrow.' She glanced up at him. 'Do you want to come?'

He had been looking up at the impressive façade above them. He shook his head. 'Oh, I think not. It might make her even more distrustful, don't you think, if you turned up with the grandson Beatrice so determinedly disowned?' His voice was light.

'Oh, Leo!'

He stopped her with another shake of his head. 'It's true, Carrie, and you know it. If you want to talk to her about Beatrice you don't need me there. It doesn't matter. Truly it doesn't. Now, come and see the church.'

She caught up with him at the door. 'How have you

spent your day?' She had absolutely determined that she would not ask.

He shrugged a little. 'Mooched about the city a bit. Stopped off for a glass of something. Sat watching the world go by. This is a very good place to do that.'

'Yes. I'm sure it is.' She smiled her very brightest smile.

'There – look – that's what I wanted you to see.' He pointed. 'The Madonna. It's della Robbia, or so they think.'

She stared fixedly at the glazed terracotta figure.

'It doesn't seem possible that she's four hundred years old, does it?' His voice was quiet.

She shook her head.

Why did she care so much? Why?

Leo, hands in pockets, sauntered towards the main altar, looking around him. For a moment he paused and his slight, graceful figure was caught by the light that fell through one of the high windows, gilding his face, his hair, the set of his narrow shoulders. And in that single moment she knew with a lucid and lacerating certainty why she cared that he had met a beautiful woman in the streets of Lucca. And – worse – had lied to her about it.

'Leo?'

He turned.

'I'm sorry,' she put a hand to her forehead. 'I've got something of a headache. Do you think we could start back to Bagni? It's quite a trek.'

He was beside her, contrite and attentive, in a moment. 'Well, of course. Why didn't you tell me? Is it very bad?'

She shook her head, despising herself. 'No. Just nagging. I'd really like to get back. A bit of mountain air's what I need, that's all.'

'Come on.' He took her hand, drew it within the shelter of his arm. 'Stupid of me. I should have realised that the journey took more out of you than you thought.'

'No, really it's nothing, it's just—' she stopped.

It's just that the lovely, raven-haired woman who puts a hand on your sleeve, who talks to you with such easy animation is in Lucca.

'It's just, I'd like to go home,' she said.

And in her strange and unnerving agitation, she did not realise precisely what she had said.

Chapter Five

'You look like her,' Maria said, unsmiling.

'Yes. So I understand.' Carrie shifted a little in the uncomfortably upholstered chair. 'Signor Bellini said the same thing. And there's a picture—' she fell to silence.

She could not pretend that this first meeting had gone well; from the moment she had arrived in the small house by the river she had been aware of that strange, wary hostility that she had sensed first in the churchyard and then again in Signor Bellini's office. Maria, certainly, had answered her questions but had actually volunteered very little, and at no time had the conversation been easy.

The silence lengthened.

'We found some journals,' Carrie said, tentatively. 'Beatrice's journals. But there seems to be one missing.'

Maria said nothing. She sat bolt upright in an ancient leather armchair, her small, dark eyes fixed, unblinking and unreadable, upon Carrie's face.

'I don't suppose you'd know where it might be? It's

the one for 1867. I've looked all over the house but can't find it anywhere. It seems a shame; they're so very interesting.'

There was a long, still moment of quiet; then Maria shook her head.

Something in the aged, sunbrowned face made Carrie ask, gently, 'But, you do remember the journals?'

'Yes. I remember well. She would show them to me.'

'Did Beatrice do the drawings too?'

'Some. Or sometimes Leonard.'

Again the silence was awkward. And again Carrie found herself feeling certain that Maria was holding something back. The mention of Beatrice's brother, and of the missing journal had, however, almost without thought, brought another question to her lips; a question that had niggled in the back of her mind ever since her conversation with Mary Webber in the churchyard. 'Maria, how did Leonard die?' she asked, and immediately wished she had held her tongue; for although the woman's face scarcely changed it was as if a shutter had closed.

'He was sick,' Maria said. 'And now – please, Signora Stowe – I am tired.'

'Oh, of course. I'm sorry.' Carrie scrambled to her feet. 'I shouldn't have stayed so long.' She held out her hand. The old woman took it, briefly. Her skin was like paper, the bones birdlike and frail. 'Thank you so much for seeing me.'

'Is all right.'

'Please – might I come again? In a day or so? There's so much I want to know.'

The woman hesitated, the austerely emotionless eyes still probing Carrie's. Then, suddenly – and to Carrie's surprise – she nodded. '*Si.*'

'Thank you.'

'*Prego.*'

Carrie stepped from the dark room into the sunshine and the glad sound of the water. It had been very cool in the house, it was pleasant now to feel the warmth of the sun on her face and shoulders. She walked back across the Ponte di Serraglio, stopping for a moment to look down into the foaming waters beneath. Maria's attitude truly puzzled her. She could think of no reason why the old lady should be so very wary of her; indeed she had hoped that she would have been pleased to have the opportunity to talk about Beatrice, of whom she had obviously been so fond. The odd and grudging reluctance to share her memories was disappointing; but then, she had at least agreed to speak to her again, so all was not lost. Maria was a very old woman; many elderly people, Carrie knew, regarded the young with some distrust. Perhaps it was as simple as that. She would take it very slowly and win her confidence. There was, as she had told Maria, so much that she wanted to know. And, too, there was the mystery of the missing journal. For the briefest of moments she had glimpsed something in Maria's face when she had asked about it. But what? From nowhere an extraordinary thought occurred; had Maria herself taken it? Or perhaps even destroyed it? And if so why? Was it something to do with Leonard's death? 'He was sick,' Maria had said. It could have meant anything. But whatever happened,

101

given her reaction to the question, Carrie would tread very carefully before venturing to mention it again.

She turned and strolled slowly to the village end of the bridge. Dark-eyed children played in the dust of the road, absorbed in a game with small sticks and stones. She stood watching them for a moment, smiling, before walking on under the trees that edged the river, towards the main street. It was market day; as she approached the small market-place the streets were thronged and busy. She edged her way through the noisy crowds towards a stall selling eggs and vegetables.

'Hello-oh. Mrs Stowe! Hello there!'

Carrie turned. Beaming and cheerfully determined, Mary Webber was pushing her way towards her.

'How very nice to see you again my dear. I was thinking of you just yesterday. How are you managing?'

'Very well, thank you.'

'Good, good. That's splendid. Now – I insist – you must come and have a cup of chocolate with me. The hotel's just across the road.' She put a firm hand upon Carrie's arm.

'Well I—'

'No excuses now. I can't tell you what a pleasure it is to see a fresh face. You must come and tell me all that you're doing up at the Villa. It's many years since I was there, but I must say that I remember it as a truly enchanting – a fascinating – place.'

Carrie allowed herself to be guided back towards the main street. 'It is. It's absolutely packed with—' she stopped, abruptly.

Mary Webber did not notice; she herself was in full

flow. 'I do believe I shall climb the mountain to visit you. I could help perhaps – there must be so much to do.'

'Yes.' Carrie watched a sleek, dark head bend to a stallholder, caught a glimpse of a high-boned, creamy-skinned face with wide, dark eyes beneath clearly arched brows. The woman was tall, and willowy. She was wearing a simple summer frock of some filmy, flowered material, with a scoop neck and dropped waist, that on anyone else might have looked pretty but unexceptional; this woman wore it with an easy and casual elegance that drew and held the eye.

'—poor Henry, of course, never did much by way of socialising. But really, my dear, you must come down to the Bridge Club. Mrs Stowe? Is there something amiss?'

'I'm sorry?'

With eager curiosity Mary Webber followed the direction of her gaze. 'What a very attractive young woman. Do you know her?'

'No. Oh, no. I was just thinking what a very pretty dress she's wearing.'

'Yes, isn't it? Ah, here we are. Shall we take an outside table? It really is delightfully warm for the time of year.'

Carrie turned her head. The woman had gone. For an instant she found herself scanning the crowds, looking for Leo. Was it sheer coincidence that the woman with whom she had seen him in Lucca was now here, in Bagni di Lucca? Had she followed him? Did Leo know?

She smiled faintly and fixedly at Mrs Webber, nodded, allowing the woman's busy chatter to pass her by. It was none of her business. Leo's life was his own.

Why did she care so much? Why, suddenly, had the sunshine gone from the day?

She became aware of silence. Mary Webber was looking at her expectantly.

'I'm sorry?'

'I asked how long you were going to stay, my dear.' There was concern in the other woman's eyes. 'I say, are you feeling quite well?'

Carrie forced a smile. 'I'm fine. Fine. The sun's a little warm, that's all. I'm not accustomed to it.'

'Well, of course not.' Mary Webber beamed again. 'But you'll get used to it, I'm sure. Now, as I was saying—'

'You're very quiet.' Leo's narrow, lazy eyes were half shut against the last of the evening sunshine. He leaned back in his chair, feet propped upon the wooden table.

Carrie shrugged a little. 'I'm a bit tired, that's all.'

He opened his eyes, fixed them upon her with a disconcerting steadiness. 'All work and no play?' he suggested gently.

'Perhaps.'

He grinned, tilted his head back again to face the sun. 'Too much climbing up and down mountains?'

She laughed. 'I enjoy it.'

'Perhaps,' he slanted a look at her through his half-closed lashes 'perhaps we should take some time off? Take the train to Florence or Siena, maybe? Spend

104

a day or two exploring the city? It seems a shame to be here and not see something of these places.'

She looked at him in sheer delight. 'Oh, could we? I should so enjoy that. Beatrice mentions Siena so often in the journals. She obviously adored it, though Leonard equally obviously didn't. Pompeii was his favourite place. He loved it. In fact he was almost obsessed with it. Have you read what Beatrice wrote?'

Leo shook his head.

The journal for 1864 was on the table in front of Carrie. She pulled it towards her. 'It seems to have been where Beatrice got the idea of creating the garden.' She leafed through the bok. 'Ah, here it is. "*Leo and I*" – isn't it funny that she used to call Leonard Leo sometimes? Do you think that's why you were called Leo? It's possible, isn't it? "*Leo and I sat upon a rock above the house on the mountainside together this afternoon, and he spoke, as he so often does, of his love for that mysterious lost city of Pompeii. So little is known of it, yet Leonard is quite passionate about it; one might almost say obsessive. He says that if he could choose a life he would choose to live in that city, and to die the day before the volcano erupted. (I asked, and he did agree that I should be there with him – though it must be said that to conspire to die upon the same day might be difficult!) I take his point. Our recent trip to those fascinating ruins was certainly most interesting and instructive. Signor Fiorelli is the most charismatic and intelligent of men. Everyone agrees that his methodic excavations of the past four years have uncovered more of the history of the city than all the blundering and plundering that has gone on for the past hundred years; he is one of those fortunate men who has the ability to convey his own enthusiasms. As we sat above the house I told Leo of my plans; that I would create here, for him – and for me – a little Pompeii. A place of treasures. A sybaritic place of beauty and of peace. A garden about the house, shaded and beautiful, terraced and vined, arboured and graced with statues. I told him that the garden was to be for him. He teased me, saying that the first bright-eyed young man who crooked a finger would soon change my plans. How wrong he is! I will never marry. I'll never leave Leo and the Villa Castellini. I told him so. He laughed at me, though gently, as always. Well, we shall see. Meanwhile, I plan my garden."* Leo, look,' Carrie pushed the book towards him, 'the picture she's drawn. Isn't it lovely? And the plan – see – it isn't unlike the way the garden must finally have looked.'

'A very determined lady, our grandmother,' Leo said, drily.

Carrie let her hands rest, flat, upon the page, looked up into the spaces of the pale, evening sky. A bird – the same bird as before? she wondered – wheeled high above the valley. 'She must have been devastated when he died.'

'Yes.' Leo felt in the breast pocket of his jacket, extracted his cigarette case. 'She must.'

'She married very soon afterwards.'

He nodded. 'We all know the story. The old family friend who had known and loved her from childhood. A strong and independent man, much older than her, who had a life of his own and who had the sense to let Beatrice stay free.'

'It's strange, though,' Carrie said. 'The last journal. The one for 1868. She was married by then, and expecting her first child: poor Uncle Henry. Yet she seems to have been living here alone, still grieving for her brother, and she hardly mentions her husband or the coming child at all. Except for the very last entry, that she writes as if addressing someone else. "*It has started my love*," she says. "*The child is coming at last. I shall no longer be alone.*" Well – something like that, anyway. Don't you think that an odd thing to say?'

Watching her thoughtfully he tapped his cigarette upon the worn silver case. 'Come on, now, Carrie. Don't make a tragedy where there isn't one. All marriages aren't the same, you know.' The words were quiet, and again the blue gleam of his eyes was wide and steady.

'I know. It's just, well, the more you read the earlier diaries the more you see what a strange, almost magical life they – Beatrice and Leonard – created here together. Enclosed and separate and – I don't know—' she closed her eyes for a moment, 'enchanted seems to be the word I'm looking for.' She got up and wandered to the low wall that enclosed the yard in which they sat. Stood looking across to the shadowed, tree-cloaked slopes opposite.

'Are you sure you aren't simply reflecting your own feelings?' he asked, softly, from behind her. 'Are you certain that it isn't your own needs, your own responses to this place that make you feel so?'

She turned, smiling. 'No. Of course I'm not sure. You're very probably right. But reading the journals, it's uncannily like getting inside the young Beatrice's mind, isn't it?' She came back to the table, closed the journal, looked again at the date inscribed upon it. '1864. She was eighteen years old, and so very happy.' She turned away from him, half sitting upon the table, her arms folded across her breast. 'She was lucky in that at least.'

He watched her, saying nothing.

'Leo?'

'Yes?'

She kept her eyes fixed upon the far slopes of the valley. Smoke plumed from a cottage chimney, drifted a little in the mountain air. Clearly they could hear the bleating of sheep, the sweet sound of a child's laughter.

'When we went to Lucca to see Signor Bellini, you met a woman – you were in the Via Fillungo – you obviously knew each other well. I saw you. I was in the office, looking out of the window—' She was aware of the sudden, still silence behind her. She swallowed. 'I know it's none of my business. Of course it isn't. But you didn't mention her. That's what puzzled me. You didn't say anything. And then today—' She hesitated, turned to him. His thin, sharp-boned face was expressionless. 'today I saw her down in the market-place at Bagni. She's very beautiful,' she added, helplessly, spreading her hands, acutely aware of the tension in the man's apparently relaxed body. She did not know why she had asked; she truly had not intended to do so. 'I'm sorry,' she said, miserably. 'I just – I just wondered – that's all.'

For a moment he neither moved nor looked at her. Then he flicked a quick glance at her, smiling a little, rueful and easy. 'Angelique,' he said. 'Her name is Angelique. She's back in Bagni, is she?'

'You didn't know?'

He shook his head.

'I saw her in the market-place. I'm sure it was her. As I said, she's very lovely. You couldn't mistake her, could you?'

'No. You couldn't.' Again that small smile.

'Leo? Who is she?'

The narrow, expressionless eyes surveyed the valley. 'A friend. That's all. A friend.'

Her heart was suddenly a leaden weight. 'A beautiful friend,' she said, lightly.

'Yes.' In that disconcerting way he suddenly looked at her, directly and openly. 'A beautiful—' he spread artless hands 'difficult friend.'

She ducked her head, making patterns on the table with her finger. 'I'm sorry. I shouldn't have asked.'

'Did you know,' he said, after a quiet moment, 'that you say "I'm sorry" all the time?'

She looked up at him in genuine surprise. 'Do I?'

'Yes.'

She took a breath. The sky was bright with light, the valley steeped in mysterious shadows. The sun glowed behind the western peak, sinking almost visibly, minute by minute. 'I'm sorry.' She laughed a little, trying to lighten the moment.

He leaned forward, poured her another glass of wine. 'It's a bad habit,' he said. 'You should break it.'

'I'm not sure I can.'

'Oh, yes. You most certainly could. If you wanted to.'

Carrie turned, half-smiling, 'I suppose—' she stopped, unable to continue the sentence, a pulse suddenly beating hard in her throat. He had stilled, and was watching her, openly and with a sudden and unnerving intentness. And helplessly she knew, as clearly as if she could see with his eyes, what was written plain upon her face, and was powerless to hide or disguise it. Just simply to look at him, to study the neat, handsome face line by line, to sustain the searching, subtle blue gaze upon her own face brought a pleasure so fierce it was close to pain. She could not look away. He opened his mouth as if to speak. Shook his head a little and said nothing.

She was aware of his hands, well-shaped and relaxed, resting upon the table.

Touch me. Please touch me.

As if she had communicated the words through her eyes he lifted a finger gently to brush her cheek.

She closed her eyes, her skin growing warm beneath his touch. She was aware that she was shaking, and that he must sense it.

'I must go,' he said, quietly.

She could neither move nor speak.

'I'll be back early tomorrow. We can make a start on the tower room.'

She nodded.

His chair scraped upon the flagstones as he stood. 'Do we need anything apart from fresh bread?'

'No.'

'Right. I'll see you tomorrow then.' Still he made no move to leave. Still he watched her.

'Yes. Tomorrow.'

Don't go. Please, don't go.

He turned abruptly and strode away from her, running lightfooted down the steps that led to the path below, his movements, as always, fluent and graceful. At the foot of the steps he stopped to light a cigarette, cupping his hands about the flame, then lifted his head to smile up at her before swiftly setting off down the track. She watched the slight figure until it merged with the shadows beneath a stand of chestnut trees. Willing him to stop. Willing him to come back.

He neither turned, nor waved.

Carrie sat for a very long time, quite still, watching the spot where he had disappeared, the wine Leo had poured her untouched upon the table before her. Then she reached for the journal and drew it towards her, bent her head to stare sightlessly at the small, battered book.

All she could see was Leo's face. His voice was in her ears.

She opened the journal at random, trying to force herself to concentrate.

Narrow eyes, blue as the skies, looked back at her.

'The garden is a project, of course, that will take many years. A project for a lifetime, I suppose, and for many lifetimes on'

A beautiful – difficult – friend. What had he meant?

'I intend that it should be our monument – Leonard's

111

and mine – our gift to the world, and to those who come after us'

Had she imagined the expression in his eyes when he had looked at her, the tenderness of his touch?

She bent her head, covered her own eyes with her spread hands. Leo looked steadily back at her, enigmatic and disturbing.

Take a grip of yourself, Carrie Stowe.

She leaned back in her chair. A breeze had sprung up, and clouds were gathering above the peaks, bruising the sky. She slipped her arms into the sleeves of her cardigan and sat on, watching them build.

What is it that you want, Carrie Stowe?

The answer came with no thought. Leo. It's Leo that I want.

And what, exactly, does that mean?

I want to be with him. I desperately want him to want to be with me. I want him not to be able to leave me. I want to listen to him, to watch him. I want to touch him.

I want him to touch me.

The thought shocked her; with a sudden and unpleasant stirring in the pit of her stomach she found herself thinking of Hastings and of Arthur. And of Tuesdays, Thursdays and Saturdays. *'You won't forget to bathe, will you?'* All at once she shivered, violently. The wind was lifting, gusting about the house, swirling dust and debris in small whirlwinds. The evening air was chill.

'He's my cousin,' she said, aloud, into the lifting wind. 'My nearest – my only – blood relative. Almost

112

my brother. And I'm a married woman. I can't feel like this about him. I mustn't.'

The silence mocked her. And the wind grew colder.

For the first time, that evening, she felt lonely in the house. She could not settle. Even Beatrice's journal could not distract her from her thoughts. Each time she tried to read it despite her every effort she found herself within seconds staring abstractedly into space, reliving those last moments with Leo. Had she imagined it? Had there truly been that sudden, electric attraction between them? Had he felt it?

Outside the wind still blew, nowhere near as strongly as it had on that first night, but hard enough to rattle the shutters and to send chill draughts through the house.

Restlessly she closed the journal and, carrying the lamp, went into the sitting room; stood surveying the untidy heaps of books, pictures and knick-knacks that were stacked upon the floor. She hadn't the heart to tackle any more of this tonight.

The room was cold; the wind whistled in the chimney.

She looked at her watch; it was early to go to bed, yet she could think of nothing else to do. Slowly she climbed the stairs, the light from the lamp sending shadows moving and leaping eerily about her. At her bedroom door she hesitated, then on impulse walked on down the passage, pushed open the door of the tower room and went in, setting the lamp upon a table by the window.

This was a large room, square and well proportioned,

with a high, decorated plaster ceiling, a stone fireplace and shuttered doors that opened onto a balcony. Within moments she knew why she had come here; very faintly the scent of Leo's cigarettes still lingered in the air. Here was the bed in which he had slept. She touched a match to the lamp that stood upon the table, looked around her, taking comfort from the stronger glow of light, the sense of warmth and safety that it brought. This really was a lovely room. Perhaps she would take it for her own for the time she had left here. She wandered round, exploring. There were the inevitable shelves full of books, and the equally inevitable walls full of paintings, mostly pictures of the mountains and valleys of the Garfagnana.

On the mantelpiece amongst a jumble of candlesticks, vases and an extremely elderly clock stood a small bronze bust of a girl.

Carrie picked up the smaller of the lamps and carried it closer. The light reflected in the spotted mirror above the fireplace, shining in her eyes. She moved the lamp a little, studied the bust intently, frowning thoughtfully. There was something about it, something familiar, that she could not put her finger on.

She lifted her head, and in doing so caught sight of her own face in the mirror, shadowed and highlighted by the lamplight. She smiled in sudden delight. Of course! Of course the face was familiar. She looked back at the bronze. This was Beatrice as a young woman; she was certain of it. She set the lamp upon the mantelpiece and turned the bust a little; the likeness was unmistakable, even more marked than in the picture downstairs.

She put out a gentle hand to touch the smooth, cool, immobile face. This above all must come home with her.

She inspected the books. They were old, leather bound and most of them seemed to be books of poetry; Donne and Lovelace, Milton and Dryden, Shelley and Byron and many others, all well thumbed. She pulled one from the shelf. In faded ink a name was inscribed on the frontispiece. *Leonard Charles Johnstone*. She turned the book over in her hands. It was the strangest of sensations to know that Beatrice's brother, so long dead, had owned this book, handled it, read it. She picked another at random. This too was marked with Leonard's name, and was Byron. A brittle and faded piece of paper marked a page. She opened it. '*She walks in beauty, like the night Of cloudless climes and starry skies*' she remembered the poem from her schooldays; learned by rote and still familiar, she had never before truly appreciated the meaning and the beauty of the words. Softly she read it aloud, '*One shade the more, one ray the less, Had half impaired the nameless grace Which waves in every raven tress, Or softly lightens o'er her face*' and then the tender, gentlest of conclusions '*A heart whose love is innocent.*'

Carrie stood, head bowed, for a long time, looking at the words. *A heart whose love is innocent.* Suddenly and with a disturbing stab of something that encompassed both excitement and fear she saw the expression in Leo's momentarily unguarded eyes when he had looked at her that evening. Innocent? No. Even in her own innocence and inexperience

115

she knew that to pretend so would be to lie to herself.

She put the book carefully back on the shelf. Had
this, then, been Leonard's room? The books inscribed
with his name seemed to prove so. Had Beatrice run
in here on a sunlit morning, perched on the bed,
chattered to her brother of poetry and gardens and
the city of Pompeii? She smiled a little at the thought. *A
heart whose love was innocent.* That surely must have
described the young Beatrice?

She went back to the mantelpiece, stood looking at the
small bronze head. Had Beatrice ever experienced the
confusing – the agonising – emotions that she, Carrie,
was experiencing now? Had she ever found her heart,
her head, her senses apparently entirely possessed by
the need to see, to hear, to touch one person, and one
person only? Had she ever stood in this room, alone,
and helpless to defend herself against the pain of it?

'What's happening to me?' she asked aloud, very
softly. 'What's happening to me?'

The house was quiet now, the breeze had dropped.
She walked to the window and opened the shutter. The
mountains were dark. Lights glimmered in the valley
and on the slopes beneath the house.

I'll see him tomorrow. Whatever happens, he'll come
tomorrow.

The thought was like a beacon in the darkness.

I don't care if what I feel is wrong. I can't help what
I feel; I can help what I do about it. And I'll do nothing.
I'll never ask anything of him. I won't ask that he loves
me. It is enough, for now, that he's here, that he'll come

116

again, that we'll talk, and laugh, and share each other's company. I'll live each day as it comes. Then we'll part, and there will be an end. But not yet. Please God, not yet. Let me have a little more time with him. Then I'll go home. Back to England, and to Arthur.

She tilted her head back and closed her eyes for a moment, pushing that thought away from her.

He'll come tomorrow.

Behind her closed lids Leo watched her, steadily, smiling in the sunshine.

She drew the shutters and latched them, turned to survey the room again. Yes, she would move in here tomorrow.

In passing, she paused to touch the bust again, running a finger down the angle of the cheek, smiling a little.

At least, now, she had Beatrice to talk to. She was smiling at that silly, fanciful yet somehow comforting thought as she left the room.

Chapter Six

When Leo arrived the following morning he brought with him a letter. The postmark was Hastings, England; the writing was very familiar, neat and precise.

'Young Pietro brought it up from the village last night. It had been left at the post office.'

'Thank you.' She took it from him, laid it on the table. 'Coffee?'

'Please.'

She poured the coffee, without looking at him, maddeningly aware that from the moment he had walked into the kitchen she had begun to shake, slightly but perceptibly. The letter lay between them. She pushed the cup across the table towards him, knowing herself unable to trust her treacherous hands. 'Did you mean what you suggested yesterday? Could we really go to Siena for a couple of days?' She picked up the envelope, turned it in her hands.

'Yes. Of course. If you'd like to?'

'I would.' She reached for a knife and slid it under the flap.

'Then we will.' He was smiling, and relaxed. 'We can go by train or – I wondered – it might be possible to hire a car? Either here or in Lucca. Would you enjoy that?'

'Oh, yes. I'd love it.'

'It would be more fun to drive, if you're ready to risk the Italian roads and my driving. And Siena's a wonderful city, whatever Leonard may have thought of it. I'm sure you'll like it.'

She had carried the letter to the door. '*My dear Carrie, Just a line to tell you that all is well here. The weather is still very cold – it will be some time before we can forgo the expense of a fire each evening. I trust you are in good health, and that the journey was not too arduous for you. I trust also that all has gone to plan in the matter of the house and its contents. I took the time to contact an auction house in London. The fellow I wrote to was most gratifyingly interested in anything of your grandmother's that might be available for sale, so do take care that anything of any value is safely packed and crated before you ship it home.*' She lifted her eyes to the sunlit mountainside, trying to control the sudden flare of her anger. '*I think it wise for you to leave the matter of the sale of the house in the hands of Signor Bellini. No doubt the man will take more than his fair share of the proceeds, but nevertheless I feel it is the sensible thing to do. When are you coming home? Soon, I hope. You will, I assume, write to tell me when to expect you? Be sure to let me know in good time. I shall, of course, take a day's leave to meet you. Your loving husband, Arthur.*'

She refolded the letter very precisely, put it in the

pocket of her cardigan. *Your loving husband.* The empty phrase rang in her head. She turned. Leo was watching her. 'Arthur?'

She nodded, half smiling. 'Yes. Very Arthur. He thinks Signor Bellini will fleece us if we let him sell the house.'

He grinned. 'He probably will.'

She stood quite still for a moment, her head lifted. 'I don't want to sell it,' she said. 'I don't want to!' And was astounded at the sudden intemperate passion in her own usually quiet voice.

He came to her gently, laid calm and friendly hands upon her shoulders. 'You have to, Carrie. You know it. It's a dream. It isn't possible. Your life is in England, with Arthur.'

She clenched her teeth. His hands were warm, his body so close to hers that the slightest of movements would have taken her into his arms. It was unendurable. She was trembling again, and knew that he must feel it. She wrenched herself away from him, shaking her head angrily, knowing that anger was her only defence. 'My life isn't anywhere. I have no life.'

'Come on, Carrie. You know that isn't true.' His voice was quiet, the words reasoned.

She walked to the door, stood with her arms folded tight across her breasts, her shoulders tensed against him. She tilted her head back, looking into the sunlit sky. 'What do you know about it Leo? What can you possibly know about it?' The words were harsh; desolate. Once again she hardly recognised her own voice, ragged and sharp with unshed tears. 'Damn

120

it look – there's that bird again. Isn't he beautiful? Isn't he lucky? Does he know it, do you think? Does he understand how lucky he is?'

He made no move towards her; she sensed his stillness, and the intent of his silence, but she would not turn to face him. She heard his movements as he took the cigarette case from his pocket, and the strike and flare of a match.

The oddly charged quiet stretched to a minute, perhaps two. The bird wheeled, drifted and dipped, great wings spread to catch the slightest breath of air.

'The letter has upset you,' he said, at last.

She turned then, with a brisk and deliberate lift of her chin. 'Yes. The letter has upset me. It has reminded me of who and what I am. But there – I know who and what I am. Why should that upset me?' She was still striving to keep the edge of anger in her voice. She glared at him, challengingly.

Disconcertingly, he smiled; and her heart all but stopped beating. 'Then it isn't just the bird that's lucky, Carrie.'

'What do you mean?'

He joined her at the door, stepped out onto the terrace. 'Not many people can say that they truly know who or what they are.'

The words arrested her, drew her from her self-inflicted anger and misery. 'What do you mean? You of all people surely know who and what you are?'

He turned his head; and she almost found herself flinching from the sudden intensity of his gaze. 'Who am I, Carrie? What am I?'

'You're Leo,' she said. 'And you are—' she hesitated, then unexpectedly found herself laughing, breaking the odd tension of the moment, 'and you are my very favourite cousin.'

'Why so I am.' The smile widened. 'So that's settled to everyone's satisfaction. Listen, I have a suggestion.'

She waited, watching him.

'Forget the house for today. We'll walk up the mountain, and take a picnic. What do you think?'

'What a perfectly lovely idea.' The mere thought was enough to lighten the black mood that had so suddenly descended upon her. Damn Arthur. Damn Hastings. She would not even think of them. She was here, with Leo. She would not waste this time. Minute by minute, day by day, she would gather the moments; a secret and precious hoard of memories, a treasure trove that would have to last her a lifetime. She took the letter from her pocket and tossed it onto the table. 'We've bread, and cheese—'

'—and a bottle of wine.'

'A positive feast.'

He stretched out a hand. Quite naturally, she took it.

'That's better,' he said, gently. 'I do so love to see you laugh.'

She dropped his hand and turned quickly, hiding her face from him. 'I'd better find some decent walking shoes. And slacks would be better than a skirt. I'll go and change.' at the door she stopped. 'That reminds me – I've decided to move into the tower room. Would you mind giving me a hand this afternoon?'

'Of course.' He cocked his head enquiringly. 'Any particular reason?'

'No. Just that it's a lovely room. It has an – an atmosphere.' She laughed a little, self-mockingly. 'And Beatrice lives in there. I have the feeling that she's lived there for a long time – it was Leonard's room, I think. I don't feel I should move her out. So,' she shrugged, laughing again, 'I've decided that I shall just have to move in with her.'

They climbed through the flowered spring woodlands, following a narrow track that took them steadily up the mountainside. Leo, in shirtsleeves and flannels, carried the picnic in a haversack, his thumbs hooked through the straps at his shoulders. Carrie took off her wide straw sunhat and shook her hair loose, looking through the bright canopy of leaves above her to the arching blue of the sky beyond. Shafts of sunlight struck like blades of gold through the branches of the trees. Every now and again a glimpse could be caught of the lovely valley below, the waters of the Lima glittering and sparkling in the sunshine.

'Oh, Leo, it's perfect! Just perfect. Thank you for having such a wonderful idea.'

He smiled.

They passed a small, nameless hamlet with its shrine to Our Lady decked with ribbons and wild flowers. Dogs barked and small children watched them with large, solemn eyes, one or two of them shyly returning Carrie's smile. Beyond the hamlet the woodlands thinned and they came out on to the high hillside that overlooked the Villa Castellini. They stopped for a while and sat upon a flat rock, warm from the sun, looking at the panorama spread beneath them.

'Do you think this might be the rock?' Carrie asked after a moment. 'The one that Beatrice and Leonard sat on? When she told him of her plans for the garden?'

He considered for a moment. 'Why yes, I suppose it could be. There's certainly a clear view of the house.' He leaned forward, looking intently down at the tiled and turreted roof of the villa. From here the disarray of the terraced garden was very obvious. As he idly inspected it Carrie allowed herself, momentarily, the indulgence of studying him. The sunlight gilded the flat planes of his face, the straight, disciplined line of his mouth, turned the fine hair to strands of gold. Despite the lightness of his build, the narrowness of shoulder – or perhaps even because of it – there was no sense of frailty about him; on the contrary the slight, muscled body conveyed an unmistakable impression of graceful, contained strength. He had turned up the cuffs of his shirt, almost to the elbow. His fair skin had darkened a very little in the sunshine. He was, she found herself thinking with lucid and painful clarity, quite the most beautiful person that she had ever seen.

He flicked the hair from his eyes and turned. She jumped up, dusting her hands and her trousers briskly. 'Time to go.'

He pulled a comical face. 'What a taskmaster! If this were the Himalayas and I were a poor hard-working Sherpa, I'd surely at least have the chance of a quick fag?'

She grinned cheerfully, not looking at him. 'Well it isn't, and you're not. Come on. Let's see if we can make it to that building up there – see it? It looks like a church.'

He swung the knapsack easily on to his back. 'My dear Carrie, this is Italy. If it looks like a bloody church, it is a bloody church.' The words were mild, amused. 'Right. Your packhorse is ready to plod on. You'd better eat this lot, you know. I'm damned if I'm carrying it all the way back down.'

The building she had spotted high above them was indeed a church. Small, stone-built, it stood sturdily upon a rocky outcrop, as if it had grown from the very fabric of the mountain. Carrie pushed open the heavy door. The interior was simple, shadowed and cool, the plaster walls white painted, their only decoration the dozen pictures, crudely painted yet potent images, that made up the Way of the Cross. The wooden ceiling was vaulted and dark with age and the smoke of candles. A small stained glass window over the marble altar glowed with light that filtered, jewel-like, into the little building, casting soft splashes of colour upon the floor and walls. On the tiny side altars stood two statues, of Our Lady and the Sacred Heart, again both primitively carved and coloured, yet both, like the pictures, compelling in their power: the still, painted faces ageless and melancholy. A brass Sanctuary lamp burned steadily upon the altar, and the smell of incense permeated the air.

They stood in silence for a long moment. With the heavy door shut behind them even the sound of the songbirds was hushed. When Carrie spoke it was almost in a whisper. 'It's beautiful, isn't it?'

'Yes.'

Something in the tone of the word made her turn. Leo was looking not at the altar, nor at the statues or pictures, but directly at her, unsmiling. 'Very beautiful,' he added, softly.

The trembling had begun again, and the hammering of her heart; she could control neither, nor could she look away.

He held out his hand. 'Come on. Let's find somewhere to eat. This damned bag's getting heavier by the minute.'

Together they walked back out into the warm sunshine. Carrie let her hand rest in Leo's, and with a lift of happiness noted that he made no attempt to release it. His skin was warm, his grip firm. 'There,' he said, pointing, 'over by the olive tree. That looks perfect.'

Perfect was the word, Carrie thought later as, with the sun dipping towards the west, they made their way back down the mountain. Leo had been the best of companions: gentle and witty, and lazily charming, he had set out to entertain and divert her; and all the while, beneath the surface of their banter and laughter, the perilous excitement of their attraction for each other had grown and strengthened, heightening their awareness of each other, making the sun brighter, the mountains more lovely, the day more beautiful. They spoke hardly at all as they followed the path back down through the woods, but there was no strain in the silence; on the contrary, it seemed to Carrie to be a silence of

126

warmth and a certain thoughtful understanding; almost a dialogue in itself.

The house was cool and shady. She made tea, and they drank it on the terrace, making desultory conversation, saying nothing of any consequence. And all the time Carrie was aware of that other, darker communication between them; a sense of waiting, of anticipation.

At last he stretched, arms above his head. 'It's getting cooler. Shall we go inside?'

She led the way back into the kitchen. 'Before you go, would you give me a hand to move my things into the tower room?'

'Of course I will.'

Upstairs the heat of the day was still trapped in the shuttered rooms. Carrie threw open the windows of the tower room and stepped out onto the balcony, stood looking across the valley.

'Lovely, isn't it?' Leo said softly from behind her.

'Yes. The loveliest thing I've ever seen, I think.'

'No. Not quite.'

She turned, leaning against the balcony rail. He was smiling; he reached to take her hand and draw her towards him. 'Come away from there. You're too close to the edge.' His hand came up, cupped her chin gently. 'I don't want anything to happen to you.'

She stood with her breath held, so certain was she that he would kiss her; but then he turned, his hand dropping to his side. 'Well. I suppose we'd better get started.' Briskly he threw open the door of the enormous old wardrobe. 'Knowing Beatrice this could be full of ostrich eggs or matchboxes or some such thing. Hello, what's this?'

'What? What have you found?'

He reached into the cupboard and lifted out a small pile of neatly folded clothes, carried them to the bed, shook them out as he laid them upon it. A dark green ankle length skirt trimmed with copper-coloured braid, two cotton blouses, high-necked and prim, one the same copper colour as the braid, the other the same green as the skirt, and a fringed shawl, faded where it had been folded but obviously matching the other things. The faint fragrance of lavender filled the air.

Carrie stared at the clothes. 'Leo? Do you think— ?' she stopped.

Leo nodded. 'I can't think of anyone else they might have belonged to.'

Gently Carrie touched the silken shawl with her finger. 'I can't believe it. I wonder—' She picked up the skirt and held it against her.

He laughed. 'It looks as though it could have been made for you.'

She shook out one of the blouses. Like the shawl it had faded in patches, but the material seemed strong and the stitching perfectly secure. 'Shall I— ? Oh, Leo, would it be all right to see if they fit?'

'Of course it would. Why are you asking me? They belong to you, remember?'

She gathered the clothes into her arms. 'Wait there. I won't be long.'

She sped along the corridor to the other bedroom, stripped off shirt and slacks and slipped her arms into the sleeves of the copper-coloured blouse. It fitted, as Leo had said, as if it had been made for her. The waist of the skirt was a little tight, and it barely reached to her ankles, but nevertheless that too was perfectly wearable. She draped the shawl prettily about her shoulders and glanced in the mirror. Frowned a little. Something was not quite right. She studied her reflection for a long moment before she suddenly realised what it was.

Five minutes later she walked back along the corridor to the tower room and pushed open the door.

Leo was standing with his back to the room, looking out of the window. He turned, smiling, as she entered, stopped dead. 'Good Lord!'

Carrie laughed, twirled on tiptoe. 'Do you like it?'

'But you could be her! Your hair – it looks marvellous like that.'

She flushed with pleasure. 'Thank you. I copied that,' she pointed to the bronze on the mantelpiece. 'It didn't look right with my hair loose.'

'You should wear it like that all the time.'

'It's not very fashionable.'

'Who cares about fashionable? It suits you, that's what matters.' Leo's voice was very soft. His back was to the window; she could not see the expression on his face. He held out his hands to her. 'Carrie. Come here.'

Still smiling she took a couple of quick steps towards him then stopped in sudden confusion as he moved a little and the light fell upon his face.

'Come here,' he said again.

There was a second when she could have refused,

when she could have deflected the moment with laughter or a flippant comment. She did neither. She stood quite still, watching him, making no attempt to defend herself, to hide what she knew he must see in her eyes.

And eventually it was he who came to her.

They were almost of a height. She felt his hands upon her shoulders, hardly had to lift her head to meet his mouth with hers. His kiss was as she had known it would be; tender, and sure and searching. She did not even lift her hands to touch him, but stood quite still beneath his hands, hardly daring to breath, aware of nothing but the warm touch of his lips on hers.

He released her suddenly, very sharply. Turned away from her, the back of his hand to his mouth. 'I'm sorry. Christ, Carrie, I'm sorry.'

'Don't be. Please don't be.'

'I wouldn't do anything to—'

'I know. Of course I know.'

There was a long and difficult moment of silence. The room had become very warm. The valley beyond the long windows was darkening. 'Leo—' she said at last, reaching a diffident hand to him.

He shook his head.

'Leo!'

The face he turned to her then was anguished, almost to the point of hostility. 'Carrie, stop it! I said I'm sorry.'

'And I said don't be!' To her own surprise Carrie heard the answering anger in her own voice, felt her chin go up stubbornly. 'Leo, don't be! I don't want you to be sorry.'

Which of them made the first move would have been impossible for either to say. For the briefest of moments his arms were fierce about her, his mouth on hers again, but this time with a force that verged on violence. And suddenly, terribly, she remembered Arthur; the hot, wet mouth, the devouring greed in the darkness – she heard the sound she made, felt her body stiffen in resistance to his.

He let her go immediately, stepped back, hands spread wide, the blaze of his eyes for a moment so intimidating that she took a quick, apprehensive breath. And then he was gone, striding from the room in silence and without a backward glance. She heard his footsteps, his rapid descent of the stairs, the slamming of the front door.

She flew to the window. Below her she saw him as he half ran across the terrace, skipped fleet-footed down the stone steps and set off at a fast pace down the track towards the woods, his hands in his pockets, his shoulders tense.

'Leo!' the wrought iron of the balcony rail cut into her fingers as she gripped it. '*Leo!*'

He did not look back.

He did not come for breakfast the next day.

Carrie had spent a restless night and had been up since dawn, watching for him. By nine, accepting at last that he would not come, and knowing that she could settle to nothing without him she decided to go down into the village to see Maria again. The alternative would have been to go to San Marco to seek Leo out; and that she would not do. One thing she had determined during the night; whatever her feelings she would not run after him. If he wanted to see her he must come to her.

The thought that he might not – that indeed there was a strong possibility that even at this moment he might be readying himself to leave Bagni – was one she tried not to contemplate.

As usual within ten minutes of starting down the mountain a cart stopped to offer her a lift. The voluble family who took up almost all the available space cheerfully shuffled along to make room for her and then after polite '*Buon giorno*'s settled back into their own conversations and left her to herself. In the market-place she jumped to the ground, calling her thanks and brushing the dust from her skirt. The children were in their habitual play spot by the bridge. Recognising her now they smiled and called greetings. She stopped for a moment, watching them, before walking across the bridge to Maria's small house.

The door stood open. The interior was dark, and quiet.

'Maria? It's me, Carrie Stowe. Are you there? May I come in?'

A mangy tabby cat stalked past her, tail in air, out into the sunshine.

'Maria?'

The silence was broken only by the rushing of the nearby river.

She stepped across the threshold and into the dim, sparsely furnished room. It was empty. The chair where Maria had sat stood in ramshackle fashion by the window, but of Maria herself there was no sign.

'Hello? Maria?' She moved across the room, pushed tentatively at an ill-fitting wooden door. It swung open to reveal a tiny bedroom, stone-floored and furnished only with a narrow pallet bed and a wooden chair. The battered shutters were closed, and through them a narrow gleam of sunlight fell across the figure huddled upon the bed. 'Maria!'

The old woman did not move. Maria's mouth was open, her breathing difficult.

Carrie knelt on the floor, took the thin, chilled hand in her own warm one. 'Maria, can you hear me?'

For a moment there was no response. Then the wrinkled eyelids fluttered, and opened.

'Maria, are you sick?'

The small dark eyes looked at her for a moment, startled, and with a look of almost joyful recognition. Carrie saw the moment when it died, and knew the cause. She gently stroked the hand she held. 'It's all right. It's me. Carrie. I came – that is – I hoped that you'd talk to me again. But if you're unwell it doesn't matter. Here. Let me make you more comfortable.' She eased the small head onto the lumpy pillow, tucked the thin blanket around her. 'You're so cold. Don't you have another blanket somewhere?'

Maria was still watching her, unblinking. She did not speak. Carrie looked around the room. She could see nothing of any warmth or comfort. Quickly she slipped her own cardigan from her shoulders. 'At least let me put this around you. Maria – I'm so sorry – why ever didn't I think of it before? There's so much up at the villa that you could have: blankets, pillows, a proper bed. A nice chair, warm shawls. Oh why didn't I think of it last time I was here?' She stood up with sudden energy. 'Have you eaten?'

Maria shook her head.

'I'll make you something. You must eat.' Anxious again she touched the old lady's cheek. 'You are all right? You don't need a doctor?'

Again the shaken head. But this time as Carrie straightened the frail hand caught her wrist with surprising strength. 'Your hair.' Maria said, softly.

A little self-consciously Carrie lifted a hand to tuck a strand into a loosening comb. 'I found a bronze bust. In the tower room—' she hesitated, fancying she had seen a sudden flicker of the old wariness in the woman's eyes. 'I copied it.' She smiled a little, hoping to coax some warmer response. 'Do you like it?'

'*Si*. I like.' The words were so quiet she could barely hear them. Maria's eyes closed.

Carrie left the door ajar and went back into the other room. She had seen before that in the corner, half-hidden by a tattered curtain, was a tiny, ancient stove, blackened by years of use. Beside it were a couple of logs and some sticks of kindling, a small stack of cooking utensils and a basket containing a few vegetables, a chunk of rock hard cheese and a stale half-loaf of bread. So far as she could see these seemed to constitute all of Maria's stock of food. She stood for a moment, considering. 'Soup,' she said aloud. 'I'll make some soup.' She looked

134

around. 'Water. There must be some water some-where.'

It took her only a few minutes to discover the pump that the hovel shared with its equally dilapidated neigh-bours in the back yard. Happy to have found something positive to do to help, and to give at least some relief from the constant and demanding presence of Leo in her heart and in her head, she lit the stove – not without considerable difficulty – and set the vegetables to simmer upon it. That done she went back into the bedroom. The old lady was dozing, her breathing quieter. Gently Carrie touched her hand. 'Maria, I'm going out for a moment. Only for a moment, I won't be long. You need some fresh bread. I'm making soup. You'll enjoy that, won't you?'

'*Si.*'

Quietly Carrie turned away.

'Signora Stowe?'

At the door she turned. The old lady was watching her with that disconcertingly steady gaze. '*Grazie. Molte grazie.*'

Carrie smiled. '*Prego.*'

The children were still there, and answered her greeting easily. She walked briskly to the bakery, the mouth-watering smell of which filled the sunny street. She made her purchases amidst a fair amount of laughter and hand-waving, and then went round the corner to the small grocery store. Since she had very little money with her she chose carefully; half a dozen eggs, some freshly made pasta, olive oil, and a few tomatoes. Before she left she would make certain that Maria had a proper meal. Tomorrow she would buy more. Despite her own lack of funds she would not see the old woman go without, and anyway food was so cheap here it would hardly cost a fortune to provide at least some of the basics. She must – she would – make sure that Maria was given enough from the sale of the house to live comfortably for the rest of her days. Arthur and his parsimony could go hang together. Maria, after all, had kept faith with Beatrice when she could have made things extremely difficult. She must be treated fairly.

Absorbed in thought she stepped from the dark interior of the shop into the sunlight. Dazzled she hesitated for a moment, blinking. The square shimmered in the midday sun. Figures moved hazily. She lifted a hand to rub her eyes, smiled and apologised as someone jostled into her from behind. Then her eyes adjusted to the brightness; and in the shadows beneath an awning not ten yards from her she saw the woman Leo had named as Angelique. Tall, slender, and apparently effortlessly beautiful she stood, watching her. And the look in the lovely eyes was such that for an instant Carrie found herself incapable of breath or of movement. In the warmth of the sun she was suddenly cold. And then the moment was gone. Languidly Angelique turned and sauntered to a nearby stall, her progress followed either openly or surreptitiously by the eyes of almost every man in the square.

'*Signora*? You buy?'

'What?' Carrie forced her unfocused eyes to the man in front of her.

He stood, obsequious, a tray of trinkets strapped about his neck. 'You buy?' he asked again, anxiously.

'I – no – I'm sorry. I don't have any money. Next time perhaps.'

He smiled, bleak and unbelieving. '*Grazie, Signora. Grazie.*'

Blindly Carrie turned and walked down the busy street towards the Ponte di Serraglio. The children still played, the shriek of their laughter lifting above the sound of the water that churned and splashed in the sunlit shadows beneath the ancient bridge.

Carrie shivered a little in the cool air that the river's swift movement generated; and in her mind's eye she saw again the malice, the undisguised venom in Angelique's eyes.

And realised that she was afraid.

Chapter Seven

The house was quiet in the afternoon sunshine. A light breeze drifted through the house, stirring curtains and hangings. Carrie counted through the small pile of things she had put on the kitchen table: two blankets, a couple of warm shawls, two large, soft pillows. At least it was a start. She would find someone in San Marco to help her take them down to Maria, and then she would work out what else could be done to make the little house by the river more comfortable. Much of the furniture in the villa was simply too big to be of any practical use, but there were quite a few smaller pieces scattered about the house that would certainly come in handy.

'Carrie?'

The softly spoken word startled her so that she almost jumped from her skin. She turned.

Leo stood in the shadows just inside the door, his figure dark against the brilliance of the light beyond.

They looked at each other for a long moment in silence. Then he came towards her with his hands outstretched. 'Forgive me?'

She cleared her throat. 'Don't be silly. There's nothing to forgive.'

'Of course there is. I frightened you. I wouldn't do that for the world.'

She shook her head. 'It wasn't your fault.'

'It won't happen again. I promise you.'

Their hands were still linked. Carrie lifted her chin, half defiantly, looked long and steadily at him. 'Supposing—' she hesitated, 'supposing I told you that I want it to happen again?'

His fingers gripped hers harder, but he said nothing. 'Well?'

'Be careful, Carrie,' he said, quietly.

She shook her head. 'No. I won't be careful. Not this time. I can't be.' She pulled her hands from his and turned from him, standing with her back to him, leaning upon the table. 'Leo, I know I shouldn't. I know it's wrong. But I love you.' She turned to face him. Asked, a little uncertainly in face of his silence: 'Leo – did you hear what I said? I mean it. I love you.'

He came to her and cupped her chin in his hand, tilting her head a little, his expression sombre. 'Carrie, Carrie. Are you sure? Are you really sure it's love that you feel? That it's me that you love?' He leaned forward and kissed her very, very gently on the forehead, 'Or is it the time, the place, the strangeness of it all? The lovely – the seductive – strangeness of it all?'

'No!'

The grip on her face strengthened. The narrowed eyes glittered in the shadows. 'I say again, Carrie; be careful.'

The trembling had begun again, and she could not control it. Neither could she look away from him.

'You quoted to me in this very room,' he said, softly, 'remember? Shaw's two greatest tragedies in life. The one, not to get your heart's desire—'

'And the other to get it. Yes. I know.'

'So, for the third time – for the last time – I say, be careful, Carrie.'

There was a daunting intensity of emotion in him, that communicated itself through his eyes and through the fierce and painful grip of his fingers. She forced herself to hold steady before it, though still she trembled. 'It is, I think, a little late for that. Leo, do you remember when I first came and found you here? Do you remember what you said, about my not having found my very own adventure yet? Well perhaps I have. Perhaps this is it. Perhaps you are my adventure. So how can I be careful? Adventures don't happen if you're careful, do they?'

He kissed her then; a long and almost painfully tender kiss that said more than any words could have expressed. When at last he drew away she reached a hand to his face. 'Leo?'

'Yes?'

'Will you, that is—' she stopped, despite every effort found herself ducking her head, avoiding his eyes, unable at the last moment to sustain her courage.

'What?'

'Will you – please – make love to me?' Her voice was a whisper. 'Please?'

He stood for a long, silent moment, waiting for her to

raise her eyes once more to his. When she did he smiled. 'Yes.' he said. 'I will.'

'Now?'

'No.'

That startled her. 'Wh-why not?'

He rested his hands lightly upon her shoulders. 'Because you're frightened,' he said.

'Of course I'm not!' The words were much too swift.

'Yes. You are. We both know it. And we both know why. Don't we?'

She looked at him in silence.

'It's Arthur, isn't it? I don't know what the man's done to you, but by Christ he's done something. Something that has made you afraid.'

'Then help me. Show me how not to be afraid.'

'I will. I promise. But not yet. It's too soon.'

'When? When will it not be too soon?'

'We'll both know that when the time comes.' He bent to kiss her again. This time she clung to him fiercely; this time she kissed him back.

Smiling now he freed himself, holding her wrists lightly. 'Enough of that, my darling. Or I might find that I can't control myself after all!'

She had lifted her head and was looking at him in delight. 'Oh, Leo, what did you call me?'

He brought her hands to his mouth, kissed first one open palm and then the other. 'My darling,' he said. 'I called you my darling.'

'And am I?'

'Oh, yes,' he said.

She slid an arm about his waist and leaned against

him, resting her forehead on his shoulder. They stood in silence for a long moment. 'Carrie?' he said.

'Mmm?'

'Will you tell me something?'

She lifted her head. 'What?'

He was laughing. 'Are you thinking of sleeping on the kitchen table tonight?'

She stared at him, blankly.

He nodded towards the blankets and pillows on the table. 'You appear to be making up a bed. I just wondered who it was for.'

Told of Maria's situation Leo quickly became briskly practical. Within the hour, leaving Carrie to collect her gifts for Maria he had gone back to San Marco and arranged transport. By the time they had gathered the comforts and the positive pyramid of small pieces of furniture that Carrie planned to take down the mountain, young Pietro was at the door with his cart. It was a gay party that set off at last in the sunshine, the rumbling, swaying vehicle piled high behind them.

Progress was necessarily slow. It was early evening before, attended by a posse of scampering, shouting children, the cart pulled up outside Maria's door. Carrie jumped down and ran into the cottage, leaving the two men to begin untying the load. 'Maria – look – see what we've brought for you. There are bedclothes, and curtains, and a comfortable mattress, and a couple of chairs.'

The old woman was sitting by the window. As Carrie entered she stood up, standing straight-backed, steadying herself with her stick. Unsmiling she nodded her head in dignified greeting. Carrie was glad to see that there was a little more colour in her face. Happily she held out a hand. 'I'm so pleased to see you looking better. Do come and see—'

'Is kind.' Maria said, firmly. 'But I don't need.'

Carrie stared at her, her hand dropping to her side. 'But Maria,' she glanced around the sparsely furnished room. 'Oh, please, don't say that. We can make you so much more comfortable.'

Maria shook her head. 'I need nothing.'

A quick, small spark of anger flared; Carrie planted her fists on her hips. 'Don't be silly. Oh, for goodness' sake, don't be so obstinate. Of course you do. And, quite apart from anything else, if you think we're turning round and hauling this load back up that beastly mountain then you have another think coming. It isn't very gracious, is it, after all the trouble we've gone to—' she fell to silence. The old woman's face was working in a most peculiar way. Concerned, Carrie stepped forward, hand again outstretched. 'Maria? What is it?' She stopped again, suddenly understanding. Astoundingly, Maria was laughing, utterly without sound, her mouth clamped tight shut, her thin shoulders shaking. 'Maria? You're – you're laughing? Why are you laughing?'

It was a minute or so before the old woman could recover the composure to speak. 'This,' she said, parodying with one gnarled fist Carrie's action. The small black eyes gleamed still with amusement. 'Is many years since I have seen this.'

Carrie laughed a little, suddenly enlightened. 'You mean – Beatrice?'

Maria nodded '*Si.*' She drew the word out; the shake of her head was more than a little rueful. 'Many times. Many, many times.' Her glance flickered then from Carrie's face, to the door behind her. All vestiges of laughter disappeared.

Carrie turned. Leo stood in the doorway, a rolled rug upon his shoulder. Eyes alight with the simple pleasure of seeing him, Carrie turned back to the old woman. 'Maria, this is—'

'A friend,' Leo said, easily, from behind her. 'An old friend of Carrie's. I'm helping her up at the villa.' He set the rug upon the floor, moved between Carrie and Maria, taking Maria's hand, bowing over it with an oddly old-fashioned gesture of deference. 'My name is Leo.'

The old woman eyed him warily.

He smiled his most charming smile. 'I'm staying in the bar at San Marco. Ask anyone. I'm her friend, nothing more. I mean her no harm, I promise you. Now,' briskly he turned to Carrie, ignoring the suspicious and searching look Maria was directing at him, 'come and tell us where you want things put. It's like a circus out there; the word has gone round – half of Bagni has come to watch!'

They had indeed. Willing hands unloaded a comfortably upholstered chair for Maria to occupy upon the pavement whilst the rest of the furniture was moved in, to much advice, admiration and comment. In no time the small house was swarming with people; the well meaning, the warmly and volubly helpful and the openly and avidly curious. Leo had a quiet word in Pietro's ear, and the boy disappeared for a few minutes, to return quickly with a small cask. The glasses and cups that Carrie had packed were quickly appropriated whilst children were sent scurrying to nearby houses for more. Carrie watched with amusement and affection as Leo, with no more of the language than she herself possessed, but with laughter and the lightest of touches, organised and diffused the energy and enthusiasm of Maria's friends and neighbours. She herself perched upon the arm of Maria's chair, a cup of wine in her hand, watching happily as her small, private gesture of thanks turned, in what she was coming to understand was typical Italian fashion, into a party.

And then suddenly, in the the midst of the noisy talk and laughter, she found herself remembering the ordered soullessness of number 11 Barrymore Walk, with its clipped hedge and straight path, its wooden gate always shut against the world, its bright lights and modern conveniences; remembering Arthur, fingers drumming, waiting for tea at five; remembering Tuesdays, Thursdays and Saturdays.

Swiftly she drained the cup.

'Carrie.' She lifted her head. Leo had materialised beside her, one hand light upon her shoulder, in the other a large stoneware jug. He was obviously enjoying himself, his slight figure alive with energy and enthusiasm. The mere sight of him brought a smile to her face. 'Have some more wine.'

'Oh, really no—'

'Nonsense. It's Pietro's cousin's very best. Awfully expensive. Works out at all of—' he pretended to think for a moment, 'oh, about tuppence ha'penny a gallon, I would guess. Don't turn it down. He'd be most put out. And at the moment he's in charge of unpacking the china. We wouldn't want any accidents, now would we?'

Laughingly she surrendered her cup, aware that she had already drunk rather more than was good for her, and that too quickly. Leo filled it, saluted her with a quick grin, and disappeared into the crowd. Carrie turned to smile down at Maria, and was astonished to see the gleam of tears in the sharp, dark eyes. A small, bony hand lifted to take hers. '*Grazie*,' Maria said softly, '*Molte grazie*, Signora Stowe.'

Carrie smiled, the wine warm and heavy and sweet on her lips and tongue. '*Prego*. And please,' she squeezed gently upon the frail hand that held hers, 'please, Maria, won't you call me Carrie?'

By the time the little house was straight, the last of the toasts had been drunk and the cask emptied, darkness had fallen. In ones and twos or in laughing groups the uninvited guests drifted off. The upholstered chair, with some ceremony, was installed by the window. Maria, utterly refusing to admit to exhaustion, sat herself firmly upon it. Carrie, by now rather more than a little unsteady on her feet, bent to kiss the withered cheek. The old lady muttered something into her ear. 'I'm sorry?'

'Come soon,' Maria said. 'There is much to tell you.'

'I will.' Carrie straightened. The world shifted a little, queasily, about her.

Then Leo was there, his hand beneath her elbow, his smile warm and teasing. 'I hate to remind you of this, but there's a mountainside between here and home. I think we should go.'

The evening was warm and humid. Somewhere in the mountains thunder rolled, distantly. Tiredly and a little clumsily Carrie began to clamber onto the high seat at the front of the cart.

'Hey, if you fell off there in this darkness we'd never find you!' A hand detained her, drew her away; bemusedly she allowed Leo, with a single easy movement to lift her onto the body of the cart. 'Come on. You're exhausted.' She was aware that he had climbed up beside her, drawn her to him, her head on his shoulder, his arms tight about her. '*Presto*, Pietro, *presto*.' She felt his cheek pressed against her hair, and through the dizzy waves of languid, unaccustomed, wine-born sleepiness heard him add, very quietly, 'My darling needs her bed.'

She smiled, dreamily. 'What did you call me? Leo? What did you call me?'

And did not hear his answer.

Carrie was aware of the storm in the night; woke once or twice with a dry mouth, thudding head and roiling stomach, then slipped back into the black depths of a deep and dreamless sleep. It was the sun that finally woke her, striking painfully into eyes that for a moment she could barely open. The air was clear and cool after the night's rain, the sky ablaze with painful light. She winced, groaned, turned over and tried to bury her splitting head beneath the pillow. She was dying. Definitely dying.

She was also, she realised, except for her shoes, still fully dressed.

She lay quite still, trying to focus mind and memory; and for the moment absolutely could not. She remembered climbing into the cart, remembered the feel of Leo's arms about her, and then – nothing. For goodness' sake, how had she got here?

As realisation dawned she winced again, mortified. Whatever must Leo think of her?

After a few moments, only too aware that the sun was high and that she could not hide beneath the pillow for the rest of the day she sat up, gingerly swinging her legs over the side of the bed. The room swung unpleasantly around her. She clenched her eyes shut. The world settled a little. She sat very still for a long time before opening her eyes again and carefully standing up. Every movement threatened, it seemed, to crack her skull. She poured water from the jug on the washstand into the basin, gratefully splashed it over her face. Her tangled hair fell about her shoulders, the ends dangling in the water. The image that confronted her when she glanced into the mirror appalled her; her face was pale, her hair a bird's nest, her slacks and shirt disgracefully rumpled. With a determination born mostly of desperation she set about repairing the damage.

It was about half an hour later that, still moving with a great deal of care, she made her way downstairs to the kitchen. She knew that Leo was there; the smell of hot coffee and toast had been drifting through the house for some time – a smell she would normally have found delicious but that, on this particular morning, was almost more than her delicate stomach could take. Trying to move her head as little as possible she pushed open the door, shading her half-closed eyes against the flood of sunlight, and leaned against the doorjamb.

Leo turned, grinning. 'Good morning, my love.' He was heinously cheerful. 'Feeling good?'

'Don't be such a heartless pig.' She managed to focus her aching eyes upon him; neatly and immaculately garbed in crisply laundered shirt and flannels he looked as fresh as a daisy. 'You're disgusting. Why haven't you got a hangover? I do assume that's what it is?'

His grin widened. 'Practice. And yes, that's what it is. Is it bad?'

'I'm dying,' she said, simply.

His smile widened. 'I'll get you something.' He reached for a glass, went to the cupboard. Carrie walked to the table, dropped into a chair, buried her face in her hands. 'God, I feel ghastly! I'm never going to touch another drop of alcohol as long as I live. I swear it.'

He laughed, 'Famous last words. Say rather that you won't try Pietro's cousin's home-made brew again – at least not until you've developed more of a head for it.'

She lifted her head. Winced. 'How the devil do you achieve that without killing yourself in the process? I swear I've never felt so bad.'

'Here. Try this.'

She eyed the awful-looking concoction in the glass with real suspicion. 'What on earth is it?'

'Prairie oyster. You knock it back in one gulp, without breaking the egg yolk. Try it. It works.'

She pushed it away, shaking her head. 'I couldn't.'

He in his turn pushed it back to her. 'Try it,' he insisted, and beneath the laughter was a warm and teasing affection that lifted her eyes to his. 'Try it, my darling,' he said, softly.

'What's in it?' As ill as she felt she could not take her eyes from his face. She rested her chin on her hand, watching him.

He perched on the table beside her, took her other hand. 'Egg. Worcestershire sauce. Salt. Pepper. And a very little of the hair of the dog.'

'It sounds disgusting.'

'It works. Try it.'

'Have you had one?'

He shook his head.

'Well. There you are then.'

'I—' lightly and laughing he bent to kiss the top of her head 'didn't need one. I promise you; it will help.'

'I think you're trying to poison me,' she said, solemnly, 'so that you can inherit the house after all.'

There was a long moment's silence.

'Sorry.' She picked up the glass and scowled into it. 'Not a very good joke.'

'No.' His voice was quiet.

She smiled shakily, lifted the glass to her lips. 'Not even a very clever one. Because you wouldn't inherit it anyway, would you? You'd have to share it with Arthur. God, what a thought. All in one swallow did you say?'

'Yes. It's the only way to do it.'

150

Obediently she gulped down the potion. 'Oh, Lord! That is truly awful.'

Briskly he stood. 'Right. That's the first part of the prescription. The second is breakfast.'

'Leo, I couldn't possibly—'

'Breakfast!' he said, firmly. 'Coffee and a piece of toast. You'll feel better, I promise. Later you can have a snooze somewhere cool and quiet. In a few hours you'll be right as ninepence.'

'You're very kind,' she said, softly. 'I'm not sure I deserve it. Did you,' she felt colour rise in her cheeks, 'did you put me to bed last night?'

He flicked the hair from his eyes, smiling, turned to reach for the coffee pot. 'Yes. You were dead to the world by the time we got back to the house. You didn't even stir. Here, try to drink at least a little of this.'

She heaped sugar into the coffee, stirred the liquid pensively. 'And you?'

He was by the stove, his back to her. 'I stayed,' he said. 'In case you needed me. I slept in the next room. Popped down to San Marco for some fresh togs this morning.'

'Leo?' In the tree beyond the open door a bird sang, piercingly beautiful, and the scent of magnolia drifted upon the air. 'Why are you so good to me?'

He turned. His laughter had died. His thin face had upon it that unguardedly intent look that so disturbed her. 'Because I love you,' he said. 'I've tried not to. You can't know how hard I've tried not to. But I do.'

Oblivious, the bird still sang. A breeze whispered in the branches of the tree.

Leo came to her, held out his hands. She took them, allowed herself to be drawn to him, her face almost level with his. 'I watched you last night as you slept,' he said. 'You looked like a child. A lovely, innocent child. I have never felt—' he stopped.

'What? What have you never felt?'

He hesitated for a moment. 'I have never felt so – touched. So protective of anyone.' The hands that held hers tightened. 'And I have never wanted anyone so much. Never.'

A sudden and unwelcome vision arose; of the woman Angelique, effortlessly beautiful. A friend. A difficult – beautiful – friend. 'Are you sure?' she found herself asking.

'Oh yes. I'm sure.'

'Then—' she stopped, the old fears, the new excitements tying her tongue.

He shook his head, half-smiling now. 'No. Not yet.'

'When?'

He gathered her into his arms, drew her head down onto his shoulder. 'When you're ready, my darling. When you're ready.' She felt a small spasm of laughter shake him. 'Apart from anything else a socking great hangover isn't exactly a recommended aphrodisiac you know. You'd be asleep before you knew it.'

She laughed a little, tiredly, her eyes closed, loving the feel of him, the smell of him, the sound of his voice so close to her ear. 'What a blissful thought!'

They stood for a very long time in silence. Then, 'It's terribly wrong, isn't it?' she asked at last, quietly.

'Yes.'

'I'm a married woman. We're first cousins; when we were children we were like brother and sister.'

'Yes.'

'Wrong. All wrong.'

'In the eyes of the world? In a word? Yes.'

She lifted her head to look at him, dark eyes wide and clear. 'Then why doesn't it feel wrong? Why does it feel so utterly, wonderfully right?'

In answer he simply tightened his arms about her. She laid her head on his shoulder again, tried to control the inevitable trembling. 'Leo?'

'Hmm?'

'Take me to bed. Please?'

She sensed his smile. 'No. Not yet. Not yet, my darling.'

Tuesdays, Thursdays and Saturdays. It must be different. It must surely be different?

'But, Leo, when? *When*?'

'When you're ready, Carrie, my love. When you're ready.'

The hours of the warm and quiet day drifted past them; and as they wore on, as Leo had predicted, Carrie felt better. In the heat of the afternoon she dozed in the green shade of a chestnut tree, woke as the sun began to dip behind the mountain peak to the west.

'Feeling better?' Leo sat beside her, watching her, a tray with two glasses on it upon the grass beside him.

'Yes, thank you. Much.'

'Here. Lemonade, nice and cool.'

She drank thirstily. He leaned to her, kissed her

lips, licking gently at the moisture on them. 'Best lemonade I ever tasted,' he said. 'It's much nicer second-hand.'

'Leo—'

'Yes?'

She laughed a little. 'Nothing. Just Leo. Leo, Leo, Leo. I love you.'

'Yes. I know.' He stood, held out a hand. She took it, and leaving the glasses where they stood they walked towards the house. Neither spoke as they moved through the shadowed rooms to the stairs. At the foot of the staircase Leo stopped, turned her to face him, his hands on her shoulders, his eyes searching her face. 'Carrie, you're sure?'

'I'm sure.'

They mounted the stairs with hands linked. In the tower room Leo closed the shutters. Carrie stood watching him. He came to her, took her face in his hands. She closed her eyes. 'Is it time?'

'Yes. It's time.' He kissed her very gently, dropped his hands to her shoulders, stroked them softly down her arms, the palms barely touching her skin.

'What – what do you want me to do?' Her voice was unsteady, her dark eyes suddenly haunted.

'Nothing, my darling. Nothing you don't want to.' One by one he undid the buttons of her shirt. 'Come now, don't shake so.'

'I'm sorry. I can't help it.'

He undressed her and laid her naked on the bed, gently but insistently preventing her instinctive attempt to cover herself. 'Don't hide from me,' he said. 'You're lovely.' Shyly then she watched as he took off his own clothes, stood smiling down at her. She held out a hand. He took it.

'It's strange,' she said.

'What is?'

'I've been married for nearly five years yet I've never seen a naked man before. You're beautiful, Leo. Beautiful.'

He settled himself beside her, stroking her face. 'Now, my love, let me show you there's nothing to be afraid of. I won't hurt you. I promise I'll never hurt you. I want to give you nothing but pleasure. There – tell me – isn't that good? and this?'

He made love to her gently and with a fierce tenderness that aroused her in a way for which nothing in her past experience had prepared her; in the end it was she who all but begged him at last to abandon his restraint and take his own pleasure. Afterwards they lay for a long time in silence. Carrie had turned on her stomach, her head on her arms, studying him, sleepily, as he lay beside her. At last he raised himself on one elbow, started to spread her tangled hair about her bare shoulders. She trapped his hand, brought it to her lips, nibbling at each fingertip. 'Wicked fingers,' she said, softly, and lifted a hand to touch his mouth. 'And wicked, wicked tongue!'

He smiled, lazily, stroked her hair.

'Wicked,' she said again, closing her eyes, smiling. 'Where did you learn such wicked tricks?'

There was a moment's silence. 'Does it matter?' he asked, very quietly.

155

Her eyes opened, huge, and calm and trusting. 'No,' she said, 'It doesn't.' And knew it for the truth.

Much later, half asleep, she asked. 'Leo? What day is it?'

He considered. 'Thursday, I think. No, Friday. It's Friday. Why?'

She smiled, dreamily, eyes closed. 'No reason. I just wanted to know.'

'Did I tell you?' he wound a strand of hair about his wrist, 'I've found a garage in Bagni that will rent me a car. Tomorrow,' he bent to kiss the small of her back, 'tomorrow I'll take you to Siena.'

They drove to Siena through the rolling hills of Chianti, taking a full day to get there – as Leo observed, whatever the new Fascist government had managed to do for the railways they had not yet managed to get to grips with the roads. They spent two days and two nights in the city – days and nights that were an utter enchantment for Carrie. The journey itself was a voyage of discovery for her as they chugged through sleepy towns and villages that looked as if nothing in them had changed with the passing of centuries. As they drove south, and away from the mountains the weather became noticeably hotter; her first view of Siena – the massive terracotta-coloured brick walls and slender, decorative towers shimmering in sunlight – was a sight she knew she would never forget. They stayed as man and wife in a small hotel near the centre of the ancient city; the days they spent wandering the cool canyons of the ancient streets and beautiful squares, exploring the magnificent buildings, sipping wine at a table in the fascinating Piazza del Campo; the nights they spent in love and laughter. Carrie had never been happier. With each moment spent in Leo's company she loved him more, and to her delight it seemed that Leo, too, became more attentive, more loving with each passing hour. Neither could resist touching the other; the brushing of hands, the meeting of eyes could spark an immediate excitement that more often than not led them back to their small, stuffy room and more lovemaking.

'What a shameless hussy I've become,' Carrie said, faint and amused surprise in her voice. She lay sprawled on the narrow bed. Leo sat on the floor beside her, the smoke from his cigarette spiralling in the still air. Their clothes lay in an untidy heap by the door. 'The man at the desk, I'm sure he knows. Why we keep coming back, I mean. And I don't care. I just don't care.'

Leo smiled.

Carrie rolled over on to her back, arms spread wide. 'No one in Hastings would believe it,' she added, solemnly, and in the way of lovers they laughed, not because the thought was particularly funny but for the sheer joy of being together, of being in love.

He took her hand, traced the lines of her palm with his finger. 'We'll have to set off fairly early in the morning,' he said. 'It will take best part of a day to get back.'

'Oh, Leo, must we? I don't want to go back. I want to stay here. For ever and ever and ever.'

He shook his head, smiling a little.

She sat up, drawing her knees to her chin, folding her

arms about them, her expression suddenly sober. 'Leo, what are we going to do?'

It was a question neither of them had asked – a question, indeed that both until now had assiduously avoided.

Leo, very precisely, stubbed out his cigarette in the ash tray.

'Leo? We have to talk about it. Don't we?'

He drew a long breath. 'Yes. I suppose we do. But not now. Not yet, my darling.' He stood up, leaning over her, lifting her chin with his finger, bending to kiss her, pushing her slowly back down onto the bed. 'Not yet.'

She slept for the greater part of the journey home, her head on Leo's shoulder, woke as they drove past the massive walls of Lucca and on up the river valley towards Bagni. The sun was dipping towards the mountains as they passed the odd and ancient structure known as the Ponte del Diavolo, a strangely constructed affair whose builder was said to have asked the assistance of the devil, and then to have tricked him out of his demanded payment – the first soul to cross the bridge – by driving a pig across first. 'Poor pig!' Carrie had said, when Leo first told her the story. 'That was hardly fair, was it?' Now they stopped for a few moments and climbed the narrow, steep path that led over the bridge, leaned hand in hand upon the parapet watching the rushing waters of the Serchio beneath.

'Leo?'

'Mmm?'

She turned her head to look at him. 'I love you.'

His smile was slow. 'And do I love you?'

She pretended to consider it. Nodded. 'Yes. Oh, yes. I do believe you do.'

The car did not have to be returned until morning, so they enjoyed the slightly doubtful luxury of driving up the mountain track to the villa. Despite her reluctance to leave Siena, Carrie was surprised and delighted to discover how pleased she was to be back in the house. Home. It felt like home. Indeed, with Leo here with her it felt like heaven. They opened a bottle of wine and took it with them to the tower room. They made love, drank the wine, made love again, and slept, with the shutters open to the cool mountain air.

Carrie woke in the small hours, frightened. Beside her Leo's breathing was uneven.

'Leo? What's wrong?'

'Nothing. I'm all right.'

'But you cried out.'

'A nightmare, that's all. Sorry I woke you.'

She leaned on her elbow, put out a hand in the darkness. His body was tense as a spring, his hair wet with sweat. 'Leo – please – what's the matter?'

'Nothing, Carrie. Nothing. I told you – a nightmare.' He pulled away from her, threw back the bedclothes, got up and walked to the washstand and then to the window. She sensed his movements, heard the tap of a cigarette upon the silver case, watched in silence as a match flared, silhouetting his neat head against the dark sky. 'Go to sleep Carrie,' he said, softly. 'I'm all right, I promise you.' His voice was strained.

Her eyes had grown used to the darkness now. She could see him, his slight figure very still, as he watched from the window. She lay quietly for a very long time before dozing off. Later she stirred sleepily and turned to him as he climbed back into bed beside her. With no word he drew her head down onto his shoulder, and within moments both were asleep again.

In the brightness of early morning the sudden and unexpected jangle of the front door bell startled them awake.

'God Almighty!' Leo sat up, tousled hair falling across his forehead. 'What the hell was that?'

Carrie was clutching the sheet to her breasts. 'The front door bell! It can't be!'

The bell rang again, insistently.

Leo groaned, head in hands. 'It bloody is.'

'But who on earth—' Carrie scrambled from the bed, grabbed for her dressing gown, pulled it on and went out onto the balcony; found herself looking down at the crown of a large straw hat decorated rakishly with flowers and a bright red scarf. As the shutter clattered behind her, the woman looked up, beaming, and gave a cheerful wave.

Carrie's heart sank.

Mary Webber waved again. 'Cooee, Mrs Stowe. I said I'd come, and here I am.' She lifted her hand, in which she held a long white envelope. 'What an adventure! The most charming young man offered me a lift up the mountain in his cart. See – I've brought a letter for you; it arrived at the post office yesterday.'

Chapter Eight

———◆———

Leo, pale and in chancy temper, did not take to Mary Webber, despite the fact – or perhaps, more likely, because of it – that she took a lively and quite open interest in him.

'Well I never, another of dear Beatrice's grandchildren! I remember now of course – Mrs Stowe mentioned you the first time we met. I wondered then how it was that no one seemed to know you were here. If I had known you were such a personable young man I'd have been even more surprised.' The woman's eyes, sharp with curiosity, darted about the kitchen, flicked from Carrie to Leo and back again. Carrie self-consciously tightened the belt of her dressing gown. At least in the time it had taken her to let Mrs Webber in, take her into the kitchen and make a pot of coffee Leo had shaved and dressed, slipped out into the garden via the drawing room windows and re-entered the house by the kitchen door; Carrie did not, however, have any great faith in the deception. The car, after all, had been standing outside the front door ever since Mary Webber arrived, large as life and twice as obvious.

'I'm helping Carrie with the business of clearing the house,' Leo said.

'Why of course. Of course.' The letter Mrs Webber had brought with her lay unopened on the table. She eyed it and looked at Carrie expectantly. Carrie ignored the look. She had already recognised the handwriting.

Leo stood. 'I've got to take the car back.' He regarded Mary Webber levelly. 'May I offer you a lift down the mountain Mrs Webber? It's a warm day for walking.'

It was the first time Carrie had seen the woman flustered. 'Er, why, I hadn't exactly planned—' she stopped. Neither Carrie nor Leo said anything. 'That is, I thought I might offer you a hand with something?' she turned to Carrie expectantly.

With Leo's eyes steady upon her Carrie shook her head. 'Thank you, but it really isn't necessary. We're managing very well.'

Leo picked up the car key and tossed it in the air, gently impatient. The woman resolutely ignored the hint. 'Tell me, how much longer do you think you'll be here, my dear?'

'I really don't have any idea.' Taking her cue from Leo Carrie picked up the three coffee cups and carried them to the sink. 'Another—' she stopped, astonished at the sudden heaviness of her heart at the thought. She cleared her throat. 'Another week or so, perhaps two. I'm not sure. There are arrangements to make.'

'To be sure. To be sure. Well you must come down to the village for supper with me. I absolutely insist.' Mrs

162

Webber's quick, brightly curious eyes flickered to Leo again, and she beamed, 'Both of you, of course.' The eyes returned to Carrie. 'Bagni has quite taken you to its heart for your goodness to Maria, you know.'

'It was the least we could do,' Carrie said.

'It was an act of great kindness.' Still the woman made no move to leave.

Leo walked to the door, held it open, courteously inviting. He glanced at Carrie, eyebrows raised. 'Is there anything I can get you in the village?'

'We—' cursing herself, Carrie stumbled a little over that, 'I could do with some tomatoes. And some olive oil.'

'I'll get them. I'll be back in a couple of hours.' He looked again at Mary Webber in polite and patient enquiry.

Reluctantly, faced with the resolutely open door, the older woman hauled herself to her feet. Still with unflawed civility Leo offered his arm.

'Why thank you. How kind. Tell me, are you well acquainted with this part of the world, Mr Swann? It really is quite lovely. What a pity Mrs Stowe has to sell the villa, she does still intend to sell it, I take it?'

The insistent voice faded at last. Carrie looked at the envelope that lay upon the table. Outside she heard the car engine roar into life, and the spin of the tyres as Leo started away on the gravel. She winced a little, allowing herself to feel some faint sympathy for Mary Webber. Something told her that with Leo in such perilously touchy mood it would not be a comfortable journey down the steep mountain track.

The letter lay, waiting, on the table.

She turned away from it, walked to the door, and then with an exclamation that was half anger, half impatience, spun on her heel and snatched it up.

It was short, brusque and dictatorial. How much longer, Arthur wanted to know, did she intend that he should run his own household as well as hold down a by no means undemanding position at the bank? Had he intended to lead a bachelor life he would never have married in the first place. People were asking questions. Surely by now she had had time enough to put her grandmother's affairs in order? Or was the task so far beyond her that she needed his assistance? He dreaded to think how much money she was spending. He commanded her home, and signed himself, '*Your loving husband, Arthur*'.

She threw her head back and yelled, inarticulately, at the ceiling, the letter crushed in her two hands. 'Damn you!' she said, very quietly. 'Damn you, Arthur. My loving husband? My *loving* husband? God Almighty! I wish—' she expelled a breath, threw the crumpled letter onto the table, 'Oh, I wish you were dead. I do! I mean it. You hear me?' She was talking to the ceiling again. '*I wish he were dead.*'

Leo returned to the house about noon. His thin face was still translucently pale and there was a quiet, a reserve about him that worried Carrie a little. 'Are you all right?' She put out a hand to him.

He took it. 'I'm fine.'

'I don't think you are. Leo, is it last night? The,

164

the nightmare, or whatever it was? It's bothering you still?'

He dropped her hand, turned from her. 'Don't keep on about it, Carrie. I'm all right, I tell you.'

'I'm not keeping on about it,' she said, reasonably, 'I just wondered, that's all. You didn't sleep well. And now you're very touchy—'

'I'm not touchy!'

She grinned.

He laughed a little, rubbed his forehead. 'I'm sorry.'

'It's all right.' With some difficulty she levered herself to her feet. He had found her in the drawing room, cataloguing books – or at least, that was the task she had set herself. Finding an old leather-bound tome on Pompeii and Herculaneum she had quickly become absorbed, and her right foot had gone to sleep. 'Ouch.' She hopped, rubbing it.

'Wine,' he said. 'Let's have some wine. Sovereign remedy for cramp, I believe.'

'Tea,' she said, firmly. 'Let's have a cup of tea. How was the redoubtable Mrs Webber?'

He directed a reassuringly subversive smile at her. 'Disappointed,' he said. 'The nosey old bat. You can have tea. I'm having wine.'

In the kitchen, true to his word, he opened a bottle. Carrie put the kettle on the stove. From behind her she heard the rustling of paper. 'May I?' Leo asked.

She turned. He had picked up the crumpled letter and was smoothing it out on the table.

She shrugged. 'Please yourself. It's – predictable.'

The room was quiet as he read the single sheet of neat, cramped writing. 'So,' he said, 'what are you going to do?'

She took a long breath. 'Answer it. Tell him—' she spread helpless hands. 'Tell him what, Leo? What are *we* going to do?'

He straightened, tossing the letter back onto the table. 'I don't know,' he said. And then again, turning from her, walking to the door, reaching into his pocket for his cigarette case, 'I don't know.'

'Well,' she said, her voice over-bright, over-controlled, 'That's reassuring.'

Again that oddly vulnerable gesture, his fingers to his forehead.

She joined him at the door, slid her arms about his waist, turning him to face her. 'Do you have a headache?'

'Yes. Sort of.'

She indicated the glass that he held. 'Is that good for it?'

'Very.' He tilted his head and drank. 'It's that kind of headache.' His smile was wry.

She leaned against him in what had become a habitual gesture, rested her forehead lightly upon his shoulder.

Your loving husband, Arthur.

Tuesdays, Thursdays and Saturdays.

How could she stand it? How could she ever stand it again?

She shut her eyes tightly for a moment. Leo's arms rested lightly about her. His eyes were distant upon the mountains.

166

'Leo, what are we going to do?' she asked again, quietly.

He drained his glass. 'We're going to bed,' he said. 'Now. Unless you have any other more pressing plans?'

'Such a headstrong child,' Maria said. 'Always so quick. No sooner did she think of something than it was done. No sooner did she want something than she must have it.' She fell for a moment to pensive silence.

'And Leonard?' Carrie asked. 'Was he the same?'

'No. He was different. A quiet boy. Very—' she pondered, 'the word is gone. *Sensibile*.'

'It's the same.' Carrie said. 'Sensitive. Intense?'

'Ah. Yes.'

'That's the feeling I get from the journals. They were quite opposite characters, yet quite extraordinarily close, weren't they? Have I got it right?'

'They were' Maria spread gnarled hands, 'brother and sister.'

'But not all brothers and sisters are necessarily as close as that. It comes out over and over again in the journals. They did everything together. It was as if, as if they lived in their own world. The villa, the garden – until—' Carrie took a long breath 'until poor Leonard died, that is.' She shook her head sadly. 'Beatrice must have been devastated.'

'*Si*. Is true.'

'But then she married.' Carrie stood and moved to the window. The afternoon was sultry, heavy and humid. Not a breath of wind stirred in the trees. Even the sound of the river was muted.

167

'Yes. She married.'

'The last journal ends on the day she had her first child. Uncle Henry. The last entry – it's an odd one. *I shall no longer be alone*, she says. A strange thing to say, don't you think? Have you read it?'

There was a long moment's quiet. '*Sì*,' Maria said, softly. 'I have read it. I remember.'

Impulsively Carrie turned. 'Maria – please tell me – do you know where the missing journal is?'

Stiffly the old lady stood. 'A glass of wine,' she said. 'Then we talk more.'

'I don't quite know why,' Carrie shifted a little, settled her head more comfortably on Leo's shoulder, 'but I feel absolutely certain that Maria knows where the 1867 diary is. Why won't she tell me? Why won't she let me see it?'

Leo picked up a strand of her hair and wound it about his finger. 'Why does it matter?'

'I don't know. But it does. She told me so much today about Beatrice when she was young, about her later life here, as a young married woman, and afterwards, when she lived here with Uncle Henry. About our parents, and about her friends, and her love of the garden. But she won't talk about Leonard, or how he died. There *is* a mystery there, I know it. And it's something to do with that missing book.'

Leo yawned.

'I'm sorry. You're tired, I know. Do you want to go to sleep?'

He turned his head on the pillow, smiling. While she

168

had been with Maria that afternoon his odd and difficult mood appeared to have dissipated entirely. 'In an hour or two,' he said. 'Or three.' He propped himself up on his elbow, looking down at her. 'Well, let's just say at some time between now and the morning at any rate.'

It was a couple of days before Carrie got down into the village again, during which time she wrote a short, apologetic but carefully uncommunicative letter to Arthur. She took it to the post office, did some shopping and then went to visit Maria.

'Maria. It's me. I've brought you some grapes—' she stopped.

Mary Webber beamed. 'Mrs Stowe. How nice to see you again. I was just telling Maria about my little trip up the mountain the other day—'

Carrie glanced at Maria. The old woman's face was expressionless, showed no sign of warmth, offered no smile of greeting.

'—and saying how grand it was to have two of Beatrice's grandchildren in the village. She's met Mr Swann, I gather, but didn't realise who he was?'

Carrie schooled her face. She said nothing.

Maria sat bolt upright, her hands folded in her lap.

'Well,' Mary Webber stood, 'I must be on my way. Do come to supper one day next week, Mrs Stowe, and bring that handsome cousin of yours with you. A charming young man. Quite charming.' She smiled her wide, bland smile. 'Though his driving, I have to say, leaves something to be desired.'

In the silence that followed her going Maria lifted small, expressionless eyes to Carrie's face.

Carrie nodded. 'Yes. Leo is my cousin. He's John's son. We know that John and Beatrice didn't get on. We know that the arrangements she made about the house were specifically to disinherit Leo. I – he – was afraid that if you knew who he was you wouldn't talk to me.'

'Is true.' Maria said.

'But why? Maria, why? Why did Beatrice hate her own son so much? What happened between them?'

'He was a bad child.' Maria said, 'And grew to be a bad man.'

'How? What did he do?'

'He took much money.'

'Took? You mean from Beatrice? He *stole* from her?'

Maria shook her head. 'Not stole. Took.'

'I don't understand.'

'He knew—' the old woman stopped, mouth pinched together.

'Knew what?' Carrie frowned. 'Maria, what did he know? Something about Beatrice?' she hesitated, 'Something – bad?'

Maria did not answer.

'Maria, please, won't you tell me? Beatrice's son – Leo's father – found out something about her, and then took money from her. You mean he blackmailed her?'

The almost lashless lids flickered. 'I don't know this word.'

Carrie studied her. 'I think you do,' she said, quietly.

Maria turned her head. 'You go now, please. Signora Webber, she has tired me.'

170

'Signora Webber is enough to tire anyone,' Carrie said, grimly. 'Maria, please. I'm sorry I didn't tell you who Leo is. Believe me, I did it for the best. Please don't let it come between us. He isn't his father. He's himself.' And I love him. She did not say it.

'The blood is bad.' Maria said.

'No! That isn't true.' The words were vehement; too vehement. Maria lifted her head, studied Carrie's face.

Carrie flushed. 'It isn't true,' she said again, more calmly. 'I'll bring him to see you, and you'll see for yourself.'

Maria shook her head, her expression obstinate. 'No.'

Still seething at Mary Webber's mischief Carrie held on to her patience and her temper by a thread. 'All right,' she said, reasonably, 'I won't. But please, don't let it come between us. I so much enjoy our talks. I may come again?'

For a moment she feared the woman would refuse. Then the bony shoulders lifted in a shrug. '*Si.*'

It was obvious she would, for now, get no more concession than that. Marshalling good sense over temper Carrie unloaded her small purchases on to the kitchen table, and left.

Maria neither thanked her nor gave her farewell.

'Do you think it's possible?' Carrie asked Leo, later, over the supper table. 'Would your father have done such a thing?'

'Blackmailed his own mother?' Leo leaned back in his chair, lifted his wine glass, surveyed it grimfaced. 'Oh, yes.'

'Leo!'

'It's true.' He lifted sombre eyes to hers. 'My father was a bastard. Of the worst kind. I hated him.'

'But – that's awful.'

He shrugged.

The silence was difficult. Then Carrie said 'So it is possible that something of the kind happened, and that's why Beatrice was so determined that I should have the house?'

He stood up, abruptly, scraping his chair on the kitchen floor. 'Carrie, for God's sake! Does it matter? What's done is done. It's over. They're both dead. We'll never know.'

'Maria knows,' Carrie said.

'*Leave it, for Christ's sake!*'

Carrie stared at him.

He turned from her, shoulders hunched, reached for his cigarettes.

'I'm sorry,' she said, at last, uncertainly.

Without a word he left her. She heard him light his cigarette on the terrace outside, saw the quick flare of the match in the darkness.

That night, for the first time, they did not make love. Carrie lay staring into starlit darkness, acutely aware of Leo's turned back, his too-even breathing. 'Leo?' she ventured, quietly.

He did not reply.

But with absolute certainty she knew he was awake.

The next day was difficult. They were careful of each other, nothing out of the way was said, but still there lingered an awkwardness, a left-over anger that was as hard to explain as it was to ignore. Heavy upon Carrie's heart was the knowledge that every precious minute wasted was a minute never to be reclaimed; soon – too soon! – she would have to leave.

Never to see Leo again? The thought was all but unbearable.

In the early afternoon he came to the study, where she was packing books and paintings into one of the large tea chests they had found in the attic. 'I'm going down into the village. I'll see you later.'

She waited, unwilling to ask what his errand might be; hoping he would tell her without her asking.

He turned.

'How long will you be?'

'I don't know. It depends.'

Anger stirred. She went back to her task, not looking at him. 'Okay.'

She heard the door close behind him.

She spent a miserable afternoon packing. As evening approached she found herself more and more often going to one window or another, hoping against hope she would see the slight, graceful figure swinging up the path towards the house. The sun slipped behind the mountain, the shadows lengthened. And still he did not come.

She tried, with less and less success as the hours wore on, not to think of the woman Angelique – Leo's beautiful, difficult friend – who waited in Bagni. Carrie had not told Leo of the encounter in the village; it had seemed best not to mention it. She had not seen the other woman since. But she was still there, of that she was uncompromisingly certain.

And was Leo, at this very moment, with her?

As the silent twilight deepened she ate alone; an hour or so later she picked up a book and carried it to the tower room. One last time she went to the window, stood for a long time gazing down the track that was by now all but lost in the gathering dusk. Then, precariously close to tears, she lit the lamp, climbed into bed and attempted to read.

Several empty hours later she heard footsteps on the gravel, and the kitchen door opened and closed. Watching the door, she waited. It was several minutes before he came. He closed the door quietly behind him, stood leaning against it, his face all but expressionless, the set of his head faintly challenging. 'You're still awake.'

'Yes.'

He stepped away from the door, slipped his jacket from his shoulders. As the lamp light fell on his face she saw how tired he looked. She held out a hand. 'Leo? What's wrong?'

'Nothing.'

'You're angry that I asked about your father?'

'No.' He sat on the side of the bed, kicked his shoes off. She smelled the wine on his breath; saw, suddenly and with a terrible twist of her heart, that his hands were shaking. Her anger left her. To have him so close and not to touch him was more than she could bear. She threw back the bedclothes and came to her knees beside him.

'Leo, I don't understand. I don't understand what's happened. Please look at me. Please try to explain.'

174

Her voice trembled on the edge of the tears that had threatened all day.

For a long moment he did not move. Then, very slowly he turned, and his eyes met hers. 'All right, Carrie. I'll tell you what's wrong,' he said. 'I knew I loved you. I have only now realised just how much. That's what's wrong.'

She stared at him in silent astonishment.

With a hand that still, very slightly, trembled he touched her cheek. 'Do you realise how little you know me?' he asked, unexpectedly.

She considered that. 'Yes,' she said, and kissed him. Then with a quick movement she slipped her nightdress over her head, shook her hair about her shoulders. 'Yes, I do realise it. But I don't care. Because I love you. Nothing will ever stop me loving you.'

He reached for her then, fiercely, his hands sliding from her waist to her buttocks, pulling her to him, his mouth at her breast. She bent above him, curtaining him with her hair.

And smelled distinctly a faint, sweet perfume that was neither wine nor the scent of tobacco.

She could not herself have said with honesty if the tears that she shed during their lovemaking that night were born of happiness or pain.

It was Maria who told her, two days later: 'He has a woman, this cousin of yours,' she said, a glint of satisfaction in her eyes, 'at the hotel. I told you. Bad blood.'

'I don't believe you.' But she did. Leo's mood swings

in the past couple of days had become more unpredictable than ever; and in her heart she had known why.

'Is true. The whole of Bagni knows. My sister's son – he works at the hotel. Ask him if you wish. The woman is very beautiful.'

'Why are you telling me this?'

The old woman took her hand, held it with surprising strength. 'Because you are like my Beatrice. Because if you love you will love too well.'

'I don't love him!' Carrie wrenched her hand away, jumped to her feet. 'I have a husband. Leo is my cousin. That's all.'

'Then why are you crying?' Maria asked, not unkindly.

Leo was sitting on the terrace with a glass of wine in his hand when she arrived at the villa. He turned, smiling. 'Caught me. I really have only just—' he stopped. Stood up. 'Carrie? What is it?'

'Tell me about Angelique,' she said, and the tears had started again, 'Tell me about your beautiful – difficult – friend.'

He drank the wine in silence. Placed the glass with great care upon the table.

'*Leo. Tell me!*' Her voice had lifted to the shriek of a fishwife; there was nothing she could do to control it.

He lifted his head sharply. The narrow eyes blazed.

'You went to her the other day, didn't you? And then you came home and made love to me. I could kill you for that, Leo. You hear me? I could *kill* you.'

Still he did not speak.

Goaded beyond reason she flew at him. He trapped her wrists, held her from him, his grip tightening as she struggled. Abruptly she stopped. Immediately he let her go, stepped back.

'Tell me about Angelique,' she said again, but quietly now.

He took a long breath. 'Someone, it seems, already has.'

'You don't deny it?'

His silence answered her.

She dropped into the chair he had vacated, put her elbows on the table, buried her face in her hands in despair.

When she lifted her head, he had gone.

She found him in the tower room, packing his small, battered leather case.

'You're going to her?'

'I'm going.'

'To her?'

He turned. 'Carrie. We have known from the start what had to happen. We always knew it would have to end.'

'But like this? *Like this?*'

He rolled up a shirt, tucked it into the case. His face was blanched, tight drawn.

'Do you love me at all?' she asked, desolate.

His movements stilled, apart from the shaking of his hands. Then he snapped the lid shut and straightened. 'Believe me, my darling—'

She flinched.

'—it's better this way. Finish here. Sell the house.

177

Then go home to England. To Arthur.' He met her eyes, levelly. 'Your husband. You never would have brought yourself to leave him. You know it.'

The tears slid unchecked down her face.

Passing her as he walked to the door he stopped, lifted a finger to her wet cheek. Then he was gone. She heard his swift, light footsteps in the passageway, running fleetly down the stairs, heard the thud of the front door behind him like the knell of death.

She flew to the window.

He did not look back.

Chapter Nine

For the first few days after Leo's cruelly abrupt departure Carrie felt physically ill; she could not eat, and sleep was all but impossible. Everywhere she looked she saw him, every sound was his voice. On the first night she could not bring herself to go to bed, but spent the night uncomfortably upon the musty-smelling sofa in the drawing room, dozing, jumping awake at the slightest sound, straining her ears for the sound of his footsteps; body, mind and heart ached for his presence, and try as she might she could not control the real, almost physical anguish of it. Dawn found her starting on her second pot of coffee on the terrace outside the kitchen; and even here she could not escape him. As clearly as if he were there she saw him running up the steps, heard his voice and his laughter, saw the bright, narrow eyes, the long mouth, the flick of his head as he tossed the hair back from his forehead. Once or twice she even fancied she smelled a drift of cigarette smoke on the air.

Infatuation? Or love? Could love, or the loss of it, hurt this much? What, indeed, was infatuation if not love taken to the extreme? And when, if the link were so suddenly and brutally broken, did the pain stop? Would it ever?

Wearily she laid her head on her crossed arms upon the table, closed her eyes against the clear, merciless light of a brightly beautiful morning; a morning without Leo. As spring moved towards summer the days were getting longer and hotter, even here in the foothills of the mountains. Suddenly the thought of it oppressed her. She wanted grey skies, and rain. She wanted the world to weep with her. For weep she did, sometimes silently, the tears simply sliding all but unnoticed down her cheeks, sometimes suddenly and uncontrollably, until she felt there must surely come a time when there could be no more tears in her; until she believed, like Alice, that this would be her punishment; to drown in her own tears.

She wandered from room to room, not bothering to open the shutters, made no attempt to order the chaos about her. Half-packed tea chests and boxes were scattered throughout the house, piles of books were on every floor, stacks of paintings against every wall. Late in the afternoon she finally went to the tower room – their room – and threw herself at last, exhausted, upon the bed, her head buried in her arms. After a moment she rolled on to her side, reached for Leo's pillow, curled herself about it, knees drawn up, like a child in pain.

And still she cried; still she could not sleep. Still she listened for his return.

The next day she could not stand the confines of the house, with its strong and recent memories, and spent the best part of the day in the garden, coming at last to the arbour with the fountain. She sat on its edge, fingers dabbling absently in the dark water.

She had to stop this, she knew it. She must do something. She was not a child. She was a grown woman; she must not indulge herself in this disgraceful way.

The musical sound of the water that trickled down the rock face and ran from the child's jar soothed her a little. It was shady and cool. All at once she found herself remembering the day she had stood in the boxroom, looking at the picture of this very spot, building dreams.

She leaned towards one of the dolphins, ran her hand over the smooth curve of its head. Some of the algae rubbed off on her palm. Pale marble gleamed wetly. How lovely this place must have been in Beatrice's day. No wonder she had loved it so. And how sad to see it now, neglected, overgrown, belonging to no one.

Would the whole world be sad from now onwards? Would there be happiness anywhere? And if she were offered a miracle – to go back in time, to make things different; never to have met him, never to have loved him, never to have suffered because of that love – what would she do?

Even unhappy as she was, without thought she knew the answer to that.

She sat for a very long time, calmer than she had been since Leo's going, though the pain was still there, raw as a fresh wound.

She was alone. She would have to make plans, get herself organised.

She would have to go home. If she did not, then Arthur

181

might well lose patience and decide to come and fetch her, and the thought of that was all but unendurable.

Where was Leo? In Bagni with Angelique? That thought was unendurable too. Surely they would have left by now? Surely they would not stay to torment her?

Then she remembered the look in Angelique's eyes, and was not so certain.

Insects scudded across the reflecting water, tiny wakes and ripples glittered. Carrie stood up, shoulders hunched, hands in the pockets of her crumpled slacks, looking about her. The nymph still gazed serenely down into the water despite the dirt and lichen that caked her, the curves of the fountain with its dolphins and sea creatures was classically beautiful as ever. 'If things had been different,' Carrie said softly, aloud, 'If I – if we – had been able to stay—' She took a long breath. Sunshine flickered and glittered through the tree canopy above her; and suddenly she knew that she could not bear it; she must leave the house as soon as possible. She must go back to England. But with Leo gone, now, she needed help. Signor Bellini must be contacted, the arrangements made to ship Beatrice's belongings back to England, the house put up for sale. That meant getting to a telephone. And that meant going to Bagni.

She heard in her head Maria's words: '*He has a woman, this cousin of yours. Is true. The whole of Bagni knows.*' And presumably, by now, the whole of Bagni would know that he had gone away with her. Well, she would have to face it sooner or later.

But not now. Not today, almost light-headed as she was with misery and lack of food and sleep and with the tears still so perilously close. She must give herself another day to pull herself together. Tomorrow. She would confront Bagni and its gossip tomorrow.

That night, unable to face the tower room she went to bed in her old bedroom; and still she could not sleep.

She walked down the mountain the following day, through a hot and somnolent afternoon. There was hardly anyone around; even most of the dogs lifted sleepy heads and kept to the shade as she passed. The village was quiet, most of the shutters closed. Not without qualms, remembering the redoubtable Mrs Webber had made her home there, Carrie made her way to the Continentiale and the telephone.

Signor Bellini, as always, was helpful charm personified. Of course he would help with the arrangements, and of course he would be pleased to take over the sale of the house for her. He would be coming to Bagni in a few days – could he perhaps come to see her? Friday afternoon would suit him best.

The arrangements made, Carrie paid for the call and slipped quickly from the hotel foyer, cheered at least a little by the fact that she had, for once, avoided meeting Mary Webber.

Her cheer was short-lived; Mrs Webber was waiting for her on the pavement outside. 'I saw you were using the telephone, my dear, and couldn't bring myself to interrupt. My goodness, isn't it hot? Summer's coming, that's for sure. You were telephoning your cousin?'

'I'm sorry?'

'Your cousin, you were telephoning him? He left on

the train the day before yesterday. Well, I suppose you must know that, of course you do, with the – the young lady.' Again that avid curiosity. Carrie could not for the life of her fathom if it were malicious or not. But at least now she knew; Leo and Angelique had left. The thought brought despair and relief in about equal measure. Fighting that she had little time or energy left for Mrs Webber.

'No. I wasn't phoning Leo. I was calling Signor Bellini. He's handling the sale of the house for me. Now if you don't mind, Mrs Webber—'

'Mary. You must call me Mary, my dear.'

'If you don't mind I really am awfully busy, and—' she cast her mind about for an excuse 'and I promised Maria faithfully that I'd call on her before I went back.'

Her arm was taken firmly. 'Oh, but I'll walk with you. It's only just across the bridge.' Mary Webber peered with those uncomfortably sharp eyes into her face. 'My dear, are you quite well? You look peaky. Very peaky. And you've lost weight, I swear.' She took on a lightly scolding voice. 'Now, I know what it is: you aren't feeding yourself properly, up there in that great rambling house all on your own. How often must I invite you to supper?'

Carrie endured the woman's company to Maria's cottage, then perforce had to tap on the front door; something she had had, in fact, no intention of doing.

Mary Webber waved cheerfully before turning and walking briskly back the way she had come. Entirely unable to resist the childish impulse Carrie stuck out her tongue at the retreating back, then turned to find Maria watching through the window, a shadow of amusement on her face.

Carrie pushed open the door.

'That woman!' Maria said, and shook the fingers of her right hand in a gesture of scorn.

'She's certainly a pest.' Carrie rubbed her forehead tiredly, then added with a brightness that was entirely spurious, 'Is there anything I can do for you? Anything I can get you?'

The old woman was watching her narrowly. She shook her head.

Carrie walked to the window, stood looking out, her back to Maria. There was a very long silence.

'You are – *triste*? Sad?' the old woman questioned at last, quietly.

Carrie nodded, unable to speak.

'Because he is gone.'

'Yes.'

'With the woman.'

'Yes.'

'Is good he is gone.'

'No!'

'Is good he is gone.' Maria repeated, stubbornly.

Carrie turned. Unexpectedly the old woman held out a small brown hand. Carrie took it.

'It will pass,' Maria said.

Numbly Carrie shook her head again. 'No. It won't.'

'Ah, yes. Everything passes, *cara mia*, everything. In time.'

'In a lifetime, perhaps.' The small endearment had

unnerved Carrie completely; the silent tears were there again. Still holding the tiny, frail hand she knelt beside Maria and, as if it were the most natural thing in the world, laid her head upon her knee. With her free hand Maria gently stroked her hair, murmuring soothingly.

'I love him,' Carrie said. 'Oh, Maria, I love him so much. Nothing has ever hurt as much as losing him does. I can't live without him. I can't!'

The stroking hand had stilled. 'No. Is not true.'

Carrie lifted her head, startled at the vehemence of the words. The small claw of a hand that held hers gripped with a surprising strength.

'Listen. Is wrong this love. Wrong! You are too close in blood. His father, your mother, they were brother and sister. There is wickedness in this. Let him go. Or God will punish you both.'

'I don't care.' Carrie was sobbing now, 'I don't care! If I could get him back I would. Let God punish us if He's really that cruel! I wouldn't care. Not if I had Leo.'

The old woman leaned close to her. 'And if the punishment falls on another?' she asked, fiercely.

Carrie fell silent, her brow furrowed, the sobs still catching unevenly in her throat. 'What do you mean?'

The old woman did not answer. Her grip on Carrie's hand loosened. She leaned back in her chair. 'You have a husband, *cara*. Go to him. Forget this – cousin. Is best, believe me. Think of him as dead.'

Carrie sat back on her heels, her face set in misery. 'It would – almost – be easier if that were true. At least I could grieve. At least I'd *know* that I could never see him again, never hear his voice. This way, each time I turn my head I fancy he may be there, watching me, waiting for me—' she choked suddenly, swallowing tears, and bowed her face to her cupped hands.

'You are young,' the old woman said. 'Pain is worse for the young, for they believe it will last for ever.'

'It will. It will!'

'No.' Maria took a long breath. 'I say again – you have a husband. Go to him, before greater damage is done.'

Carrie lifted her tear-wet face to look directly into the old, tired eyes. 'I hate my husband,' she said. 'I love Leo. I don't care how wrong it is. I won't deny it. I love him.'

'Then you are in danger. You must go. Leave this place. Go home.'

'Home.' Carrie repeated, bleakly. 'Home?'

Maria's claw hand reached again, gently, drew her head back down onto the musty black material of the skirt. 'Life is hard, *cara mia*, life is hard.' Maria said.

Half an hour later, calmer, Carrie left. She had opened her heart to Maria, talked of Leo, and the simple pleasure of being able to speak his name had eased the pain a little.

The old woman sat, eyes distant, hands idle upon her lap for a long time after the door closed behind her young and troubled guest. Then with some difficulty she eased herself out of the chair and reached for her stick. It was a full minute before she could steady herself enough to walk across the room to where a largish, flat box lay on top of the bureau that had been one of Carrie's gifts to her. With some difficulty she opened it, gnarled hands shaking, and lifted out a book.

A book that Carrie would have recognised instantly.

Maria carried it with her, back to her chair, laid it upon the small table, and contemplated it with pensive eyes.

At least knowing that Signor Bellini was coming on Friday gave Carrie some purpose, some goal towards which to work. And work she did, deliberately to the point of exhaustion, dragging cases from room to room, wrapping and packing and making lists that sometimes seemed a mile long. She worked into the night, until her strength was gone, and then was up at dawn, starting again.

And still, every time she passed a window in the front of the house, she found herself pausing for a moment, eyes searching the mountainside, hoping against all reason to see him; and never, of course, seeing him.

She was standing at the window of the tower room, three days after her conversation with Maria, when she noticed a small cart labouring around the bend that led up to the house. With her heart hammering in her throat she stepped out onto the balcony; but it took only the most cursory of inspections to dash her hopes. The hair of the young man who drove the cart was very dark, his shoulders broad. Beside him, diminutive in black, her head shaded suffocatingly by a heavy shawl, perched a figure that looked remarkably like Maria. A few moments later, when she went downstairs to greet her unexpected guests it was to discover that this was indeed Maria, come to call upon her. She introduced her companion as her great-nephew. He shook Carrie's hand, smiling, an enormous young man with an infectious grin. He spoke no English, Maria explained, dismissively, and would be spending the afternoon with a cousin in San Marco. She let fly several sentences in rapid-fire Italian. The young man grinned again, kissed her dutifully and affectionately on the cheek, saluted Carrie and swung back onto the cart. As Maria and Carrie turned away he called, obviously asking a question, gesturing to something that lay beside him on the seat. Impatiently Maria shook her head, and replied sharply. He shrugged goodnaturedly and raised a hand, clucked to the pony, and the cart pulled away.

Carrie, in honesty, was nonplussed. 'Maria, may I get you something? A cool drink? Something to eat?'

'Later.' Maria said. 'First my wish is to see the house. It will be the last time, you see.'

The simple words touched Carrie. Gently she offered her arm. 'Of course. Come in. You're more than welcome. I'm just sorry that everything's in such a mess.'

The afternoon was not an easy one. Maria said little as they moved from room to room; yet still, occasionally, the odd illuminating observation made Carrie wish it had occurred to her to ask the old woman up to the house earlier.

'Here Signorina Beatrice would sit for hours,' Maria said, standing at the window of the drawing room. 'Here she would read, and sew, and sometimes sing to herself.'

Carrie smiled, 'Sing to herself?'

'But yes. All the time. Until—'

'Until?'

Maria shook her head. 'Until she no longer sang.'

'Was the kitchen terrace here in your time?' Carrie asked, standing looking out to the mountains, suppressing memory.

Maria shook her head. 'This was later. When the children—' she stopped, 'when Signorina Beatrice and Signore Leonard were young this was a place to grow – things for the kitchen?' she opened her hands in a typical Italian gesture, looking at Carrie in enquiry.

'Vegetables? Fruit?'

'Ah, *si*. Vegetables.'

'Ah. *Il studio*. In this room they learned, my little ones.' The library was perhaps the most chaotic room of all. Maria stood in the doorway, declining to enter. Carrie, in conscience, could not blame her. An agile cat would have found difficulty in manoeuvring its way round the obstacle course of the floor. Maria chuckled, the sound dry. 'They had a—' she hesitated, '*precettore*, ah, a teacher.'

'A tutor?' Carrie suggested.

'Yes. A tutor.' Again Maria spread gnarled, expressive hands. 'Poor man,' she said.

Upstairs she showed Carrie the two rooms, entirely empty now, at the far end of the main corridor, which had been hers. 'One to sleep and one to sit. It was a good life.' She smiled. 'They never left me alone. Never. *Cattivos!*'

At the door of the tower room she baulked. 'I know this room. I don't need to see it.'

'But please, Maria, there's something here I'd really like to show you.'

190

The woman's reluctance was obvious. Carrie was puzzled. 'This was Leonard's room, wasn't it?'

'Si.'

'Most of the books have his name in them.' Carrie pushed open the door, 'Look. This is what I wanted you to see.' She walked to the mantel and took down the bust. 'It's Grandmother, isn't it?'

Maria nodded. For a moment Carrie fancied she saw her blink against tears; but when the other woman spoke there was no sign of emotion in her voice. 'Was Leonard's favourite.'

'I thought it might be. That's why I left it here. I'm going to take it home with me. To keep for myself. I couldn't bear to sell it.'

'Is good that you keep it.'

'Is there anything here that you would like? Some keepsake – something for yourself?'

Maria shook her head. 'No. I have memories. I need nothing else.' She stood looking around the room, her face sombre. 'I need nothing else,' she repeated, quietly.

At no time during the tour of the house had Leo's name been mentioned. It was not until they were seated on the terrace with a cool glass of lemonade that Maria asked, abruptly, 'You are feeling better?'

Carrie lifted her eyes to the astute, wrinkled face. 'No,' she said, 'I'm not. I don't think I ever will.'

Maria shook her head, exasperated, and muttered something in Italian.

Carrie, unable to sit still, stood and walked to the balustrade. 'It's not that I'm not trying,' she said, 'I am. I simply can't believe that he's really gone. That I'll never see him again. He loves me. I know he does. And I love him.'

'And the other woman?'

'Angelique. Her name is Angelique. I don't know. I don't understand. All I know is that I love him. And if I saw him – if he lifted one finger – I'd go to him. I couldn't help myself.'

She heard the old woman sigh behind her.

'I know what you said the other day is true; it's wrong. On all counts it's wrong. But—' she turned to face the other woman, 'Maria, haven't you ever loved like this? Don't you know what I'm saying? It's as if he owns me, body and soul. I have no control over the way I feel for him. Can't you understand that? Can't you understand that right and wrong simply don't come into it?'

'*Si*. I understand. Very well I understand.'

A sound made Carrie turn. 'Your nephew is coming.'

The woman sighed again. Her face looked suddenly careworn. 'I have something for you,' she said.

After the cart had set off again down the mountain Carrie took the journal into the kitchen and laid it upon the table. 'Read it well,' Maria had said, 'and understand.' She had offered no word of explanation or apology, and Carrie had not expected one. She stood pensive for a moment, her fingertips resting on the leather cover. *Read it well. And understand.* What had the old woman meant by that? She opened it to the first page. The first entry had been written in London. '*Rain, rain, nothing but rain! Oh how I long for the blue skies*

192

of Italy! Drizzle, drizzle, drizzle! Where are the storms of the mountains?'

Behind her the kitchen door snicked shut, very quietly.

Catching her breath she spun round.

And there, on the one occasion she had not looked for him, stood Leo.

There was a very long moment of silence. Then both moved at once and within an instant were in each other's arms.

'Carrie, Carrie. My darling, darling love forgive me,' he said into her hair. 'I'm sorry. I'm sorry, I'm sorry!' his arms were so tight about her she could barely breathe.

She could not speak. She clung to him, her wet face buried in his shoulder. The feel of him – the dear, exciting, familiar feel of him – as always had set her trembling. He put a hand beneath her chin, lifted her face to his. 'Tears, my darling? Don't cry. Please don't.'

'I have never cried so much,' she said. 'Never.'

He kissed her then, fiercely, and his hands were on her body. 'Let me love you,' he licked her wet face, tasting her tears, 'let me love you now. Let me dry your tears and make you happy again. Please. Let me love you.'

'Yes,' she said. 'Yes.'

The sun went down and the mountains grew quiet as he made love to her. She cried again, but the tears this time were different. The night was warm, the crickets called, woodsmoke drifted in the air and through the open window; and still he loved her, tender and sometimes savagely fierce, coaxing and sometimes ruthlessly demanding, taking possession of her, binding her to him once again. And she, racked with pleasure, did nothing to defend herself from him. Past and future slid away. What had happened, what was to happen became meaningless. There was only now, only the slaking of hunger and thirst; only the joy of being together again.

It could not last, of course, this ecstatic obliteration of the world. Dawn came, and with it the knowledge that reality had to be faced, questions asked, explanations offered. They lay together and watched the light seep into the clear sky beyond the window. In the tree outside the kitchen a bird sang, sleepily.

'Why did you come back?' Carrie asked.

His breathing was very quiet and regular, his body utterly relaxed. 'Because I love you,' he said. 'Because I want you. Because I couldn't bear to be parted from you,' he came up on one elbow, looking down at her. 'Because I would starve without you.'

'Then – why did you go?'

He studied her face, gravely. 'Because I am bad for you. Because I fear I'll hurt you. Because there is Arthur, and England. Because I have never loved anyone as I love you, and that frightens me more than anything has ever frightened me.'

'And Angelique?'

'Angelique was a side issue. She's gone.'

'Gone?'

194

'We quarrelled.' His lashes veiled his eyes.

'What about?'

'You. I told her I was coming back.'

'Are you certain she won't follow you again?'

'Yes.'

She traced the line of his mouth with her finger. 'And if she does?' she asked, softly.

'I told you. She won't.'

'What are we going to do?' How often – how often? – had she asked it?

'I don't know. I only know that I can't live without you. Without seeing you. Without loving you. Without knowing that you love me. If you go back, I'll follow you. I won't let you go. I'll see you if it kills me. I told you – I love you too much. Once a week, once a month, once a year, I don't care! I will – I must – see you, my darling.'

'Don't!' She closed her eyes. 'Please don't!'

He leaned to kiss her. 'You're going to have to choose, my darling. You're going to have to choose.'

'Choose? How can I choose? You know what I want. I want this house. And you. But the self-same law that Beatrice so carefully circumnavigated to disinherit you means that the house isn't mine. It's Arthur's, too. He won't let me keep it. I know it. He won't let me leave him; he'll never allow me to leave him. And how would I live if I did? I've nothing. Nothing of my own. And even you—' She turned her head away. 'I know that you love me. But in reality you aren't mine, either. Are you?'

He buried his face in the tumble of hair that nestled in the curve of her neck.

*   *   *

195

'What day is it?' she asked, much later.

He stirred. 'Thursday. No. Friday.'

'Oh, blast it. Signor Bellini's coming.'

'When?'

'This afternoon. About three.'

He reached a lazy hand. 'Then there's time—'

Despite herself she laughed as she tried to wriggle away from him. 'Leo, do stop it!'

'—to make love again. Come here.'

Signor Bellini arrived, unexpectedly, very much earlier than the hour agreed. Fortunately Carrie and Leo were up, decorously dressed and taking tea on the terrace when the only taxi in Lucca pulled up with a self-important spray of gravel in the drive.

Smiling, Carrie ran down the steps to greet him. 'Signor Bellini how nice! You've come in time to lunch with us – my cousin and I—' She stopped.

The man's face was troubled. He gripped the hands that she held out to him. 'Signora Stowe. I'm so sorry. I don't know how to tell you this. I am the bearer of bad news. Very bad news.' He glanced up at the terrace, where Leo sat, watching. 'Please. You wish to sit?'

She searched his face, puzzled. 'Why should I sit? Signor Bellini? What is it? What's happened?'

'Signora, you have my sympathy. I have had a communication from your husband's employers. They did not know how else to get in touch with you. There has been a tragic accident. Signora Stowe – there is no easy way to tell such things – your husband, he is dead.'

Chapter Ten

The worst thing – the very worst – was the immediate, unacceptable and shaming sense of relief. Guiltily she tried not to feel it, tried to focus her mind on a life lost, a life wasted, a tragic and senseless accident that had cut short a man's living, breathing existence; but she could not. Try as she might she could not conjure up anything but the most superficial feelings of grief, nor could she, deep in her heart, as she accepted condolences from virtual strangers – the news having run round the English community in Bagni like wildfire – and made hasty plans to return to England, repress the knowledge of what Arthur's death actually meant to her. Awful though the thought was she could not escape it; in the moment that he had tripped and fallen on those steep, space-saving stairs in the modern box of a house of which he had been so proud, she had been set free. Whilst far from rich she was financially independent. The Villa Castellini was hers, and hers alone. No one now could force her to sell it.

And there was Leo.

She surprised herself by, at first, refusing his offer to accompany her to England for the funeral. 'It's all right. I can manage, I promise.'

'I wasn't suggesting you couldn't, my darling,' he said, mildly, 'I just thought you might find it less of a strain with me there. Travelling alone isn't much fun at the best of times. And there'll be a lot to do. I'd be happy to help, that's all.'

In the end the temptation openly and legitimately to have him with her proved too much; less than twenty-four hours after Signor Bellini had delivered the news of Arthur's death they set out together for England.

They arrived at Number 11, tired and cold, in the chill April dusk two days later, having been held up on the French coast by storms. Carrie pushed open the door against a small pile of letters, bent to pick them up. The house was oppressively silent, and ice-cold.

The newel post and banisters at the foot of the stairs were broken. Someone had made some attempt to tidy them; the broken pieces were stacked neatly in the corner of the hallway.

Carrie swallowed against a sudden terrible stirring of guilt. She had wished him dead: and here he had died. Faint nausea made her mouth dry. 'I'll make a cup of tea.' She passed the stairs and went into the familiar, clinically clean kitchen.

Leo put down the cases he was carrying and followed her. 'Carrie.'

She turned, sobbing, and buried her head in his

shoulder. 'Leo, it's horrible. Horrible! I didn't realise how awful it would be.'

'You can't stay here,' he said, firmly. 'No one would expect you to. You'll come to the hotel with me – no!' She had lifted her head and started to speak. 'I won't hear any argument. I won't let you stay here on your own. It's out of the question.'

'But what will people— ?' She stopped, ashamed of her swift and automatic reaction to his suggestion.

'What will people think? People will think nothing at all my darling. What do you take me for? We'll have perfectly respectable separate rooms. I'm your cousin, remember? Your only blood relative. What could be more natural than that I should be here with you? Until the funeral is over and your affairs are in order we will behave impeccably. After that, what we do is our own business; for we certainly won't be doing it here. Now, take that damned kettle off. I'll use the call box up the road to find a taxi.'

Ironically, it was in the comfortable panelled office that Arthur had always aspired to occupy that Carrie heard the full story of her husband's death.

'On the first day we simply assumed that he was unwell.' Mr Simpson, the bank's manager, though sympathetic was clearly – and not unnaturally – finding the interview far from easy. 'On the Wednesday, however, when again he didn't come to work and we had no word, it did seem strange. Stowe,' the man blinked owlishly and awkwardly behind wire-rimmed glasses, 'Arthur, that is, was such a—' he

199

hesitated, 'such a punctilious man. As you know of course.'

'Yes,' Carrie said.

'So that evening I sent young Marlborough round to find out what was wrong.'

'That was very kind of you.'

The man made a small dismissive gesture with long, bony hands. 'He could get no reply. He left, but called again in the morning. And this time—' Mr Simpson cleared his throat, 'this time he looked through the letter box. What he saw – well, he called the police.'

'Arthur had fallen down the stairs.' Carrie's voice was quiet but steady, 'That's what Signor Bellini told me. And the banisters are broken.'

'Yes. So it seems.'

'There is to be an inquest of course. At the end of the week.'

'Yes. So I had heard. But there seems to be little doubt. A carpet-rod had come loose at the top of the stairs. His neck was broken. The doctor said he must have died immediately.'

'That's something, at least. I shouldn't like to think—' Carrie did not complete the sentence.

'No,' the man said.

There was a short silence. Mr Simpson stirred a little in his chair.

'As I said, the inquest is at the end of the week,' Carrie continued at last. 'I have to wait, of course, for that, before I can make any definite arrangements. About the funeral, that is. Would you like me to let you know the day?'

'Oh, of course, of course. Yes. And if there is anything I can do, anything at all?'

Leo came out of his chair, held a hand to Carrie as she too stood. 'We'll let you know,' he said. 'Thank you for your time.'

'Simpson detested Arthur,' he said, later, over tea in the hotel lounge. 'It's perfectly obvious.'

'Yes. He did. And Arthur detested him. Sad, isn't it?'

Leo lifted a shoulder. 'I must say I'm becoming happier by the minute that I never met your husband.'

'Leo! You shouldn't—'

'—speak ill of the dead?' He regarded her levelly for a moment. 'Don't fall into that trap, my darling. You spoke ill enough of the living.'

She lowered her eyes, fiddled with the spoon in her saucer.

'Don't,' he said.

'What?'

'Feel guilty. It isn't your fault.'

'I know. It just feels as if it is.'

The verdict was accidental death; the funeral service was short, and ill-attended. It was a bright, gusty late April day, still cold but full of the fresh promises of spring. 'Perhaps I should have hired some mourners,' Carrie said. 'Isn't that what people used to do?' She was leaning against the parapet that separated the front from the beach. Grey, white-capped rollers washed onto the sand and swirled, foaming, towards the high tide mark. Two small children, wrapped against the wind, dug sturdily, building a castle, watched over by a uniformed nanny. A shaggy black and white dog rushed in and out of the swelling waves, yelping maniacally. Carrie took off her black felt hat with its wisp of widow's veil, turned it in her hands. 'God, this is a horrible hat, isn't it? I look awful in it. Why did I buy it?'

'I told you not to.'

'Yes. I know.' She squashed the thing flat. 'Arthur would have liked it. It's not exactly flamboyant, is it?'

She had not cried. Not once. She wondered if anyone had noticed. She thought probably not. She was certain that the two neighbours who had been the only other mourners, if such a word could truly be used, and poor put-upon Marlborough, who had represented the bank, had been altogether too anxious to get away after the depressing service to analyse or even consider the bereaved widow's apparent fortitude.

Leo removed the hat from her fingers, dropped it neatly in a nearby litter bin.

'Leo! The beastly thing cost seventeen and six.'

'Will you ever wear it again?'

She shook her head. The wind caught her hair where the pin had slipped from it and whipped it across her face.

'Well then.' He leaned, with easy grace, sideways on the parapet, facing her. She kept her eyes on the moving water, but could feel his on her, as tangible as a touch. As a caress. She felt slow colour lift in her cheeks.

'When can we go home?' he asked, softly.

Carrie turned her head at the word, looked at him in

a kind of wonder. 'Home,' she repeated. 'Yes. That's what it is, now, isn't it? Home.'

He nodded.

'The solicitor said everything's absolutely straightforward. Needless to say Arthur's affairs were in perfect order. There's no problem with the insurance. And as you know Mr Simpson has offered to take charge of the sale of Number 11 and its contents. So—'

'So we can go back to Italy when? Next week?'

'I – yes – I don't see why not.'

He had lit a cigarette, turned to face the sea. 'Carrie?'

'Mm?'

'Do me a favour?'

'Of course. What is it?'

He did not look at her. 'Leave your door on the catch tonight?'

'Leo, no!' She was truly shocked. 'Not – not tonight of all nights! I couldn't.'

'Oh, yes you could. If you wanted to.' He slanted a look at her and she caught her breath, heart hammering. 'What's so special about tonight?'

'Leo, we've only just buried him!'

'And are you grieving?'

She ducked her head.

'Little hypocrite,' he said, gently and with his sudden smile, touching her gloved hand with a long, stained finger. 'Oh, what a little hypocrite you are.'

As they travelled south a week or so later it was indeed, Carrie thought, like going home. The weather, that in southern England and northern France had turned damp and grey improved with staggering suddenness. They took the night train and woke to find skies that had cleared and taken on a burnished depth of blue that dazzled the eye. The hedgerows and meadows of rural France were full of flowers; farms and small villages basked in the sunshine. Slow moving cattle gathered beneath the spreading shade of the new-leafed trees. There was snow still on the towering mountain tops of the Alps. 'Like icing on the biggest Christmas cake in the world!' Carrie said.

And then they were in Italy, chugging through the dusk across the flat, green valley of the Po towards the mountains that guarded Tuscany.

They arrived in Bagni, as Carrie had on that first occasion, that seemed now so very long ago, in full darkness; but this time it was the warm darkness of early summer. The hotels and bars were lit and noisy. People sat in their open doorways, calling to each other. Leo deposited Carrie and their luggage at a table outside one of the quieter cafés. 'Have a cup of coffee or something. I'll go and organise some transport.'

He was back fifteen minutes later, with driver, cart and a brown paper bag.

'What's that?' Carrie asked.

'Supper. Bread. Ham. Wine.'

'You don't want to eat here? Before we go up the mountain?'

He waited until she lifted her face to his. Then 'No, Carrie,' he said, very firmly. 'I don't want to eat here. I want to eat at the house. Later. After we've made love.'

She opened wide eyes that were suddenly very bright. 'Leo! We've just been travelling for twenty-four hours. I'm exhausted.'

He swung her case up onto the cart. 'Then all I can say is that you'd better get some sleep in the back of the cart, my darling. I'm tired of hotel beds and thin walls and holding hands on the night sleeper. We're home. I'm going to prove it to you. And if you don't get a move on—' the quick grin flickered in the lamplight, 'then I'm going to kiss you, here and now, in full view of at least half the village. How long do you think it would take Mary Webber to hear about that?'

Collectedly Carrie stood, smoothing her skirt. 'About three and a half minutes, I'd guess. All right, you bully. I'm coming. Did I say I wanted dinner?'

They made love in their room, the tower room, and drank wine that made them sleepy. Carrie woke to a pearl-pink sky and a smiling face above her. 'For goodness' sake,' she murmured, lifting her arms, 'don't you ever give up?'

It took two full days for the fact to sink in; the house was hers. The cases could be unpacked, the rugs laid back on the floors, the pictures put back upon the walls, the books on the shelves. And the garden! The garden too was hers, and no longer a sad heritage of neglect but a joyous challenge, a hope for the future. Why should it not again become what it had once been? She could not get used to the fact that there was no longer a time limit on her life in the house; it was truly hers. She could live here. No one, now, could order her back to England.

Leo, discreet to the last, booked his old room at the bar in San Marco, but in fact spent very little time there. He too was the one who came up with the practical answers to the different set of problems that now faced Carrie.

'You need help. A woman to clean the house before we set it back to rights. A couple of young men to do the heavy work in the garden.'

She frowned a little. 'I'm not sure I can afford it, Leo. I'm getting rather short of money. Until everything's settled I'm not certain—'

'It will cost next to nothing. And anyway, don't worry about money.' He laid an arm across her shoulder and turned her to face him. 'I have a little. A small allowance. It's all we need.'

'No. Leo, I couldn't possibly—'

'Only until everything's sorted out.' He was soothing. 'Then you can pay me back. Just don't worry. Everything will be all right, I promise you.'

And so the days were spent in cleaning and reorganising the rooms and planning the work on the garden, and the nights in the tower room making love, sleeping, making love again. The only thing that marred those first days was that twice Leo woke, shaking and pale, from a nightmare, and on each occasion he disappeared down into San Marco the next day for hours on end. When he returned each time he was nervy and in too high spirits and the smell of wine was heavy on his breath.

*　　*　　*

206

So busy was she that it was almost a week after her return before Carrie found time to pay a visit to Maria; and the old woman's first question threw her entirely. She asked not about Arthur, nor the journey to England, nor the funeral, nor Carrie's plans for the future. She asked, simply, 'You have read the journal?'

Carrie looked at her blankly.

Something like anger flickered in Maria's eyes. 'The one I brought to you. The one you wished to read.'

Read it well. And understand.

She had forgotten the journal entirely. From the moment that Leo had walked through the door behind her that day she had forgotten everything but the fact that he had returned to her. And then there had been the news about Arthur. She could not for the moment even remember what she has done with the book.

'You have not read it,' Maria said.

'Maria – I'm sorry – but truly, I haven't had time. The news about my husband – you must surely understand? There has been so much to do.'

The old woman leaned forward in her chair, hand clenched upon the knob of her walking stick. '*Read it!*' she said.

When Carrie returned to the villa it was empty, windows and doors standing open to a cool mountain breeze. One of the lads who had begun to help her in the garden was digging on the terrace above the house, whistling cheerfully. He waved and called a greeting.

Carrie walked into the house. Already it was beginning to look like a true home; she had brought a rug from the drawing room and laid it upon the hall floor, there were flowers on the table and a smell of polish in the air. The kitchen, too, looked different. Isabella, the plump and cheerful woman who came from San Marco each morning, had helped Carrie rearrange it and had then spent two full days scrubbing and cleaning. The tiled floor positively glowed, the wooden table had been scraped almost white, even the squat black stove shone smugly in the corner. Carrie stood in the middle of the room looking around. She had been inspecting the journal here, on the table, when Leo had come back. At some point it must have been moved; and presumably Isabella had tidied it away. But where?

She wandered round opening cupboard doors, poking in drawers, but the book was nowhere to be seen. She was on the point of giving up, intending to ask Isabella the next day – they had of necessity swiftly managed to evolve a laughter-provoking but relatively efficient means of communication, involving much hand-waving and an idiosyncratic mix of English and Italian words – when she noticed the small stack of books that was being used as a doorstop. The journal was on the top. With an exclamation of satisfaction she picked it up and carried it out onto the terrace.

Read it well. And understand.

At first she did not. As Carrie dipped into it, the journal seemed little different from the others, a clever and entertaining diversion chronicling the brother and sister's happiness at being away from cold England, their always-busy parents and from the constant company of others and back in the Italian house for the summer with Maria, their books, their poetry, the garden and each other. Most of all, each other. There was an account of another trip to Pompeii, of a visit to the picturesque high mountain village of Montefegatesi, of walks, and picnics, of conversations and inventive and complicated games, all, as always, illustrated by sketches and snatches of poetry.

And then she found the pencil sketch of Beatrice.

It was pasted into the journal under the date 20th June, 1867 and signed by Leonard; a delightful study, lovingly executed. He had made his sister beautiful; wide of eye, soft of cheek, a small, secret smile on her lips. And beneath the sketch, in what Carrie immediately recognised as Leonard's writing, a quotation from the *Song of Songs*:

'*A garden inclosed is my sister, my spouse;*
A spring shut up, a fountain sealed.'

She spoke the words aloud, softly. Beneath them Beatrice had capped them with:

'*This is my beloved, and this is my friend—*'

And then again, in Leonard's hand:

'*I sleep, but my heart waketh: it is the voice of my beloved that knocketh, saying; Open to me, my sister, my love, my dove, my undefiled—*'

She had come across this game before, in the other journals. But never these words. Never quotations from what surely must be the greatest love songs ever written.

Pensively, frowning a little, she touched the smiling lips of the portrait with her finger. '*Open to me, my sister, my love—*'

Read it well. And understand.

Slowly she turned the page.

The sun was westering to the mountain rim and the breeze had dropped by the time she read the last dark and terrible entry, the last anguished piece of verse. She sat for a very long time, looking into space, her hands loosely linked upon the closed book and its harrowing secret. The words Beatrice had written, sprawling and tearstained across that last page spoke themselves in her head, and she could not stop them. No *Song of Songs* this time, but the plea of a desperate, desolate child:

'*Oh! Call my brother back to me!*
I cannot play alone:
The summer comes with flower and bee—
Where is my brother gone?'

To his death. By his own hand.

Because Beatrice, his sister, his love, his dove, his undefiled, had quickened with his child.

Henry. Poor, demented Henry whom Beatrice had loved and favoured all of her life over her other children, who had lived out his blighted existence here in the very house in which he had been conceived in illicit and incestuous love.

And if the punishment falls on another? Maria had asked her.

Moving like a sleepwalker she found herself climbing the stairs, pushing open the door to the tower room. She had not yet made the bed. The sheets were rumpled,

210

the pillows tumbled. She and Leo had made love that morning, as they occasionally did, with a ferocity, a violence almost, that had left her bruised and aching, and begging him to love her again: she and Leo had made love that morning, as they had from the start, in the very bed that Beatrice had shared with Leonard.

The bed in which their love-child – their punishment – had been conceived.

The bed in which Leonard, unable to face the consequences of their sin, had died, of a self-administered overdose of laudanum; the bed in which his sister had found him, too late to save his life. *'Oh! Call my brother back to me! I cannot play alone—'*

Tears ran down her face, and she made no attempt to stem them. *'The summer comes with flower and bee – Where is my brother gone?'*

She walked to the mantel. The little bust, serene and inscrutable, gazed into the distance. Gently she picked it up, cradled its weight in her hands. 'Poor Beatrice,' she said. 'Poor, poor Beatrice. How very much you must have loved him. And how very long you had to live without him. Knowing he had killed himself because of you. Because of your love. Knowing the agony of his spirit when he died. And then, Henry; how did you bear it? How did you survive?' Very carefully she set the bust back upon the shelf, stood gazing at it with eyes still burning and blurred with tears. 'Leo isn't my brother,' she whispered at last, the words echoing in the quiet room. 'He is my cousin. It's different. It is different.'

She walked to the window. Leo, straight and slight,

211

hands in pockets, neat, bare head bright in the sunlight, was running up the steps to the kitchen terrace. As always the mere sight of him stirred her; she was helpless to prevent it. 'He is not my brother,' she said again. 'It is different. It is!'

'My darling, my darling. Don't upset yourself so!' Leo cradled her, rocking her gently and soothingly.

'But, Leo – it's such a horrible, horrible thing. I can't bear it! They loved each other so much. Oh, I know it was wrong – of course it was wrong – but there was something so beautiful about them, so different! And for it to come to such an end – it's so terribly cruel.'

'Life is,' he said.

She turned her tearstained face to his. 'Do you really believe that?'

'Yes. I do.'

'Then what of us? Leo, what of us? Will we be punished? Maria thinks we will. That's what she's been trying to tell me. Or will the punishment fall on someone else? Has it? Leo, what of Arthur? Did he die because of us?'

He took her firmly by the shoulders. 'Carrie, stop this. Now you're truly being silly. You're overwrought. Arthur died because the time had come for Arthur to die. It was an accident. Accidents happen. How could it possibly have had anything to do with you and me?'

'I don't know. I'm afraid; perhaps I willed it to happen,' she whispered, remembering. 'I wished him dead. I did!'

212

His hands tightened. 'Stop it! You're talking non-sense – sheer, superstitious nonsense – and you must know it. Darling, I know you feel guilty; I even under-stand why, though I don't think there's any reason in the world why you should. And now this damned journal has upset you and made things worse. But Carrie, Beatrice and Leonard have nothing to do with you and me, can't you see that? Look at me – will you look at me? I'm not your brother.'

'But your father was my mother's brother. And Henry – poor half-witted Henry – was brother to them both.' She rubbed her forehead tiredly. 'Oh, it's all so muddled.'

'No,' he smiled a little, 'it's you that's muddled. And I want you to do me a favour; I want you to get unmuddled just as quickly as possible.'

Sniffing still she could not help but return his smile. 'Why?'

He gathered her to him. 'Because,' he said quietly into her hair, 'I want you to marry me. And it seems to me that the last thing a fellow needs is a mud-dled wife.'

Chapter Eleven

She was adamant; she would not marry him. 'We mustn't,' she said, time and time again. 'I just know that we mustn't. I can't explain it.'

And time and again, at first with patience and at last, inevitably, in anger he argued with her. 'Carrie, my darling, you aren't making any sense. Why shouldn't we marry? We're both free. We love each other. For God's sake, we're more or less living together already. What's the difference? Why won't you marry me?'

Still, stubbornly, she stuck to her guns. 'I can't. Leo, I'm sorry, I just can't.'

'You don't want to,' he said one day, angrily, 'that's it, isn't it? You don't love me. You think you'll tire of me—'

'No. *No*! How can you say that? You know how much I love you.'

'Then marry me!'

'Leo – please. Why do you keep on about this? Why can't we just stay as we are?'

'Because I want you as my wife, that's why. Can't

you understand that? It's very simple. It's what people do when they're in love.'

'Not necessarily,' she said very quietly. 'I married Arthur, remember?'

'And now I'm to be made to suffer for it? Does that make any sense?'

'Leo, we're cousins—'

'Ah! Now we come to it. It's those damned diaries, isn't it? Beatrice and precious bloody Leonard. Poor benighted Uncle Henry. And that blasted old witch in the village with her superstitious nonsense about bad blood and punishment. Use your head Carrie, for Christ's sake. It isn't against any law for cousins to marry; the upper crust do it all the time.'

'Give me time. Let me think about it.'

'What will thinking change?' He picked up his jacket, slung it over his shoulder.

'Where are you going?'

'Down to the bar for a drink.'

She bit her lip. 'You'll – Leo, you'll come back?'

'Later.'

It was indeed much later when he returned; Carrie had already gone to bed. She went downstairs the next morning to find him, still fully dressed, asleep on the sofa in the drawing room. 'I didn't want to wake you,' he said, unsmiling, when she questioned him at breakfast.

She put a hand on his. 'Leo – please – don't let's quarrel like this. It's hateful.'

He regarded her levelly. 'There's a simple way to stop it. Marry me.'

She shook her head. 'I don't know. I really don't know. Perhaps it's just too soon.'

'The grieving widow,' he said, coldly. 'The role hardly suits you.'

'So,' Maria said. 'At last. You read it.'

Carrie nodded. 'Yes.'

'And now – *eccolo!* – you know.'

'Yes.'

There was a long moment of silence.

'It was a dreadful thing to happen,' Carrie said.

'*Si.*'

'You were there? On the day that Leonard – on the day that Beatrice found him?' Carrie spread her hands.

'*Si*,' the old lady said again, softly, 'I was there.'

'It must have been terrible.'

'It was, it was, *odioso.*' The single, whispered word was disturbingly self-explanatory.

Carrie wandered to the window, and perched on the sill. 'Maria, what happened next? How did Beatrice come to marry Grandfather Swann?'

The old woman shifted a little in her chair, rested her cheek upon her hand. 'She – my *bambina* – she shut herself into her room, their room, for three days. She would not speak, even to me. She did not eat. She did not sleep. She grieved. And I believe she considered—' Maria stopped.

'Following her brother?' Carrie asked, softly.

'Yes. But then they were different, those two. Different. She was the stronger, always. Even though she

216

tried, she could not will herself to die. And she had the new life within her. She would not, could not, destroy that. She came from the room. And she wrote to your grandfather. He was an old and much loved friend. He used to come to see the children – Beatrice and Leonard – often. She trusted him. He saved her. He married her, protected her. He loved her. I think, perhaps, he had always loved her. I think she knew it. I think that was why she turned to him.'

'But did no one suspect? That Henry wasn't Grandfather's child?'

Maria shrugged, looking into the distance. 'Who knows? There is always gossip, in Bagni. Always talk.'

There was another long silence. Then, 'Leo wants me to marry him,' Carrie said, quietly.

The old woman's head turned sharply. '*No!*'

'I know. That's what I said. But he doesn't understand. He says it's because I don't love him.'

'But you do? Still? You are sure?'

'Yes. Oh, yes. But—'

'You must not marry him.' Maria leaned forward in her chair, her eyes fierce, '*And you must not bear his child.*'

Startled and uncertain, Carrie stared at her.

'The blood is bad. Is bad!'

'No. Maria you mustn't say that. I told you, Leo is himself, not his father—' Carrie stopped, aghast. 'His father,' she repeated. 'Henry. Beatrice and Leonard. Leonard's death. That's what John found out,' she said, suddenly and flatly. 'Wasn't it? He discovered the story – read the journal? Somehow he found out

217

about Henry and he blackmailed Beatrice – blackmailed his own mother! Oh, God, that is truly awful.'

Maria's face was set in grim lines. She said nothing.

'That's it, isn't it? That's what happened? That's why Beatrice – and you – hated John so much. That's why you both went to such lengths to prevent Leo from inheriting any part of grandmother's estate?'

Still the woman neither moved nor spoke.

'And if I marry him, all of that will have been for nothing.' Tiredly she dropped her face into her cupped hands for a moment. 'I don't know what to do. I just don't know what to do.'

'*You must not marry him.*' The intensity of emotion in the words made Carrie flinch a little. 'Is a sin!'

'No! Oh, I don't know—'

'Your love is a sin,' the old woman spoke more quietly now, watching her steadily.

'No,' Carrie said again, shaking her head fiercely. 'No Maria, please don't say that.'

Maria sat back in her chair, folding her hands upon her lap. 'If you marry him,' she said, 'you will be punished. As she was punished. Best to send him away. Best to let him go to his other woman.'

'I can't. Maria, don't you understand? I love him. I love him so very much. And he loves me. I know he does. He wouldn't go, even if I could bring myself to try to make him. And as for Angelique, he's finished with her. He told me so.'

The small eyes regarded her with something close to sympathy. 'The woman has been seen again.'

Carrie's heart all but stopped. 'In Bagni?'

'*Si.*'

'I don't believe you.'

'Is true.'

'I tell you I don't believe you!'

Maria made a small, dismissive movement, but said nothing.

'You're – you're just trying to come between me and Leo. You're trying to make me believe he lied to me, trying to make me distrust him. Aren't you?'

In reply, unexpectedly, the old woman held out her hand. Carrie took it, dropped to her knees beside her, searching the wrinkled face with unhappy eyes. 'Maria, please don't hate him so. I keep telling you, he isn't his father. He's himself. It isn't his fault, what his father did, horrible though it was.' She tightened her grip on the frail hand. 'That was what happened, wasn't it? John did discover Beatrice's secret, and blackmailed her?'

The woman nodded, once.

'But how? How did he find out?'

For a moment the woman did not answer. She took a long, sighing breath. 'I told him,' she said.

Carrie stared, eyes and mouth wide. 'You?' she asked, faintly, '*you* told him?'

'*Si.*'

'But why? Why would you do such a thing?'

The woman sat pensive for a moment, searching for words. 'He was a young man of great – persuasion. He had a tongue that flattered. His words were soft, though his heart was black. He came one summer, when his mother was in London.' Her thin-lipped

219

mouth tightened, and her eyes glinted real anger. 'He became my friend.' There was a terrible bitterness in the word. 'There had been, as I said, much gossip in the village, even for many years after. John heard it. He came to me, worried, he said, for his mother and his brother. Wanting to help. He brought wine. We talked. He was – what do you say? – he had much sympathy for his mother. He spoke of love, and of pain.' The old woman laid her head back for a moment and closed her eyes. 'I was a fool. I showed him the book.'

'The journal?'

'Yes. I wanted him to understand. As I wanted you to understand. How much they loved. And how great was the pain.'

'And he used the information to extort money from Beatrice.'

Maria nodded. Her eyes opened. 'And now his son is here. In her house. With you.'

'The sins of the fathers,' Carrie said. 'I never did understand that. And I won't accept it now. Leo's done nothing wrong. He didn't even like his father.' She stood up, still holding Maria's hand. 'Please try to understand. I love him.'

The small, bony hand gripped hers. 'Don't marry him, child,' Maria said. 'Promise me.'

Carrie shook her head, gently disengaged her hand. 'I can't do that. I can't promise. I have to think.'

She turned and walked to the door. Her hand on the latch she stopped, looked back at the old woman. 'Maria, is it true? Is Angelique back in Bagni?'

'Is true.'

'And – has Leo been seen with her?'

The old woman shrugged, her eyes suddenly sly.

'Maria? Has he?'

She hesitated. Then, with a small, almost regretful sigh, 'No,' she said. 'My nephew at the hotel, he says no.'

'Perhaps Leo doesn't know she's here?'

'Perhaps not.'

Carrie opened the door. The blaze of the sun dazzled her. 'Then perhaps I'd better tell him.'

'Oh, Christ,' Leo said, 'that's all I need.' He ran his hand through his already disordered hair. 'Angelique? Here? She swore, she promised—' he stopped. 'I might have known, I suppose.'

'She loves you,' Carrie said.

He lifted his shoulders, helplessly. 'Yes.'

'And you?'

He said nothing.

'Leo? And you?'

His head came up, his eyes met hers. 'Once, yes. Since you, no. There's a simple way out of this, my darling. Marry me. Then she'll know. Then she'll have to understand.'

'No. More than ever, no. If you stay, stay because you want me. Not because we're tied together.' Carrie was astounded at her own words, at the sudden strength of her own conviction. At her own courage in expressing it. 'Leo, I love you. I want you. I want you to stay with me. But I won't be rushed into marriage. There are so many things to take into account.'

221

'What if there were a child?'

The silence was long.

'There was no child with Arthur.'

'Your fault? Accounted your fault?'

'Yes.'

'Of course.' His smile was wry. He walked to her, bent to kiss her lips, gently at first, and then with less control.

'Leo!'

His fingers had found her breast 'My darling. My poor confused darling. Come to bed,' he said.

They spoke, later, about his father.

'How could he do it?' Carrie asked. 'How?'

'With ease, I should imagine.' Leo turned on his belly, laid his head upon folded arms. 'Knowing him.'

She reached a hand to stroke his hair.

Abruptly he twisted from her, sat up, knees drawn to his chin, arms linked about his slim, bent legs, his face brooding. 'He was a gambler. We were always either in money or out of it. An awful lot of the time out of it. I lost count of the number of schools I got pulled out of. The number of houses we lived in. The number of excuses I used to think up to explain it. The moonlight flits. The bailiffs. The friends who came when the money was there and went when it wasn't. The tears my mother cried. And still, off he'd go to the race track. Dressed to the nines. He was a dandy. A handsome man. And one for the women, too.' He flicked the hair back from his eyes.

'And all with Beatrice's money.'

'Apparently so. Yes.' He reached for his cigarette case.

Carrie trapped his hand in hers. 'Leo, it isn't your fault. It's nothing to do with you.'

'I know that.'

She watched him as he lit the cigarette and blew smoke thoughtfully towards the ceiling. 'Leo?'

'Mm?'

'What are you going to do about Angelique?'

'Do about her? What can I do? It's a free country. I can't forbid her to stay in Bagni di Lucca, now can I?'

'I suppose not.'

'If I stay away from her she'll get tired and leave.'

'And if you don't?' she asked, softly.

He glanced at her, lifted his narrow, naked shoulders in the slightest suggestion of a shrug.

'What does she want of you?'

He smiled, with not the faintest trace of humour, slid from the bed and walked to the window, stood with his back to her looking out across the valley. 'She wants what you apparently don't. She wants me to marry her.'

'Leo—'

Swiftly and impatiently he turned. 'What? Leo what? I won't marry you because I've had this crazy idea put into my head that something that happened upwards of fifty years ago somehow has to be atoned for? I won't marry you because some crazy old woman has convinced me that I'll be punished for it if I do? Or is it, Leo, I won't marry you because I don't love you enough to give up new-found freedom? To promise to share my life with you? A lover is one thing, a husband quite another. Is that it?'

'No! You know it isn't.'

'Carrie, I know no such thing. From where I'm standing Beatrice, Leonard and Henry seem a very, very long way away. They have nothing to do with us. You love me or you don't. It's as simple as that.'

'It isn't. You know it isn't.'

'Beatrice didn't want me to have this house. Is that it? If you marry me I'll have a share in it.'

'You have a share in it already,' she said, very quietly.

'Do I?' There was a bitterness in the words that twisted like a knife in her flesh. 'Do I?' He reached for his clothes, shrugged his shirt on, stood looking at her. 'Marry me,' he said.

She bowed her head, and her tumbled hair hid her face; when she lifted it, he had gone from the room.

The quarrel that led to his leaving was as savage as it was unexpected.

For days Leo had been his normal, affable, loving self and had not again mentioned marriage; tentatively Carrie began to hope that he had come to terms with her refusal, or at least that he was ready to give her the time for which she had asked. Peace had apparently re-established itself between them. The tea chests had been returned to the attic, and the house, beneath Isabella and Carrie's ministrations, had come into its own again, lived in and loved. Carrie never tired of wandering the rooms with their smell of polish and the lovely, faded colours of the rugs and shawls and worn, comfortable furniture. It seemed to her that every day she discovered a new delight: a picture she had not noticed before, a tiny silver thimble, a piece of Venetian glass.

The garden too was showing some signs of the attention it was at last being paid, though progress there was slower, for there was a huge amount of work to be done and her young helpers, though cheerful and obliging as it was possible to be could not exactly be said to be over-industrious. Yet still, slowly, under Carrie's supervision the terraces were being rebuilt and the weeds cleared. She spent hours studying Beatrice's sketches of the layout; was surprised to see how much of the original plan could still be discerned on the ground.

In a shed at the top of the garden she discovered several large pots, which she planted with some of the brightly coloured geraniums that, now that the hot days of true summer had arrived, ran riot all over the tumbledown terraces. Most of these she set about their favourite sitting area, the terrace outside the kitchen. The others she put on the balcony of the tower room – something that turned out not to be such a good idea as she had thought, since a couple of days later one of them, set less carefully than the others on the uneven coping stones, crashed to the ground not a yard from where she was standing, giving her the fright of her life and causing Leo firmly to remove the others and put them in a safer place, shaking his head in gentle exasperation at this latest illustration of the impracticability of some of her notions.

At Leo's suggestion they set off at dawn one day to ride into the mountains, travelling by donkey, to visit the high and improbably picturesque village of Montefegatesi. Carrie was utterly enchanted. The air was cooler than in the valley and the fields beyond the tree line were still profuse and bright with the wild flowers of late spring. With them, in panniers, they carried a simple picnic, which they ate sitting on an outcrop of rock in brilliant sunshine beneath a lucent sky. The air was as intoxicating as the wine that Leo, as always, poured with a generous hand.

'What a lovely, lovely day!' Carrie spread her arms as if to encompass the world. The pretty little village perched on its peak opposite where they sat, the only sign of habitation in the wilderness of the mountains. A small herd of goats grazed beneath it; distantly through the clear air the tinkling of bells reached them.

Leo pointed to where a narrow track wound further upwards. 'Are you game to go a bit higher? The view from the top must be absolutely magnificent.'

Carrie eyed the track a little doubtfully. 'It looks awfully steep. Are you sure it actually goes anywhere?'

'Of course it does.' He jumped to his feet, held out his hand. 'Come on. Let's try it. We can leave the donkeys here. They're perfectly safe. Come on! Don't be a spoilsport.' His eyes were bright with laughter, the breeze blew his hair into his eyes. She came to her feet and into his arms. His mouth was cool, and demanding, and tasted of wine. 'Careful,' he said, softly, as she drew away from him at last, 'careful, my darling. If we can see the village over there it's a fair bet that the village can see us. We don't want to shock anyone, now do we? Come on, let's try the path. Who knows what we might find?'

They set off together, hand in hand. The goat-track climbed slowly at first and then, suddenly, very steeply over a tumble of rocks. Carrie pulled back. 'That's more of a climb than a walk. I don't think—'

'Oh, do stop it.' He drew her on. 'I'm here. No harm can come to you.' He pulled her to him and kissed her again, undisguised excitement in his eyes. 'I've never made love on a mountainside before. Let's do it. Let's make love on top of the world!'

The air, the warmth, the wine she had drunk, the sheer pleasure of his company had induced a reckless happiness; had he suggested that they jump from the ledge where they stood and attempt to fly she might well have agreed. She took his hand.

Halfway up she truly wished she had shown more sense. The climb was steep and dangerous, the footing unstable. Her head for heights had never been particularly strong; twice she had to stop, eyes shut tight, to regain her uncertain balance. But always Leo was there, unhurriedly encouraging, his hand strong in hers; and when they reached the top, even breathless and trembling as she was, Carrie had to admit that it had been an effort worth making. 'Leo! Oh, Leo – it *is* like being on top of the world.' Still unsteady on her feet she took a step. Small stones slid from beneath her foot and she stumbled a little.

'Carrie!' Laughing he grabbed her, pulled her to him. 'Will you for goodness' sake be careful? Stay away from that edge. Here,' he drew her towards a cleft in the rock. 'Look, the perfect place. Waiting for us.' He slipped the small knapsack he had been carrying from his shoulders, pulled from it a soft woollen rug which he spread on the rock. She stood watching him, unmoving, pulse suddenly hammering, eyes very wide. He straightened. Took her face in his hand, brushing the silky web of her hair from her shoulders. 'Take your clothes off, my darling,' he said. 'All of them. I want to take you here, in the sunshine, in the sky. And I want to see you while I do it. Please. Take off your clothes for me.'

The wine-fed excitement heightened. With a small smile she challenged him. 'You first.'

He spread his hands, his eyes warm. 'With pleasure.' With swift, graceful movements he stripped whilst she watched him, stood easily before her, his skin very smooth and very white except for the golden vee at his neck and the even tan of his face and arms. 'Now,' he said, gently. 'Your turn.'

They made love not once, but twice, and lay sleepily together as the sun moved across the sky, and the high breeze drifted coolly upon warm skin. At last Carrie stirred, rolled over, lifted herself on her elbow above him and kissed each of his closed eyes in turn. 'Leo. We have to go. It'll be dark before we get down the mountain otherwise.'

He grinned and shook his head, groaning. 'Why can't we stay here?'

She kissed him again. 'Don't be silly.'

'We've got a bed,' he said, opening one aggrieved eye. 'What else do you want?'

'Supper,' she said. 'I'm hungry as a hunter.'

He groaned again. 'God, woman. Where's the romance in your soul? *Hungry?*'

She laughed delightedly. 'Hungry,' she insisted firmly, and sat up, reaching for her shirt. 'Come on, for goodness' sake. Or we really will be here all night. And what about the poor donkeys? They must be wondering what on earth has happened to us!'

The quarrel the next day blew up so very quickly that she never could remember exactly how it started. They had reached the house in the last quiet light of dusk. Leo had insisted on opening another bottle of wine. She had gone to bed, tired and muzzy-headed and slept like a log until she had jumped awake to find Leo threshing beside her, drenched in sweat; another nightmare. As she had done so often before she held him as he woke, muscles corded, jaw clenched so that his teeth ground together. And as so often before, as consciousness had returned he had turned away from her, tense as a coiled spring. The next morning, as always, he looked drawn and tired.

'Leo, what is it? What do you dream?' she asked, her heart aching for him.

He shook his head, eyes fierce and guarded. 'I don't know. I can never remember afterwards.'

She looked at him for a long moment. 'I don't think I believe that,' she said at last, quietly. 'Was it – is it – something to do with the war? I've heard that some—'

229

'Leave it, Carrie. Just leave it.' His face was white and hard as bone.

'Leo, please. I'm only trying to help. I thought that perhaps if you talked about it—'

He ran his hand tiredly through his hair. 'I'm sorry. But I don't want to talk about it. I really don't. Leave it. Please.'

As the day wore on he became shorter and shorter of temper; she was positively relieved when he said in the early afternoon that he was going for a walk to clear his head. When he came back a couple of hours later, however, the relief was dissipated; perfectly obviously his 'walk' had taken him directly down into San Marco, and to the bar. She recognised the signs now; for all the absolute steadiness of hand and tongue, for all the unchallenged grace of movement, he had been drinking heavily.

She managed to avoid him for an hour or so. The house was very quiet. She felt as if she were walking on eggshells. She did not remonstrate when he refused tea in favour of another glass of wine. She tried to thank him for the trip up the mountain the day before. 'It's I who should thank you,' he said; but this was that other Leo, with no ready smile, absolutely no expression in the narrow eyes, an almost ruthless set to the straight mouth.

Whatever insignificant, inevitable spark it was that set the quarrel off, Carrie never ever forgot the sudden blaze of it; always, later, she thought of it as a bush fire that sprang to vicious life in a blustering wind, that fed upon itself, becoming ever more frightening

230

and destructive, defying any attempt to control it. By the time the disputed subject of marriage came up she was as angry as he, but infuriatingly and demoralisingly in tears.

'Leo, please! I've tried to explain—'

'Explain?' He was suddenly cold as ice. 'Explain? What have you explained? Nothing. You have put forward no rational reason for not marrying me. You've put forward a hodgepodge of excuses, most of which seem to be grounded in bloody superstition. Forgive me, my darling,' that last word was chill, and she physically flinched at it, 'I find it hard to believe you. There seems to me to be only one reasonable and rational explanation. You don't love me.'

'No!'

He ignored her. 'You don't' he repeated evenly, 'love me enough to trust me. To marry me. So where does that leave me? Have you thought of that? Have you even considered it?' He reached for his jacket. The hard, bright gaze did not leave her. 'You said Angelique is at the hotel in Bagni?'

'Leo please!'

He stepped forward, unexpectedly caught her wrist in a grip so strong that she could not disguise the pain. Watching her, knowing that he hurt her, he did not relax his hold. 'I know where I'm wanted,' he said, very steadily. 'And I know where I'm not. Do you think I'm stupid? Tell me now; will you marry me?'

She opened her mouth to say Yes. Anything. Anything to stop you from going to her, and then Maria's words – *Don't marry him, child. Promise me* – were there, positive and clear as a bell in her head. And driven by something beyond control she found herself saying, 'If you must go, you must go. I won't be coerced.' Tears ran unchecked down her cheeks. Her tangled hair was damp with them. 'Go. If that's what you want, go! Go to Angelique. She's beautiful, why wouldn't you want her? She wants you.'

The brutal grip tightened. 'And you?'

'I want you too,' she said, and her tears were helpless. 'You know I do.'

'Not enough.' He shook his head. Stilled. And then, very deliberately, he opened the hand that had held her so strongly, releasing her. He stepped back, shaking his head. 'My darling, not enough.'

Nursing her bruised wrist she watched him go, heard him run up the stairs, and then some moments later come down again. She waited, hoping against hope that he would come back to her; surely he would not leave with no word?

She heard the front door close.

From the kitchen door she watched the light, erect figure, the small suitcase that was his only luggage in his hand, run down the steps of the terrace and walk off along the track. She watched through tears until he disappeared into the trees.

Predictably, he did not once look back.

Chapter Twelve

She told herself that this time she would not let herself care; often she told herself that. This time she would get over him. She had what she wanted – the house, the garden, her freedom – often she told herself that, as well; too often by far.

But as before, the pain of his loss was all but intolerable. She ached for him. Ached for his presence, in the house, at the table, in her bed – to her shame, especially in her bed.

She would not – could not – consider where he might have gone, or who he might be with; tried not to remember the clear inference of that last bitterly angry exchange. Leo was not a man to live without a woman, and Angelique was beautiful.

Let her have him then, Carrie told herself stubbornly; I'm better off without him.

There were indeed times when she came close to convincing herself of that; for much as she loved him, and beguiling and gentle as he usually could be, there were those other, disquieting times when it was as if an unpredictable stranger inhabited his skin, a man she could not reach, no matter how hard she tried. A man she did not know. A man in whom, no matter how she attempted to excuse or deny it, she caught a disturbing glimpse of cruelty. A man, she admitted to herself now, for the first time, who occasionally frightened her. Of course she was better off without him.

But still she cried.

She spent long hours in the garden, working from dawn until dusk, heavy work, man's labour, trying to exhaust herself – trying, if truth be told, to ensure at least a couple of hours' sleep. Her young helpers were genuinely concerned; the Signora must not lift rocks, drag logs, dig the stony ground. The Signora must take care in the sun. But the Signora simply shook her head, smiling her thanks, and ignored them. The Signora tore her hands and all but broke her back, the Signora burned her skin in the bright hours of the Tuscan day and spent the early hours of darkness studying plans and writing notes by lamplight.

And still, she did not sleep.

She became a virtual recluse. She would not go down the mountain to Bagni; at worst there was the possibility of seeing Leo and Angelique together, at the very best – the village being the same as any other village the world over – she would have to face knowing looks and sympathy. She could not bear the thought of either. Isabella shopped for her and visited Maria, taking Carrie's small gifts of comforts or money. If Maria sent a message then Carrie never knew it; her system of communication with Isabella was of the most basic kind, and did not extend to such sophistication, whilst Maria of course could not write.

In the first couple of weeks that followed Leo's departure Mary Webber called twice. On both occasions Carrie quite unashamedly hid in the garden and absolutely refused to show herself. To her relief the woman had the grace to take the hint, and did not come again.

And then, five long and unhappy weeks after Leo had left – five weeks spent struggling to come to terms with the fact that she would never see him again – Carrie came in from the garden, hot and tired and dying for a cup of tea, to find a neatly folded note upon the kitchen table.

Leo's handwriting. She would have recognised it anywhere.

She stood for a suspended moment, looking at the folded scrap of paper before she stretched a scratched and dirty hand to pick it up. The note was short, and quite brutally to the point: '*I'm in San Marco. If you want me, come. I'll wait until this evening. No longer.*'

She lifted her head. *If you want me, come.*

She dropped into a chair, elbows on the table, bowed her face into her hands.

If you want me, come.

In the darkness behind her closed eyelids she saw his face, laughing. She saw him watching her, eyes narrowed; wanting her. She saw him bending his head to light a cigarette, the lines of his face lit by the flame, saw the negligent flick of the head when his hair fell over

235

his eyes. Saw the slight, graceful ease of every movement he made.

If she wanted him?

I'll wait until this evening. No longer.

Oddly, an obstinate part of her brain fought her instinctive urge to run to him. Think, it said, think! What is it you really want?

Leo, she answered, as she had answered before, knowing all her fine, self-deluding defiance defeated. I want Leo.

It was perhaps a ten minute walk down into the hamlet of San Marco. The afternoon was hot and still. Cicadas rasped and chirped, dust rose from beneath Carrie's feet. The smell of rosemary and thyme hung in the warm air. She could see the roofs of the houses through the trees beneath her. The sky was a bowl of light, bright and harsh as hammered metal.

The tiny village was quiet, shutters and doors closed against the heat. The bar stood back a little from the rutted track, a small, ramshackle building set in the shade of a huge chestnut tree. She had never before been inside it. As she stepped through the door, from the glare of the sunshine to the cooler shadows of a single, shuttered room, she was blinded, and she stood uncertain, trying to get her bearings in the dim light. After a moment her vision cleared; and suddenly her cheeks burned.

The room was untidy, far from clean, and stiflingly hot; the air thick and acrid with cigarette smoke. Flies buzzed at the windows. There was a small, stained counter and a few tables, covered with ragged oilcloths. Why in the world she should have assumed that the place would be empty of anyone but Leo she could not imagine; but she had.

It was not.

There were upwards of a dozen dark-faced men lounging about the tables, glasses in hand. The barman leaned upon his elbows on the smeared and pitted surface of the bar, his eyes bright and interested upon her. In fact every face but one was turned towards her; she was quite openly the focus of every pair of eyes but Leo's. Conversation had stopped. A chair scraped as someone lowered the front legs onto the floor and sat forward, the better to view her.

Leo sat, solitary, at a table on the far side of the room, his long fingers lax about a half-empty glass, upon which, beneath lowered eyelids, his gaze was fixed. He did not look up.

For the space of several heartbeats the tableau held. Carrie's legs were trembling; in an agony of embarrassment she willed Leo to look at her, to speak, to smile, to hold out a hand. To help her.

He did not stir, though he must have known she was there; and with a sudden lift of anger at the unnecessary cruelty of it she understood. This time, she was to go to him. For a moment she was tempted to turn on her heel and leave him. If she had believed for a second that he would follow she would have done it; but she knew with certainty that he would not. As the others in the room stirred back into life and conversations were resumed she walked steadily to where he sat, aware that for all the movement and talk every eye, sly, inquisitive, was still upon her.

She was standing in front of him before, with a studied coolness so obvious that it cut her to the heart, he lifted his head. The narrow, bright eyes were inscrutable. 'You came.'

'Yes. Did you think I wouldn't?'

He lifted a shoulder. 'I didn't know.'

'Leo, did you deliver the note yourself?'

'Yes.'

'Then, why? If you were at the house why not speak to me there? Why make me come down here?'

'I needed to know. I needed to see if you would make the effort.'

'Well, I have. So now you do know. So, please, won't you come back to the house? Won't you come back home?'

He shook his head, slowly. 'Not yet.'

'But why not? Leo? Why not?'

He did not reply, but sat watching her steadily. And Carrie, suddenly, recognised his purpose.

'Come upstairs,' he said softly.

'Leo no! Don't do this, please.'

'Upstairs.' He tossed back the rest of his drink, stood, and walked past her to a door on the other side of the bar. One of the watching men said something in an undertone, and another laughed and made a gesture that Carrie did not understand, but that nevertheless heightened the colour in her already burning cheeks.

Without looking back Leo pushed open the door and

238

mounted the dark and narrow staircase it revealed. Carrie was left to follow or not, as she chose.

Humiliatingly aware that every knowing and amused eye in the room was still upon her, she followed.

He was waiting at the top of the stairs in a dim-lit, ill-smelling, airless landing. As she appeared, he pushed open a door. The room beyond it was claustrophobicly small and sparsely furnished: a narrow, uncomfortable-looking bed, roughly made, the bedclothes none too clean, a washstand containing a chipped jug and bowl, one rickety chair. Leo's small suitcase stood, neatly placed, in the corner. It was very hot. Leo walked to the window and threw wide the shutters, turned to face her.

There was a long moment of silence, and even now, even here, he would not make the first move. Carrie it was who went to him: it was without thought or volition that she found herself in his arms, and then his mouth was ferocious on hers. There was little of gentleness here, no tenderness. There was force and there was need. There was violence. Hands and mouth bruised her, and when she bit his lip he bit her back, fiercely, making her catch her breath in pain; she tasted blood in her mouth. They had played rough games in their lovemaking before, but never like this. He pinned her beneath him and he took her in anger and with savage lack of care.

'I'm hurting you?'

'Yes.' She almost spat the word.

'You like it.'

She gritted her teeth and would not reply.

239

He tightened his grip on her wrists, making her flinch. 'Tell me to stop.'

She could not.

When it was done she found that she had cried, and could not remember doing so. They lay quietly for a long time before he lifted himself onto his elbow beside her, put a finger to her still-wet cheek. 'I'm sorry. Carrie, I'm sorry,' he said, quietly, all violence spent.

She shook her head. 'You don't have to be.'

'Are you all right?'

'Yes.'

He turned from her, slipped from the bed, reached as always for a cigarette. She watched as he lit it, sat on the bed, blew smoke to the cracked ceiling.

'Leo – why? Why did you make me come here? Why wouldn't you come back to the house? Why did you make love to me like that? Did you really want to hurt me?'

'Yes.' He had his back to her. Through the smooth, fine skin she could see the straight and delicate line of his spine.

'But why? *Why?*'

'I don't know. If I say because I love you it would sound absurd.'

'I don't think so.' Her voice was quiet.

He smoked in silence, his face sombre.

'Leo?'

He turned his head.

'Do you still want to marry me?'

He watched her for a long moment. Then 'No,' he said.

Her eyes widened a little in question.

Leo took her hand. 'You were right. There's no need. What difference does a scrap of paper make? You came to me of your own free will today. You let me make love to you here, knowing that everyone downstairs knows what we're doing. You let me hurt you. It's enough.'

'This was – some kind of test?'

'I didn't actually think of it in that way but, yes, I suppose it was.'

She put her finger to his marked lip. 'And did I pass?' she asked, softly.

He smiled. 'Oh, yes. You passed. With flying colours. And now—'

'Now?'

'now you have to be a very brave girl, make yourself respectable and run the gauntlet of the bar downstairs.' He stood up, pulled her to him, held her, his face resting on her tangled hair. 'Then we'll go home.'

She tilted her head to look at him. 'Home? Do you mean that? Is that really how you think of it?'

'Yes.'

She put her hand in his, smiling more than a little wryly. 'In that case why waste time making myself look what I'm not? Respectable indeed! After the show you just made of me? Come on. Take me home. Please.'

They slipped back into the old ways so easily that it was almost as if the quarrel had never happened. The days were long, the nights scented and warm. Leo, suddenly, was at his kindest and best; it seemed that there was nothing he would not do for her. It was full summer now, and very hot; Leo was insistent that she stay in the cool of the house out of the noonday heat. If they needed something from the village he went himself, whistling blithely down the track, hitching a ride back up the mountain, trying out his very bad Italian on anyone who cared to listen. On one such occasion he brought back an English paper, tossing it on the table in front of Carrie, bending to kiss the top of her head. 'There you are. Catch up on the news. It's over a week old, but never mind. I'm sure the world won't mind that we're a few days behind it.' He grinned cheerfully. 'In fact I doubt it will even notice.'

She picked up the paper, watching him, loving the smile, the warmth of his hand on her shoulder. 'So what is happening out there? Anything interesting?'

He shrugged a little. 'Dock strike at home. Stalin has apparently taken over the Communists in Russia. The Fascists have finally taken over entirely here. There's hyperinflation in Germany – so what's new? And,' he bent to her ear, lowering his voice, 'I hate to tell you this, my darling, but the big news in Bagni isn't in the paper.'

'What do you mean?'

'It's us. We're rumbled. In the doghouse. *Persona non grata*, and all that.' His smile was quizzical.

'Why? What happened?'

He kissed her again, hitched himself onto the table. 'I was completely ignored by three people this morning. Looked straight through me. It seems we are disapproved of. Severely disapproved of.' He was laughing aloud now. 'Idiots!'

242

She blinked. 'Ignored you? You mean, deliberately ignored you?'

'Oh, yes. It was made quite clear. We, my darling, are living in sin. And the world doesn't like it. The expatriate Anglo-Saxon world that is.'

'Well,' Carrie composedly spread the newspaper before her, smoothing the creased pages. 'The expatriate Anglo-Saxon world knows what it can bloody well do. Doesn't it?'

He was silent so long she looked up. He was standing beside her, looking down at her intently, his eyes warm. 'I love you,' he said. 'Oh, how I love you!' He caught her hands, pulled her to her feet, kissed her and hugged her hard. 'Come to Florence with me.'

'What?' Laughing she struggled free. 'Now? This very moment?'

He shook his head. 'Of course not. Don't be silly. Tomorrow.'

'Tomorrow? Just like that?'

'Just like that. Come on. Don't hang around, I might change my mind. Yes or no?'

'Yes.'

'You know the trouble with you? You're just so indecisive. It's maddening.' He laid his face against her hair. 'Carrie?'

'Mm?'

'You're sure you don't mind?'

'What? Going to Florence? No, I don't think so.'

'You know what I mean.'

She leaned back to look into his face. 'Yes, I know what you mean. And no, Leo. I don't mind. I have what

243

I want. I have all that I could possibly want. I told you; the world can go hang. It's none of their business. Now. Tell me about Florence.'

'It's wonderful. You'll love it.'

She did. They stayed in a small, picturesquely run-down hotel on the city side of the lovely old Ponte Vecchio. The city enthralled Carrie. She wanted to visit every single palace, museum and church, explore every single street, sit in every single piazza. She marvelled at the Cathedral and the Baptistry with its wonderful bronze doors known as the Paradise Portals, she insisted on climbing to the top of the Campanile to survey one of the most famous views in the world.

'Oh, Leo – look! Isn't it wonderful? It's like having the city laid out on a tray. And the roofs are such a beautiful colour.'

Leaning beside her he smiled at her enthusiasm.

She slipped her arm about his waist, rested her head for a moment on his shoulder. 'Thank you for bringing me.'

She felt the brush of his lips on her hair. 'Thank you for coming. Florence has never been so lovely before. Have you seen enough?'

'Yes.'

'Good. Because I have suddenly realised that there are several hundred well-worn steps between me and the next glass of wine. And after that—'

'After that?' she asked, smiling into his eyes.

'After that,' he said, firmly, 'we're going back to the hotel for a siesta.'

'But I'm not tired,' she said, innocently.

'Did anyone, my darling, say anything about being tired?'

When they got back to the villa there was an unexpected break in the weather; a series of violent storms lashed the mountains, and they were housebound for a few days. It was during this time that Leo's nightmares returned. For three nights running Carrie awoke to find him tossing and sweating beside her, and during the day he was tense and quarrelsome. This time she neither questioned him nor allowed herself to be provoked. Unable to work in the garden she sat at the kitchen table looking through the notes she had made in the past weeks, and planning future projects.

'Did I tell you that originally Beatrice intended the fountain arbour to be further down the hill, closer to the house?' she asked. Thunder murmured in the mountains again, the air was sultry. 'I'm half tempted to have someone come up to see if we could resite it. It would be nice if we could actually see it from here, and if it were less of a struggle to get to I'm sure we'd use it more.'

Leo, frowning, lifted his head from the book he had been reading. 'I don't think that's a good idea.'

'Why not?'

'For goodness' sake, Carrie, think about it. The effort of moving those statues? Don't be daft. It's totally impractical. They're perfectly all right where they are.'

'I suppose you're right. Though I still think it would

be nice. I'll think about it. The fountain needs attention anyway. Next time I'm in Bagni perhaps I'll see if I can find someone to come up and look at it.' The thunder had moved closer. Leo winced and put a hand to his forehead, closing his eyes. She moved to him, laid a hand on his shoulder. 'Would you like a cup of tea?'

He shook his head. The first heavy drops of rain splashed on to the terrace outside, and a sudden gust of wind tossed the branches of the pear tree. He stood up, walked to the cupboard, took out a bottle. She watched in silence as he poured the dark wine into a tumbler, shook her head at his look of enquiry. 'No, thank you.'

'Sun not over the yardarm?' The words were tart; self-mocking.

'Something like that.'

He tossed his drink back, poured another, came to her. She recognised the look on his face, and shivered.

'Come to bed,' he said. 'Now.'

'Leo—'

His hand closed on her wrist. 'Now.'

Thankfully, this time, the mood did not last. Within days he was himself again, in fact if anything suddenly he was as animated and ebullient as she had ever known him. A week passed, and then another, and his nights were calm. Obviously anxious to make amends for his ill humour he planned outings, picnics and expeditions, laughing her out of any excuse. 'For goodness' sake, leave the damned garden alone for a bit! You've years

246

to do it. Come and enjoy yourself.' And on one thing he was determined; that they should go up the mountain again, to Montefegatesi, and make love on the rock above the village. This was an expedition he planned with extra care; they were to take a picnic, and wine and rugs and cushions. This time they would be prepared; this time, he told her, everything would be perfect. Their day, a day they would never forget. He hired the donkeys and he packed the picnic basket, and on a gloriously warm August day they set off to ride the eight miles of track that led into the mountains and to Montefegatesi.

Leo was in a fever of high spirits. He sang, he teased her, he told silly jokes. Long before they were anywhere near their destination he had opened one of the bottles and was drinking from it as he rode. The sun rose higher, dazzling, in a sky blue as cornflowers. The track began to lift, winding through woodlands that rang with birdsong towards the treeline they occasionally glimpsed high above them. When they rode through the thinning scrub and trees onto the mountainside the sun hit them like a blow; and in the distance they caught their first sight of the tiny village, clinging to its peak, that was their goal.

Leo eyed the much depleted bottle from which he was drinking. 'We'll go into Montefegatesi first, to replace this. Then we'll go on up the mountain to the place we found before.' He leaned across to kiss her; his mouth tasted of the wine. 'And then, my darling, we'll do what we did before, only we'll do it for longer, and in much greater comfort.'

Carrie tilted her head to watch the swifts and swallows that swooped above them, high in the brilliance of the sky. 'Is it true that swifts make love on the wing, I wonder?' she asked.

He laughed, throwing his head back, the sound bright and unrestrained. 'It's a nice thought. Perhaps we should try that too!'

They rode down the steep and narrow track that led into the tiny, tree-shaded cobbled square in the centre of the village just before noon and were greeted by a small pack of wildly yapping mongrels that skittered about the donkeys' hooves in a frenzy of excitement, shattering the sleepy peace of the day. Shutters opened. Voices called. An old man sitting on a bench brandished a stick, his eyes sharp with curiosity on the newcomers. The dogs scattered and ran, still yelping, down an alleyway. Leo slid a little stiffly from his donkey's back and turned to help Carrie from hers. 'I don't know about you, my sweetheart, but I'm ready for a quiet sit on something that doesn't move. Come on. Let's have a drink.'

The bar they entered was almost a carbon copy of the one in San Marco, but smaller, cooler, and empty of customers. The landlord came round from behind the battered counter, beaming, setting a chair for Carrie, speaking volubly.

'*Una caraffa di vino, per favore,*' Leo said, cheerfully, 'In fact *una caraffa grande*. And that's about my limit in the conversational stakes.' He reached to take Carrie's hand. 'My darling Carrie you look wonderful, do you know that? I could eat you.'

She could not resist laughter. 'Are you absolutely sure you should drink any more? You have had quite a lot. We don't want you falling off your donkey!'

He poured the wine the landlord had brought with a steady hand. 'No chance of that, my darling. No chance at all.' He handed her a glass, clinked his against it in salute. 'Here's to our day.'

They drank the carafe and Leo, over Carrie's half-hearted protests, ordered another. The somnolent calm of high summer had returned to the village. The donkeys dozed, standing, beneath the shady trees. At last Leo leaned forward and took Carrie's hand in his, lacing their fingers. Suddenly there was no more laughter, no more flippancy. His face was disturbingly intent. 'Are you ready to go? Are you ready to climb the mountain?'

'Yes.'

He paid for the wine, and they walked into the warm afternoon in silence.

As they turned the donkeys' heads and urged them forward into the sunshine the old man on the bench lifted a hand and nodded in dignified farewell.

They picnicked on the lower slopes of the peak; bread, cheese, ham and fruit washed down with strong red wine. A quiet had fallen between them. Leo sat cross-legged on a rock, cigarette between long, stained fingers, eyes remote and distant upon the magnificent, towering crags that stretched before and above them. An eagle soared, great wings spread to catch the slightest breath of air. Silence drummed in the ears; it was as if no world existed but this, of rock, and stillness, of heat and of light. Carrie tilted her hat to shade her eyes and studied the man's profile, etched clean and sharp against the bright furnace of the sky; and something she saw prompted her to ask, suddenly, 'Leo? Are you all right?'

For a moment he neither moved nor answered. Then he turned upon her his most brilliant smile, and her heart all but stopped. 'Yes. Of course I am.' He straightened his legs, swung them from the rock, stood up with that grace that seemed second nature to him. Held out a hand. 'Come on. Time to go on up.'

She had forgotten how steep, how vertiginous the climb was in parts; and the wine she had drunk – that Leo, she suddenly realised had been insistent that she drink – made nothing easier. And this time, oddly, Leo did not help her. He forged ahead, sure-footed and confident. Twice she had to swallow her pride and call him back to offer his hand. Stones and shingle slipped and rattled beneath her unsure feet, bounced down the cliff face and scattered into the space that she was suddenly frighteningly aware yawned and beckoned beneath her. Halfway up her legs were trembling and her hands clammy despite the warmth of the rock to which they clung. When at last she scrambled onto the ledge her relief was tempered by the thought that there was no way back to safety except by the path she had just trodden.

Leo had dropped the knapsack he had been carrying and was waiting for her; slim, straight, unsmiling.

Dangerous. The word clicked into her head from out of the blue. Dangerous.

'Leo?' Her voice was uncertain. The perilous trembling had not stopped. She stepped slowly away from him, backing into the rockface. 'There is something wrong. Isn't there?'

He watched her.

'Leo, don't be silly. Please don't be silly.' She heard the precarious edge of panic in the words; forced herself to an untrustworthy calm. 'I'm sorry to be so stupid. But I'm frightened. Please, let's go back down.'

He held out a hand. 'Come here.'

She shook her head, pressing back against the rock.

'Carrie. Come here.'

There was a very long, very tense moment of silence. Carrie did not move.

He came towards her then, unhurried, reaching for her shoulders, drawing her to him, bending his head to kiss her. And for a moment the fire that was always there when he touched her flared again; this was Leo. She loved him. This was no dangerous stranger to be feared, from whom she had to escape.

The moment she relaxed to his kiss she knew her mistake. In a second he had twisted her around; when he lifted his head he it was who had his back to the rock. This time when she stepped back from him, heart pounding in terror, she stepped towards the edge, not away from it.

He moved forward.

Despite herself she backed away again. Gravel slid

from beneath the soles of her shoes. 'Leo. *Leo!* What are you doing?'

'I think you know what I'm doing, my darling,' his voice was very soft in the quiet. 'I'm killing you. At least—' he stopped.

'But why? *Why?* I thought you loved me.'

'Ah, yes. Love. A chancy thing, love. I should have known that. Shouldn't I?' He took another step towards her. This time, terrified, and uncertain as to how close she already was to the edge she stood her ground.

'Love,' he said again, and for an instant closed his eyes, as if against pain.

The instinct for survival took even Carrie herself by surprise. In that moment's distraction she sprang at him, forcing him back against the rockface, nails clawing at his face.

Quick as a cat he caught her wrists, holding her from him, his wiry strength as always overwhelming her in seconds. But in that desperate instant of surprise she had managed at least to slip beneath his guard. The rockface jarred against her back, and she gasped with pain; felt the sudden wet stickiness of blood. For a moment they stood still, face to face, his hands locked about her wrists, as they had so often been before.

Then he stepped back.

She froze. 'Leo. *Leo!*'

'Love,' he said again. 'Whoever would have believed it possible?' Another step.

She was sobbing now, uncontrollably, shaking with shock and with horror. 'Leo, don't!'

His voice was oddly detached, the narrow blue gaze

252

distant. 'They loved, I suppose – some of them, anyway – the men I left dead in the night.' He spread his hands, looked down at them thoughtfully. 'Do you know how many ways there are to kill a man with your bare hands?'

'Leo – please – come away. You're sick. My darling, you're sick. Please come away, please don't do this.'

'Sick. Yes, I suppose so. But isn't the world? And when the world takes you, and twists you, when the world encourages you to do the things that I have done and when it is done with you, abandons you – leaves you with nothing but the nightmares – isn't it reasonable to try to take the things you want, the things you need, using the methods that world has taught you?'

'Leo, I don't know what you're talking about.'

'No.' He stepped back again. Stood, face shadowed, body limned in sunlight, balancing. 'No, I know you don't. And I pray you never will.' He moved very slightly.

'*Leo!*' The scream tore her throat.

'So which is the greatest tragedy of life, my darling? Not to get your heart's desire? Or to get it, and to find yourself so tainted, so fatally flawed, that you know that you will inevitably destroy the very thing you most love?'

'Leo, please!'

His last movement unbalanced him entirely. Stones and small rocks showered into the abyss. And Leo was gone. He screamed once, as his falling body hit an outcrop of rock; then there was nothing. Nothing but the sunlit and echoing silence.

253

Chapter Thirteen

The sun still shone, though low now, dipping behind the village, blinding her; the tears – hysterical, terrified – came as she stumbled down the mountain track towards Montefegatesi. By the time she reached the square she was sobbing uncontrollably.

The village, perched on its peak, had known such accidents before. The shocked and bereft young woman was comforted, as best as was possible, the body of the young man recovered, decently shrouded, and arrangements made to transport both the living and the dead back down the mountain to Bagni di Lucca.

No one questioned that it was anything but a tragic accident. In her account of what had happened Carrie made no mention of Leo's attempt to kill her. What would have been the point? To have done so would merely have brought questions she could neither face nor answer.

Why? *Why?*

The villa rang to her footsteps, the rooms stifling, airless, utterly empty.

Why?

The British community's disfavour did not, it seemed, pursue its victim after death. In any case, predictably, Mary Webber's busybody inability to keep out of anyone else's affairs was strained to the limit by events, and for once Carrie was grateful for it. Within a day the woman had braved the mountain track to the villa and with her usual staunch and indefatigable energy had taken over entirely.

'Well, of course, you can't possibly stay here alone. I won't hear of it. Come, my dear, I'll pack a bag for you. It will be much the best if you join me at the Continentiale for a few days, at least until after the funeral. The place is really quite comfortable and I'm sure I can get you a special rate – I am Signor Donitello's longest-staying guest, after all. You've suffered a tragedy, a terrible tragedy; you need people about you, people to help you, to share your grief. You mustn't stay here to brood, you really mustn't. So come along, my dear, chin up. Come and tell me what you want me to pack for you.'

Dazed with grief Carrie allowed herself to be crisply bullied into leaving the house. Once settled in the hotel, however, she found the sense of horror and confusion heightened rather than eased. At least the villa had been familiar, and associated with Leo. Now she found herself amongst strangers and in strange surroundings. And no matter how kindly the strangers and how pleasant the surroundings the dreadful, almost surreal sense of loneliness, of isolation, was simply made worse.

She fled to Maria.

'He tried to kill me. Maria – he was going to kill me! I saw it in his face. And then—' she had begun to shake again. She clenched her hands together to stop their trembling, 'And then, he stepped back. Over the edge. I couldn't stop him. I couldn't stop him!' She buried her face in her spread hands. 'It was horrible. Horrible!'

Maria said nothing. There was a terrible and impotent sympathy in her eyes. She looked very old today; frail and fatigued, her desiccated skin all but colourless.

Carrie lifted her head. 'Why?' she asked, for the hundredth, perhaps the thousandth time. 'Why?'

Maria shook her head. 'The blood was bad.'

'No! I don't believe that. Maria, he loved me – I know he did. That's why he couldn't do it.'

'He wanted the house for himself, *cara*. If you had died he would have inherited it.'

'No. I've thought of that. But, Maria, it simply doesn't make sense. He had the house – and everything in it. I told him, he could take anything he wanted. He could have had it all, simply by asking. He knew that. I loved him. I would have given him anything he asked.' She shook her head in despair. 'It doesn't make sense,' she repeated.

Maria leaned her head back tiredly upon the cushion, closed her eyes for a moment. 'Perhaps you will never know, *cara*,' she said, softly. 'Perhaps you will never know.'

Carrie came to her then, knelt beside her and took the claw-like hand. 'Promise me you won't say anything to anyone about what I've told you. Please, Maria, promise me. I couldn't bear it.'

The small head moved in assent. 'I promise.' The old woman's eyes were still closed.

Carrie looked at her in sudden concern. 'Maria? Are you all right?'

The eyes opened. 'I'm old, *cara*. Old and tired. I have seen too much.'

Carrie tightened her grip. 'Maria, come and live with me. In the villa. I can take care of you, you'll be much more comfortable.'

'No,' Maria shook her head, still resting upon the cushion. 'I am too old for such changes, *cara*. Much too old.'

'It would help me, Maria, to have someone to care for. Someone else to think about.'

To her surprise the faintest of smiles touched the thin mouth. 'You will have, *cara*. You will have.'

'No. I'll never love anyone ever again. I know it.'

'Ah, the young!' Maria said, gently. 'How fierce they are.'

Maria did not attend the funeral. The day was a beautiful one. The tiny cemetery, shaded by cypress trees, lulled by the sound of the river, was, to Carrie's surprise, packed with mourners, most of whom she was certain had never even met Leo. It was Mary Webber who pointed out that in this expatriate community, it was simply not the done thing to miss a fellow-Englishman's funeral. In consequence Carrie found herself once again surrounded by well-meaning

257

strangers, mouthing thanks for their quite genuine condolences, accepting invitations to vaguely timed lunches and dinners, and with little time to dwell upon the occasion. It was only after the simple service, held in the tiny chapel at the top of the hill, when the coffin was carried to the quiet corner of the churchyard that was to be Leo's final resting place, that the enormity of what had happened hit her again, with a force that brought a wave of nausea and a sudden dizzy roaring of blood in her ears. She stopped for a moment, swaying, fighting faintness.

'My dear,' Mary Webber's arm was firm about her shoulders, 'lean on me. That's right. Close your eyes for a moment. Mr Wallace – a chair for Mrs Stowe, please. Quickly.'

'No,' Carrie shook her head a little to clear it. 'No. I'm all right, I really am. I'm sorry. I just felt a little faint, that's all.'

The other woman did not relinquish her grip. Carrie lifted her head and the world rocked again. She squeezed her eyes closed. 'I never faint.' Her voice sounded distant. Detached.

'There's a first time for everything, my dear. And in this case it really can't be counted surprising—' Mary Webber broke off, rather suddenly. Then, 'Good heavens!' she said, a faint, disapproving shock in her voice. 'Well, I'll be jiggered!'

'What?' Carrie asked, bemused.

'Nothing, my dear, nothing at all.' The briskness was forced. 'I just thought I saw someone, that's all. Must have been mistaken.'

258

But Carrie had opened her eyes, and this time the world had steadied.

And through the crowds she too saw the figure that had arrested Mary Webber's indignant attention. Tall, slim, elegant, dressed entirely in black, her face hidden by a wisp of black veil, Angelique stood, unmoving and graceful as a statue, watching as Leo's coffin was carried slowly, shoulder high, through the sunlit cemetery. Then as if feeling Carrie's eyes upon her, very slowly she turned her head, lifted the veil to reveal the cold, beautiful, pale-skinned face. For a moment it was as if the two of them were alone.

Carrie shivered.

'Come, my dear,' Mary Webber was gentle, 'they're waiting for you,' and she ushered Carrie towards the grave and the last farewells. When Carrie turned her head again, Angelique was gone.

She knew that, sooner or later, she would have to go home; that, sooner or later, she had to confront the emptiness, the loneliness. The unanswered and unanswerable questions. For three days she allowed herself to listen to Mary Webber's persuasions, but then she knew that enough was enough; she would have to face the house. There would never be an easy time; it might as well be done now.

She arrived at the villa in the late afternoon, as the sun clipped the edge of the mountain and the long shadows started to fall across the valley. It was very warm. Maria's nephew, solemn and courteous, handed her down from her seat. They had not been able to communicate during the tortuous ride up the mountain, yet she had felt his sympathy, and as, after saluting her with a dignified nod of the head and a quiet '*Arrivederci, Signora*' he swung himself back up onto the cart and clicked his tongue at the stolidly patient mule she felt a sadness to see him go. She stood and watched him move out of sight under the thick green canopy of the chestnut trees before turning with heavy heart to the door and fitting the key in the lock.

The first thing she smelled as she pushed open the door and stepped into the hallway was cigarette smoke.

Fresh cigarette smoke.

Carrie stood rooted to the spot, heart hammering.

Upstairs, clearly and distinctly, a door shut, clicking sharply.

'Who's there?' Her voice cracked a little. She cleared her throat. 'Who's there?' she asked again.

Footsteps clipped upon the floorboards of the landing. A figure appeared at the top of the stairs, stood for a moment looking down at her before starting slowly down the stairs.

'What are you doing here?' Fear turned to a sudden, shattering fury. 'What the hell do you think you're doing here? How dare you come into my house.'

Angelique paused, halfway down, narrow white hand on the banisters. The smoke from the cigarette she held drifted about her. She was wearing a white silk blouse tucked in at her narrow waist to softly flattering black slacks. About her neck was a casually tied scarf, a scarlet splash, red as blood against the skin of her throat. She looked as always, cool and beautiful.

Carrie almost choked with rage. 'Get out of my house. Now!'

The dark head shook. 'Oh, no. I think not.' Her voice was husky, and attractively accented. 'I think it's time we talked.'

'I don't want to talk to you. Not now. Not ever.'

The other woman resumed her slow descent of the staircase. 'But I want to talk to you, Carrie Stowe,' she spoke the name as a curse; and with the same sudden shock she had experienced in the square in Bagni all those weeks ago Carrie once again recognised that she was encountering real hatred. 'I want to talk to you.'

'What about?'

At the foot of the stairs Angelique dropped her cigarette on to the wooden floor and very deliberately ground it out with her heel. Then she lifted her head, and once more Carrie had to force herself not to recoil from the sheer malevolence in the great, dark eyes. 'About the fact that you and I both know who killed Leo,' she said. 'I want you to tell me about it. All about it. I need to know. I'm sure you understand?' Without waiting for an answer she turned and walked along the passage that led to the kitchen. Carrie stood for a moment, still shaking with shock and rage, before following her. When she entered the room Angelique was standing by the open door, lighting another cigarette.

The taller woman turned. 'Well?' she asked, very softly.

'I don't know what you're talking about.'

Angelique made a small, scornful sound. 'Why play games? You killed Leo. We both know it.'

'No!'

The other woman took two quick steps to the table and slammed her open palm on it, fiercely. 'And I say yes! You killed my Leo. *You killed him!*'

'No! It isn't true. It isn't!'

'Don't lie to me. Don't lie!'

They were suddenly screaming at one another, faces distorted and on the verge of tears.

'I'm not lying. I swear it!' Carrie folded her arms across her breasts, gripping her upper arms, forcing herself to be calm. 'Angelique, listen to me. I didn't kill Leo. I didn't. He—' she stopped.

'What?' Angelique had become still, the lovely, luminous eyes fixed upon Carrie's face. 'What did Leo do?'

'He tried to kill me.'

To Carrie's horror the woman threw her head back and laughed. 'Well of course he did! That's what he took you up the mountain to do. Are you really so stupid?'

'Why? Angelique, *why?* Why would Leo want – why would he need – to kill me? Please, tell me.'

There was a small, venomous smile on the pale, lovely face. 'You don't know,' Angelique said. 'You still don't know.'

Carrie shook her head numbly.

Once again the laughter.

Carrie covered her ears with her hands. 'Stop it. Stop it!'

Angelique rested her hands upon the table, leaned

forward, a predator, tooth and claws bared. 'What I want to know,' she said, softly, 'what I intend that you shall tell me, is what went wrong? How did you kill him? A man so experienced in death?'

'I didn't! I keep telling you Angelique – he killed himself. He just stepped back. Off the ledge. Yes, he was going to kill me. I'm certain that was what he intended. But he couldn't.' The words that had haunted her since the day on the mountain rang clear in her head, as if Leo were beside her, and speaking. *Love. Whoever would have believed it possible?* 'He loved me,' she said, quietly. 'He told me so. He killed himself because he loved me.'

'You're lying.' Angelique's voice was flat, implacable. 'You're lying, you bitch.'

'No. I'm not. I didn't kill him. I couldn't have. I loved him.'

'Love? You? You little fool! You don't know the meaning of the word!' For a moment, the mask slipped, and Carrie glimpsed the suffering, the utter despair.

'We both loved him,' she said, quietly. 'I know that. But I didn't kill him, Angelique, I swear it. I've told you the truth. He loved me. And because of that he died.'

Angelique straightened, the mask in place again. She stood for a long moment in silence, drew on the cigarette, threw back her head to blow smoke to the ceiling, watching Carrie through half-closed eyes. 'You must be a jinx, my dear,' she said, at last, softly and with mocking spite. 'The men in your life seem to die with quite monotonous regularity. Don't they? Doesn't that strike you as being a little – strange?'

Carrie stared at her. 'What do you mean?'

Angelique said nothing.

'Angelique, what do you mean?' Carrie's heart had begun to beat heavily, slow and suffocating.

The other woman kept her gaze steady and that hateful smile was back; deadly, vindictive. Knowing.

'Arthur's death was an accident,' Carrie said. And even she heard the sudden, awful uncertainty in the words.

Angelique shook her head.

'It was! He fell down the stairs.'

The smile widened a little.

'I tell you he fell down the stairs!'

Angelique's hand hit the table so suddenly and so sharply Carrie all but jumped out of her skin. 'You silly little bitch! An accident? An *accident*? My God, Leo said you were naive. He didn't ever tell me how stupid you are. How could he have borne it?'

'Stop it! Get out of my house. You hear me? Get out!' There was an edge of hysteria in the words.

'Tell me this, my silly Carrie,' Angelique was completely in control now. Her husky voice was very low, totally calm. 'Where was Leo when your husband died?'

'He was here. Of course he—' Carrie stopped.

Angelique shook her head again, still smiling. 'Think again, little fool. Think again. I asked not where Leo was when news of your husband's death arrived. I asked, where was he when he died?'

There was a very long moment of silence. 'With you,' Carrie whispered. 'I thought he was with you.'

Again the shaken head.

'No.' Carrie said. 'No!'

'Yes.' The word was flat and brooked no denial.

The sun was well behind the mountain now; a shadow had fallen across the door. The cooking fires of San Marco were sending their fragrant message to the sky. A dog barked.

'Leo killed your husband,' Angelique said. 'He broke his neck. And threw him down the stairs.'

Carrie dropped her face into her spread hands. 'No. I don't believe you.'

'Believe me. The banisters were broken, were they not? And a stair rod at the top of the stairs. Leo did that too. He was experienced in such things. He knew he must make the accident' she put a dry emphasis on the word, 'look authentic. Your husband was a big man, was he not? Much taller than my Leo. You see? He told me. Why do you cry? You wanted him dead, did you not?'

'No!'

'Yes.' The word was absolutely implacable. 'Face yourself, Carrie Stowe. Even Leo, in his own way and by his own code, was a little more honest than that. Was that, perhaps, why you killed him? Did he tell you he didn't love you? There is, they say, no fury like a woman scorned. It would not be the first time that even such a man as he has been taken by surprise at a woman's sudden strength in such circumstances.'

Carrie lifted her head. 'No! Why won't you listen? No Angelique, I didn't kill Leo. I keep telling you – I swear it – he killed himself.'

'So now we are even; for now I don't believe you.' The woman's voice was perfectly controlled. 'He would never have done such a thing. I know it. He was a survivor. If nothing else, he was that. Always. Don't expect me to believe he had changed so much.' She flicked the cigarette through the open door out on to the terrace.

'I don't understand any of this,' Carrie said.

'It is my only consolation.' The other woman's voice was soft.

'Leo? Leo killed Arthur? So that I would inherit the house?'

Angelique watched her.

'And then tried to kill me because—' there was a certain awful logic appearing in this nightmare of an equation, 'because—'

'Because he was your only relative, and because under Italian law – you had made no other arrangements – the house would have come to him.'

'But he *had* the house. He knew I would give him anything he asked.'

Angelique turned and walked to the door, stood surveying the peaceful scene. 'Well, perhaps, or perhaps not. Or maybe, little bitch – has it not yet occurred to you? – maybe he did not wish to share it with you? Perhaps he wished to share it all with me? Have you not thought of that?' She stepped through the door, and turned, her face in shadow, the light brilliant around her. 'Tell me, did Leo ask you again to marry him? After he returned?'

Numbly Carrie shook her head. 'No.'

'Of course not. Because he realised he did not need to. Because he had come to understand that already, by the tie of blood, he was your only living relative, so there was no need to commit yet another crime.'

'What do you mean? What other crime?'

'The crime of bigamy.' The woman paused, savouring the moment, watching her. 'Leo couldn't marry you, little bitch, though even that, to begin with, he was ready to do. He could not have married you because he was already married. To me. To me, my so silly Carrie. To me.' She pushed back a lock of hair that had fallen across her forehead. 'And do you think that any man who had me would leave me for you?'

'I don't believe you.'

'Believe me.'

'He loved me. He did! He told me so.'

'But my poor Leo always was a liar, didn't you know that?' Angelique leaned against the doorjamb, arms folded. 'He told you, did he not, that he loved his grandmother?'

Carrie stared at her numbly.

Angelique shook her head. 'He hated her. Hated her for leaving everything to you and to him, nothing. He told you, of course, of his gambling debts? Ah, I see not. Poor Carrie, there does seem to be a very great deal you don't know, doesn't there?' She let the silence linger. Beyond her Carrie caught a glimpse of the great bird of prey wheeling and turning in the still sunlit sky. 'He told you he had been to his grandmother's grave, did he not? A pilgrimage of love?' The woman laughed, softly.

Carrie turned away, closing her eyes for a moment,

267

leaned against the table. 'I guessed he hadn't,' she said, 'when I talked of the cemetery. He got everything wrong. He obviously hadn't been there.'

'Ah? So perhaps you aren't always quite so stupid? Why did you not challenge him?'

Carrie bowed her head. 'I didn't want to embarrass him. I didn't want to let him know I'd caught him in a lie. It was such a small, silly lie. It didn't seem to matter.'

Again the soft laughter. 'How wrong you were. How wrong. Tell me; what else did you guess? What else did you not challenge?'

'What do you mean?'

'Did you for instance know that it was Leo who found your grandmother's clothes, Leo who put them in the wardrobe? And then pretended to discover them, encouraged you to wear them?'

'Why? Why would he do that?'

Angelique shrugged. 'A game. That's all. Just a game. He wished later he had not; after you had read those stupid books, after you had met the old woman, you came to identify too closely with your grandmother. The game was spoiled.'

'A game,' Carrie whispered.

'Yes. A game. And tell me, the pot that fell from the balcony?' Angelique shook her head mockingly. 'It might have killed you, might it not? Do you really believe in so many accidents?'

Carrie closed her eyes for a second. There was a long moment of silence. Carrie lifted her head. 'What else don't I know? Is there more?'

'Oh, yes. There is more.' Angelique pushed herself from the doorjamb, slipped her hands into the pockets of her slacks. Smiled. 'But you'll never know what it is. Never. That, too, is my consolation. You killed Leo. And you'll never know why. I hope it haunts you for the rest of your days.'

'Angelique, I didn't—'

But the woman had turned, and was gone. Carrie heard her footsteps on the flagstones, on the steps and then, faintly, on the gravel.

Just before the footsteps faded, she thought she heard an echo of laughter.

She tried not to believe it, tried to tell herself that Angelique had lied out of bitterness, a desire to hurt. But the more she thought about it – and she thought about it almost obsessively – the more uncertain she became. That Leo would have had few qualms about killing Arthur she did not doubt. And the time scale fitted Angelique's story; Arthur had been dead for two days before his body was discovered; it had taken another twenty-four hours for the news to reach her. There was no doubt that Leo could have done it, and still managed to return, as he had, to be with her. And, worse, the things he had said the day that he had died on the mountain now made a dreadful sense. *'Isn't it reasonable to try to take the things you want, the things you need, using the methods the world has taught you?'* And then *'To find yourself so tainted, so fatally flawed, that you know you will inevitably destroy the very thing you most love?'*

The very thing you most love. These were the words that, through all her agonising, she returned to time and time again. *The very thing you most love.* Angelique had been right; perfectly obviously there had been many, many things about Leo she had not known. Hateful things. Hurtful things. But in one particular, no matter what Angelique might profess to think, Carrie knew she was wrong; Carrie had not killed Leo. He had chosen to die rather than harm her; and that could surely only mean one thing. He had loved her. In his own strange, contradictory, complex manner he had loved her. If Carrie were certain of anything, it was that; and the knowledge at least made the burden she carried easier.

She did not see Angelique again, neither at the house nor in Bagni; to Carrie's relief after that single visit the woman had vanished, as if she had never existed. Only her words stayed to haunt Carrie, and her reference to other secrets, other lies, about which Carrie knew nothing. Carrie, determinedly, shut her mind against the thought. Any other secret, any other lie, could only be painful. It was, she told herself, best not to know. There was in any case, she thought, no possible way to discover what they might be.

She was wrong.

One morning, some three weeks after Angelique's visit she forced herself to face the tower room for the first time since Leo's death; and discovered, tucked neatly under the bed, a painfully familiar small leather suitcase.

She put it on the bed, brushed the dust from it, stood

looking at it for a very long time. Her eyes burned suddenly, and she blinked fiercely against tears. This had been the only piece of luggage Leo had ever carried; it had gone with him when he left her, come back with him when he returned. It had stood in the corner of the room when he had made love to her that day six or seven weeks ago – a lifetime ago – in the bar at San Marco.

With gentle fingertips she stroked the scratched leather that he had touched, slipped her hand about the worn handle, where his hand had so often been. Then with suddenly determined movements she pulled the thing towards her and clicked the catches open.

Five painful minutes later, she found the letter.

Chapter Fourteen

'Signora Stowe.' The dapper, expensively dressed young man advanced upon Carrie, footsteps crisp and echoing upon the marble floor, 'Welcome to the gallery of the Lasale brothers.' He took her hand in thin, soft-skinned fingers, bowed over it, brushing the knuckles with his lips. Carrie, with hard held restraint, resisted the temptation to snatch it back. The sleek, pomaded black head lifted and she found herself the recipient of a wolf's smile. 'I am Giuseppe Lasale. We were very pleased to receive your letter.' Again the sharp gleam of teeth. 'I understand you had our name from Signor Swann?'

'Yes.'

'I had hoped he might come with you. We had wondered what was happening, we had not heard from him for so long. Please, come upstairs to the office. You would like a glass of wine, I'm sure?' He led the way through the gallery towards a sweeping marble staircase, the strong, flamboyant scent of the haircream marking his passage. 'You enjoy Florence, Mrs Stowe? You know the city well?'

'No, I don't. Know it well, I mean.' The lonely journey, the sight of the lovely city that last she had so happily visited with Leo had been a harrowing experience. Nothing but a dedicated determination to discover what lay at the root of Leo's actions would have brought her back to this place. 'I've only visited it once before, and that briefly.'

'It's a beautiful city. You are staying long?'

'No. No, I'm not.' Carrie had stopped, her attention arrested by a painting.

The young man came back, stood by her side. 'It's very fine, no?'

Carrie nodded. The lean-faced young man in the portrait looked out from his frame, brooding and powerful. The fingers of his clasped hands gleamed darkly with jewelled rings, gold thread glittered on shoulder and sleeve.

'You are interested in art?'

Carrie shrugged a little. 'Interested, yes. Informed, no, I'm afraid. Is this by someone famous?'

The faintest flicker of a smile brought the unsettlingly sharp teeth to her notice again. 'Yes,' the young man said, softly. 'It is indeed by someone famous. They all are. Now,' he laid a hand upon her arm, 'please. We have a glass of wine, and we talk. Yes?'

The room into which he showed her was palatial, the high ceiling a masterpiece in itself, a miracle of carved and decorated beams and plasterwork. A great gilded mirror above a marble fireplace – filled at this time of the year with flowers – dominated the room, and the view from the tall windows, of the city with its spires, its campaniles, its ancient roofs and the majestic dome of the Cathedral, was breathtaking.

'Please. You take a seat.' The young man indicated a large carved wooden chair upholstered in worn velvet that Carrie found herself thinking would not have been out of place in any self-respecting palace. She accepted the slender-stemmed glass she was offered and gingerly sipped its contents, half afraid to put her lips to the fragile, beautiful glass. The wine was magnificent.

The young and wolfish Signor Lasale settled himself opposite her. 'Signor Swann, he is well?'

'Signor Swann is dead.' She never afterwards knew how she found the composure to speak the words so collectedly. 'An accident in the mountains a few weeks ago.'

'Ah, Signora, I am so sorry. A tragedy, for such a one to die so young.' The hard, dark eyes had sharpened. 'He was – a friend?'

'He was my cousin.'

The smooth head nodded. 'I see. And, he had spoken of us? Of our, shall we say, shared interests?'

She hesitated for a moment before shaking her head. 'No. He hadn't spoken of it. I found a letter, after he died. That's when I wrote to you.'

'I see.' The atmosphere had changed; there was a wariness, a small prickle of tension in the air. The young man rose, carried his glass to the window and stood with his back to her looking across the city. Eventually he turned. 'So. You don't know of the arrangement that we had with Signor Swann?'

'No,' she said, bluntly. 'That's why I'm here.'

He nodded, thoughtfully.

'Signor Lasale, what is this all about? The letter I found – your letter – was cautious, but it did mention a very large sum of money. What was your connection with my cousin? What was this – arrangement – you had made?'

The man still said nothing. He picked up the bottle from the table and walked to where she sat. 'Another glass of wine, Signora?'

'No, thank you.' She set her glass down, and rose. 'Signor, I insist. If my cousin was dealing with you in respect of something from the Villa Castellini – and I can put no other interpretation on the letter I found – then I have to tell you that in fact he had no right to do so, not without my agreement. The villa and its contents are mine. If you wish an "arrangement" as you call it, then, whatever it is, it has to be with me.'

He stood watching her for what seemed a very long time, one long, very clean and too-well-manicured nail tapping against those sharp teeth. Then, as if coming to a decision he straightened, briskly, and put down his own glass. 'Come, Signora,' he said, 'I have something to show you.'

Carrie followed him out into the corridor, down the wide staircase and through to the back of the gallery, where he drew aside a curtain and opened the door it disclosed. Stepping through it at his courteous invitation she found herself in a very different atmosphere than the quiet and elegant gallery. This was a workshop, or perhaps more accurately a studio. The air was pungent with the smell of turpentine and of the

275

sweet and oily scent of paint. As she hurried to keep
pace with her escort she glanced about her. Though
the large room was empty of any human occupancy
several easels were set about the room upon some of
which half-executed paintings rested. There were tables
upon which paint-stained rags, palette knives and pots
and jars full of brushes of all shapes and sizes vied
for space.

'This way Signora.'

Another door; and this time she found herself in a
huge room that was flooded with light. Dust motes
danced in the shafts of sunlight that fell through the
tall, open windows. Again, the purpose of the place was
immediately obvious. This was a sculptor's studio. In
the yard outside rough slabs of stone and marble were
stacked. To one side of the room stood a bench upon
which several small busts and statues stood, some of
them covered with sheets, and in the centre of the
floor the figure of a woman, rough-hewn as yet, but
nevertheless already wonderfully lifelike was emerging
from a block of marble as if being liberated from her
prison of stone.

Again she was given little chance to take in her
surroundings. The young man led her swiftly the length
of the room to a wooden door that was barred and
studded with iron. He drew a key from his pocket,
inserted it into the lock and pushed the small, heavy
door open.

This seemed to be some kind of storeroom. It was
darker, and very cool. It took some moments for
Carrie's eyes to adjust to the dim light. Paintings were

stacked neatly along one long wall, and everywhere there were statues, covered with dust sheets. The young man took her arm and guided her to the far corner of the room. Carrie watched, puzzled, as he reached to pull the shrouding sheets from a group of statuary.

There was a very long, very still silence. Carrie looked at the statues. The young man, hard eyes veiled, looked at her.

'I don't think I understand,' she said, at last.

These figures did not look new; on the contrary they might have been as old as those that stood in the arbour in the garden of the villa. And they were, in every apparent respect, identical. The nymph's hands reached to catch the water, her head turned to smile at the dolphins that tumbled at her feet. Beside her the little water carrier shouldered his jar. 'I don't understand,' Carrie said again; and even as she said it, knew that she did, at least in part.

'Come.' The young man was brisk again. He threw the dust sheet back over the statues, turned and led her back into the gallery and up the stairs. Once in the office he poured wine and handed it to her. She took it with no thanks, held it, watching him, waiting. He poured his own wine, sipped it, set the glass upon the table. 'Are you coming to understand, Signora?' he asked at last, softly.

'Not entirely – but,' she stopped. 'May I ask you a question?'

'Of course.'

'Did Leo – did Signor Swann – get in touch with you? Or did you contact him?'

He shrugged. 'We contacted him. The name you see – Swann. It is unusual. And we have our methods of tracing people.'

'I'm sure you do.'

He pulled out a cigarette case, opened it, offered it to her with a questioning expression. She shook her head. Looked down into the amber depths of her untouched wine as with neat movements he extracted a cigarette, tapped it upon the lid of the box and lit it. 'For years there had been rumours,' he said. 'Rumours of the kind that we listen to. When the old man died we followed them up.'

'And found the statues.'

'Yes.'

'Are they very valuable?'

'Signora Stowe they are almost priceless. In America they will fetch a fortune.'

'America,' she said.

'Yes. That's where the money is, Signora. We already have several interested buyers.'

'But – if they are what you say they are – it's illegal to export such things. Isn't it?'

He blew smoke to the ceiling.

'So. The plan was to substitute the new ones for the old, and smuggle the originals out of the country?'

'Smuggle is not a good word, Signora.'

'It's the honest one.'

He shrugged.

'Explain to me, Signor; why did you even bother to contact my cousin? Why didn't you simply steal the statues before anyone arrived?'

278

'Signora, please!' the words were pained, almost shocked. 'Be careful what you say. The Lasale brothers are not thieves. We are reputable dealers in fine art. Yes, on occasions such as this we—' he spread narrow hands 'we may evade the law a little. The law is ridiculous. Everyone does it. But steal? Ah, no. That is not our way. We made our bargain with Signor Swann. The replicas were almost ready. And then we heard no more.'

'Because I arrived out of the blue.' She remembered, suddenly, a rain-soaked packet of cigarettes lying in the arbour; the arbour her cousin had said he did not remember and had not visited; and another piece of the puzzle clicked into place. 'What an idiot I've been,' she said, quietly. And then, after a moment, 'Tell me, Signor. Just how old are the statues?'

He sipped his wine, his face impassive. 'Very well, Signora Stowe. Since as you say it appears that we must deal with you now, I shall be honest.' He ignored the wry lifting of Carrie's brows. 'We have reason to believe the figures are very old indeed. In fact it is virtually certain that they came from the excavations at Pompeii.'

'Is that possible?'

'Ah, yes. More than possible. A generation ago anything was possible. It is only now, for our sins, that we have these busybodies to invent restrictions and pass laws.'

'And would anyone who had some knowledge of such things suspect how valuable they were if they saw them?'

He shrugged. 'Any such person would know how fine they were, yes. And any close inspection would cause interest.'

279

She heard, in memory, a distant grumble of thunder. And her own words to Leo: *'Next time I'm in Bagni perhaps I'll see if I can find someone to come up and look at it.'* Was that when he had decided that she had to die? He would have known – must have known – that much as she loved him she would have had no part of this, even for him.

'What were your arrangements with Signor Swann?' she asked, quietly.

'The same as we always make under these circumstances. The same as we are ready to offer you. The deal is fifty-fifty. And as I said, there is a great deal of money involved. You are going to be an extremely rich young lady, Signora Stowe.'

She set her untouched wine on the table and straightened to face him. 'No, Signor Lasale. I'm not. Because neither you nor anyone else is going to touch those statues. Make your squalid little deals with others, not with me. If you want to sell damned statues sell the ones downstairs.' The rage that burned in her was so great that she trembled with it.

His face had hardened. 'Signora, I think perhaps you need time—'

'No, Signor. I need no time.' Carrie had turned and walked to the door.

'Signora Stowe!' His voice cracked like a whip behind her.

She turned.

'It would be – unfortunate – for any word of this discussion to become public. You do see what I mean? We have our interests to protect. I can assure you that

280

any false allegations laid against us would not proceed far, and might only rebound upon those who made them. The Lasales have friends in very high places.' The long fingers flicked again. 'Remember. This is Italy. And you, Signora Stowe, are an outsider.'

'Keep your sleazy little secrets, Signor Lasale,' Carrie said calmly. 'But stay away from me. I want nothing of your schemes.'

He sighed a little, and raised pained brows. 'A pity,' he said. 'A very great pity.'

On the long, hot train journey back to Bagni she stared unseeing at the rolling hills dotted with the dark fingers of cypress trees, the tiny villages that dozed beneath the sunny sky and looked back, with eyes now clear and open, over the past months. How Leo must have cursed her untimely arrival. To have been so close to a fortune and then to have been frustrated; how it must have angered him. And then – slow uncomfortable colour lifted in her cheeks at the thought – and then he had sensed how attracted she was to him, and another plot had hatched in his fertile brain. He must have known that she would never have agreed voluntarily to the export of the statues. And even if he had simply helped her to clear the house and sent her packing back to England, by then too much attention had been drawn to the Villa Castellini. Signor Bellini had become involved. Mary Webber had her inquisitive nose in the business. Half of Bagni and all of San Marco were watching. Leo had needed time. And he had needed to own the statues.

So he had manufactured the quarrel, gone to England, killed Arthur, and then been ready, if Angelique were to be believed, bigamously to marry Carrie; until it had dawned on him that as her only living relative he would, on her death, inherit the house and its contents anyway.

A brutally simple way to a fortune; except that, for Leo, something had gone wrong.

'To find yourself so tainted, so fatally flawed, that you know you will inevitably destroy the very thing you most love?'

He had loved her. Despite himself and against his will, he had truly loved her. She knew it with a certainty that could not be shaken. The contradictions, the complexities of his character – the dark side of the man – notwithstanding, he had loved her. And in the end he had proved it: he had chosen his own death over hers; and in doing so had surely gone some way towards atoning for those other deaths, that had so haunted him.

She turned her mind from the deceits, the betrayals; remembered the touch of his hands, the blaze in his eyes when he had looked at her. Remembered the laughter and the lovemaking, the quarrels and the tears.

He had loved her. No one and nothing could take that from her.

Carrie tilted her head back against the straight, hard-backed seat, closed her eyes, and surprisingly, lulled by the movement of the train and the steady, hypnotic clicking of the wheels, she slept.

*   *   *

The first thing she did, the following morning, was to visit the arbour. It was a wonderful morning, clear and bright and with the first hint of autumn in the mountain air; the great acacia – Beatrice's acacia – that sheltered the grove was tinged with gold. In wonder Carrie stroked the smooth, almost translucent marble of the statues, as she had done so often before. She knew, of course, that she must have someone come to see them, to evaluate and authenticate them. That this might mean that she would have to give them up she regretted but well understood; the Italian government jealously guarded its heritage, and in truth these precious things had no real place in a Tuscan garden – though in a small corner of her heart she found herself harbouring a hope that in the circumstances she might be allowed to keep them in situ and restore the garden around them.

But all of that was for tomorrow. For today, calming and beautiful in the dappled shade, the lovely, ancient things were still hers.

She stretched a little to ease the nagging ache in her back and then sat on the rock beside the fountain, as she had on that first morning with Leo. A dragonfly swooped upon gauzy wings, its body the green of emeralds and the blue of sapphires.

The child within her stirred.

Carrie laid her spread hand gently upon her belly, feeling the movement.

Maria, in the way of wise women, had guessed. And had, apparently, relented. '*It would help me, Maria,*' Carrie had said, '*to have someone to care for.*' And '*You will have, cara,*' Maria had said, '*you will have.*'

'It has started, my love,' Carrie said, softly, aloud, her eyes distant. 'My dearest love. Our child is alive, and growing, and will come in his own good time. And yes, I do know now – I am not Beatrice, and our son will not be as Henry was. The punishment is done. It won't fall on him. And though you are gone, and I shall miss you for ever, I – I shall have at least a part of my heart's desire, my darling, and will no longer be alone.'